LIMBO

LIMBO

THE DOOR ABOVE THE LAKE

ROBERT-BRIAN SMITH

Matador
9 Priory Business Park,
Wistow Road, Kibworth Beauchamp,
Leicestershire. LE8 0RX
Tel: 0116 279 2299
Email: books@troubador.co.uk
Web: www.troubador.co.uk/matador
Twitter: @matadorbooks

ISBN 978 1838594 909

British Library Cataloguing in Publication Data.
A catalogue record for this book is available from the British Library.

Typeset in 11pt Adobe Garamond Pro by Troubador Publishing Ltd, Leicester, UK

Matador is an imprint of Troubador Publishing Ltd

To the wonderful team at SWR
To everyone I worked with at Selco
To a bunch of deviants named Andy, Brian, Ray and Fella
To the lovely staff in Starbucks on Maylands Avenue
To a crazy Greek man called Havoc
To Mum, Dad, Annie, Megan, Richard
To my biggest fan Charlie
To Trev and Louis
To the wise and trusted Martin and Carole
To the beautiful and unbelievably patient Aimée
And to you for reading these words
Thank you
Please know that without any of you
I never would have got this far
I hope you will find some joy and entertainment
in the madness that is my mind.

“Everybody wants to go to heaven.
But nobody wants to die.”
– *Unknown*

PROLOGUE

◀▶

Deep in the Gora Chimtarga mountains of Tajikistan, a private military sniper team had set up in a position overlooking a long valley. Their exact mission details were classified. They were, however, aware that they were there to oversee an exchange between militia groups. Amongst one group of militia was a friendly informant that the sniper team were there to recover should the exchange go wrong. As the sun began to fade it shone with a thick orange glow, which cast long shadows of the various rocks and shrubs that littered the ground of the clearing. The sniper team were zeroed in on a patch of dirt road a few hundred yards away, where the exchange was due to take place.

The two young men of the sniper team were both in their mid-twenties, wearing black-and-white urban camouflage uniforms that were well suited to the snowy peaks of the mountains above them. Their legs were covered by thin metal plates that hid the hydraulic mechanisms of exoskeleton suits.

Call sign Zero was the leader of this operation; he lay flat on his back with his combat helmet and assault rifle lying beside him. His hair was a ghostly white that made him look much older than the young man actually was. Beside him was Sharpe, the shooter of the team, who lay very still with a crystal-blue eye staring down the scope of his sniper rifle. Zero held up a hand to shield his eyes from the sun.

"I thought albinos weren't supposed to sit in the sunlight for too long," Sharpe croaked in a low, lazy voice that carried with it a thick and clear English accent.

Zero rolled over and tapped the rim of Sharpe's boonie hat in an attempt to get on his nerves. Sharpe didn't so much as flinch or even blink in a deliberate move to deny his friend the satisfaction.

"I'm not a fucking albino. Besides ya'll are paler than me!" Zero retorted with a strong Texan accent.

Sharpe didn't respond. He continued staring down the sight of his weapon and slowly reached up for his scope to make a very slight adjustment.

"What's the distance to the target, four hundred?"

"Five," Sharpe croaked.

"Think you can make the shot from here?" Zero teased. His taunt hit a nerve with Sharpe, setting him off into a rant Zero had heard several times before.

"This is a custom-made SR-25 sniper rifle, I've spent years perfecting its design, swapping out springs, barrels and sights to create the perfect long-range weapon, not to mention since we've been lying here I've made all of the calculations to land aimed shots from here to five hundred yards from the target zone. With this rifle, and this data, I can hit a man-sized target in the chest at one kilometre."

"Yep and that is exactly why ya'll don't have a girlfriend."

Zero gave Sharpe a wide grin as the sniper glanced over at him for just a second before returning to his scope.

"Look, I get that you'd much rather be somewhere a little more interesting but can you please stay focused."

"Yeah, sorry."

Zero looked down at his unsteady hands and took a long breath before he spoke again.

"Why are we even out here, man? Why do our countries have a stake out here? These people were fine long before the West came into the picture and now they're sandwiched between us, the Russians and the Chinese. So many lives ruined and for what?" Zero spat on the ground.

"Oil," mumbled Sharpe. "And we're out here for three times the wage of the average US soldier."

The clearing below them suddenly came to life. A shiny black SUV with tinted black windows rolled in from behind the sniper team's position, kicking up the dust as it went.

"What's the chances of that thing having armour?" Zero mockingly questioned as he slid back down into cover, grabbing his rifle in the process.

"About as likely as my shot bouncing off, if it does," Sharpe murmured as he shifted his aim to the SUV.

"Fuck's sake."

The vehicle entered the clearing, pulling to a halt five hundred yards away. The two front doors opened; the driver and another man exited the vehicle. Each of the men were dressed in a green uniform with a tan bulletproof vest. The passenger produced a gleaming Kalashnikov assault rifle. The two men then moved to the front of the car.

"That's a little bit high-tech for them isn't it?" Zero pointed out. "These guys must be on some heavy-duty payroll – that car isn't standard issue."

The two men stood patiently by their SUV for a few minutes. One man took the opportunity to light up a cigarette, neither of them aware of the crosshairs hovering over their heads. Zero put one hand to his ear, activating the radio hidden inside.

"This is Whisky Oscar One, we have Yankee Two in range, no sign of Yankee One, over."

Zero's radio crackled into life as a female voice with an English accent belonging to Operator 'Sam' came through clearly.

"Whisky Oscar One, this is Whisky Oscar Two; be advised Yankee One has entered the field."

As she finished her sentence a second vehicle entered the valley, this time from ahead of the sniper team's position. This one was a dirty white sedan that screeched through the valley kicking up dust and dirt into a thin cloud that followed the car. The sedan slid to a halt twenty yards from the first group. Three men exited the car, moving fast, frantically yelling to the two from the first car, waving Kalashnikovs. They moved round to the back of the sedan, opening the boot and pulling out a badly beaten fourth man in a blood-soaked white shirt.

"Shit, that's our guy!" Zero cursed.

The beaten informant was thrown to the ground in front of the first two men. The leader of the trio began to angrily converse with the two men waving a large silver handgun around in the air. Zero raised his voice as he spoke into his mic again.

"All teams mission critical, they're about to execute our man. Sam, I need you to reposition and prepare to engage on my mark. Wolfman, when we hit them, I need you to get down there and grab our guy. We shoot first and ask questions later. I'll take the heat from Big B."

Zero was greeted with an assortment of affirmatives from the other members of the team.

"No time, Zero, they're going to execute him now," Sharpe croaked.

Sharpe levelled his sights over the leader who was pressing the silver handgun into the back of the informant's head. The other team members weren't in position. The informant was crying on his knees begging for his life.

Wolfman, another private military soldier, had positioned himself amongst the rocks just a hundred yards from the exchange. Wolfman slowly and cautiously levelled his own assault rifle at the chest of the executioner. The younger Spanish soldier's less experienced hands trembled as adrenalin began to flood his system.

The informant cried out as the leader of the second militia group started to squeeze the trigger. The handgun clicked. The informant screamed as he fell to the floor and the executioner stepped back, trying to pull back the slide and clear the jam. Zero looked over to Sharpe.

"Send it."

Sharpe exhaled; he slowly squeezed the trigger of his rifle. A 7.62mm bullet left Sharpe's rifle and disintegrated the left eye of the executioner as the man turned back to finish the informant. The back of the executioner's skull exploded as the bullet tore clean through his head. Before the other militiamen could realise what was happening a second shot tore into the chest of one of the leader's guards. Wolfman opened fire as well, firing his weapon on single-shot mode with expert precision. He put two rounds into the third uniformed guard and then began firing at the last two men, who started running for cover. The informant scrambled behind the SUV while the two remaining men were finished by a combination of rifle fire. Wolfman raced across the open ground to the SUV. He moved so fast he had to dig the heels of his boots into the ground before he slammed into the side of the vehicle. He held his rifle in one hand and used the other to slam the informant against the SUV.

"Star!" Wolfman yelled.

The informant, however, kept snivelling and crying. Wolfman released his grip and took hold of his rifle with both hands, keeping the barrel at the head of the informant.

"Star or I will shoot!"

The informant managed to stutter out the word.

"T-Texas."

Wolfman lowered his weapon and checked the frightened man over. Zero let out a sigh of relief before patting Sharpe on the back a couple of times.

"Remind me to never doubt you again!"

Suddenly Zero's earpiece crackled into life as Sam's voice came through again.

"Boys, get out of there, we've got technicals incoming."

Two civilian pickup trucks fitted with long fifty-calibre machine guns raced into the valley. From two thousand yards away, they opened fire. Too far away to be accurate, the rounds impacted the ground around the SUV that Wolfman was hiding behind. Zero looked over at Sharpe and extended his arms as if to say 'do something'.

"Out of range," Sharpe coldly answered.

Sharpe still didn't flinch from the rifle's scope. He once again made an adjustment and shifted his aim slightly higher.

Zero reattached his rifle to his sling and started rapidly making his way down the hill, cursing loudly with every step.

"Big B, we're in trouble, enemy armour closing on our position! Requesting immediate exfiltration!" Zero barked the words into his microphone but received no answer.

Zero reached the bottom of the valley and took aim. The truck was still out of range, leaving his weapon useless. Bullets from the trucks snapped at the air around his head and tore into the rocks of the cliff behind him. Zero dropped to his belly and returned fire, in a desperate attempt to suppress his enemy. Wolfman tried to run to him but another burst of gunfire forced him back into cover behind the SUV. The technicals closed to nine hundred yards of the exchange, which was also the precise point Sharpe had set his sights on. A volley of high-velocity rifle rounds slammed into the windshield of the first vehicle, one hitting the driver in the chest. He slumped down onto the wheel, forcing the truck into a sharp turn. The move was too fast, the vehicle violently flipped over, crushing the gunner as it rolled to the side of the road. The second vehicle hit the brakes hard, skidding to a halt just ahead of the first, leaving the crew an easy shot for the overlooking sniper. Sharpe delivered the remainder of his twenty-round magazine into the gunner, who felt the impact of a sledgehammer against his chest as a pink mist of blood and bone filled the air.

The driver attempted to leave the truck but took a round to the face sending fragments of bloody skull and teeth across the hood of his machine. Zero ran over to Wolfman and the informant, checking the two men were okay. Sharpe reached the bottom of the hill shortly after, his exo-suit allowing him to clear the distance to his comrades with immense speed. He dropped to his knees beside the SUV and expertly swapped his empty magazine for a new one.

"So that's why they call you Sharpe, then!" Wolfman exclaimed with a wide grin.

Sharpe smiled back, his voice taking a slightly more upbeat tone as he spoke to the newest member of the team.

"Don't thank me too much, if they had known how to shoot you'd all be dead." Sharpe looked back past the two machines. There were two more technicals as well as three large trucks now driving into the valley.

"We need to go, can he walk?"

Wolfman looked down at the wounded informant, then back to Sharpe and shook his head. Zero cursed under his breath. He ran around to the front of the SUV. The engine was shredded. Fifty-calibre rounds were originally designed to destroy tanks. Even at this range the SUV's armour did little to stop the shots.

"Contact rear!" Wolfman shouted.

The three soldiers spun their weapons around as two urban-camouflage Humvees screeched to a halt behind them. The doors flew open allowing three older soldiers wearing the same uniform to exit. The squad's leader rushed over to Zero. Big B, more commonly referred to as 'Boss', was an ageing ex-Navy SEAL. His hair had lost almost all of its colour and his face was covered by thick stubble. He held an AR-15 in his hands and wore no headgear. His voice was low and commanding when he spoke.

"Get inside now," he barked.

The soldiers raced into the Humvees, piling themselves into any free space they could find. Zero emptied his rifle's magazine as the vehicles pulled away. The rounds didn't seem to have any effect on the oncoming forces but it made him feel a little better.

Zero and Sharpe were sitting in the back seat; they'd left their doors open allowing the second sniper team to jump in a few yards down the road. Sam, an athletically built woman in her late twenties, jumped into Sharpe's lap with a smile. Her blonde hair was cut short with a few lines shaved into the side for decoration.

"Hey, big boy," she said, raising her eyebrows.

Sharpe pushed her over to the middle seat while her spotter, a young man of about the same age, jumped onto the side of the truck using the door as cover. Call sign Sev was of Russian origin with a shaved head and a red cross on his arm showing he was the team's field medic. The two jeeps beat a hasty retreat, now satisfied they had everyone on board. The Humvees tore up the dirt of the road as their powerful engines easily opened the distance between them and the carnage left in the valley.

◂▸

SONS OF ODIN HEADQUARTERS, TEXAS

Sons of Odin was a private military contracting agency that had made great strides for itself over the last ten years having been established in 2017 by a wounded Navy SEAL. Austin D. Spencer sat in his favourite room in the building. It was a mission briefing area that he often used as his office, claiming he didn't enjoy the cramped space with his name above the door. The room had been nicknamed the Roundtable thanks to the large circular table that sat in the centre. Behind it stood a large projection screen. Austin himself was in his late fifties; he was sporting a slimming grey suit and walked with a cane. He sat at the far side of the table sipping brandy from a lead crystal tumbler. At the opposite end of the table sat Boss with his feet up fidgeting with a similar glass. Boss had traded his urban camouflage for a smarter black uniform, this time devoid of the exo-suit and weapons. At the far end of the room a blank steel door opened and Zero, the silver-haired soldier from the previous mission, stepped through the opening, closing the door behind him. Like Boss he too was wearing the same sleek black uniform now. His hair had been cut shorter to more of a soldier's length. Zero did his best to keep eye contact with Austin, his father.

"Zach, sit down, we have some things to discuss," Austin instructed.

Zero took a seat beside Boss, making an effort to sit up straight.

"The mission I gave you was not easy, son, I'm sure you know this was deliberate. Like any military operation things went wrong and you very nearly lost an HVT and endangered the lives of your team and yourself through your actions. This is not ideal behaviour for an operator of your calibre."

Boss took over.

"The positioning was good, you were able to cover the exchange point nicely and were even able to sneak Wolfman close enough to the target to apprehend our man. However, you did not account for hostile reinforcements or cover their potential entry points. You screwed up and people could have died because of that."

The two old soldiers looked to Zero awaiting his answer. Zero got back to his feet, stepping away from Boss.

"Yes, sirs, I am aware of my mistake. I would like to include however that I set the design for this run as a snatch-and-dash mission. We eliminated the threat on the ground, acquired the target and Sharpe was able to eliminate the enemy reinforcements before they could inflict any casualties on our team."

Austin and Boss looked at each other. Austin spoke again this time with more authority and anger in his voice.

"Regardless of this, Zach, people nearly died because of you. Had Boss not been operating so close to bail you out, you would have had no exfiltration. In fact, you didn't have an exfiltration plan in your report so had the target been incapacitated, your team would have lost combat efficacy. Had you been dealing with an organised military instead of a few militia, your plan would never have succeeded. The mission would have failed. And their blood, assuming you made it out alive, would have been on your hands. Not only that but a large portion of the operation depended highly on the marksmanship of a single man!"

Zero lost his temper. He slammed a fist into the table and spoke louder, almost shouting at his commander.

"Actually, Dad, I analysed the combat effectiveness of the militia before we started. I looked at their potential inventory and was well aware we were not dealing with an organised military. I took a calculated risk, which last I checked ended with our informant alive along with my full team heading back home without a single scratch."

Zero recomposed himself. He retracted his hand and leant back in his seat knowing he had overstepped the line. Boss had moved one hand over his mouth to hide his smile, having now realised something regarding Zero's plan.

"Zero, how exactly did you plan on getting out of there?" Boss finally asked.

The young man looked over to the Boss with a slight smile.

"It was established in the mission briefing that Boss and a small team were standing by to pick us up should anything go wrong. It made much more sense to me to use them as the extraction force should anything go wrong, that way minimising potential casualties and resources in use for this operation. I, of course, ran my team through this plan and they all agreed it was a wise course of action."

Boss and Austin shared a quick glance.

"Why didn't you think to mention this to us before the mission's start? What if Boss's team were based further back than you calculated?" Austin questioned even though he already knew the answer.

Zero gave him a quick grin.

"Because I know you, Father, and I knew you'd have the Boss close at hand in case something went wrong."

CHAPTER 1

◀▶

THE EYE OF A WARRIOR

Terra Kisaragie, a nineteen-year-old Japanese-English student stood amongst the shuffling crowds of Moi International Airport of New Mombasa. Terra's flight, along with every other, had been grounded. The crowd had gathered below a large screen broadcasting the local news report. A news reporter on the screen was speaking the local language, which Terra couldn't understand. However, the images on screen, showing a missile hitting a passenger airliner, gave her all the information she needed.

Terra brushed a strand of dyed black hair from her eyes and pushed through the growing crowd until she reached the safety of the terminal's glass wall, which provided a clear view of the aircraft across Moi's runways. She clutched a leather satchel that hung around her hip making sure that nothing had been taken; fortunately, the bag's strap remained securely buckled. She was distracted briefly as a pair of children came rushing past her, laughing and chirping to each other in a language she didn't recognise. A woman who was presumably a parent called out after the children before returning to her heated discussion down her mobile phone. The terminal was littered with small such incidents; a newlywed couple sat at one of the benches rubbing noses and giggling excitedly much to the displeasure of the overweight man sitting beside them who was desperately trying to lose his thoughts in his newspaper. In an attempt to distract herself, Terra looked out at the runway again; not a single plane was in the air. A couple of large commercial aircraft had been towed to the side and one sat with its engines running, but clearly none of them were going anywhere anytime soon.

Terra's deep-brown eyes fell upon an unusual sight sitting across the main runway: two small jet aircraft that didn't match the rest of the large passenger airliners. They were smaller, clearly designed for one person, with sleek surfaces and wide wings. The aircraft were painted a pale grey and were guarded by military-looking personnel on either side.

"F-22 raptors, one of most advanced fighter jets on the planet right now."

The voice belonged to one of Terra's classmates, Billy. Billy's hair was short and brown, and he had a warm smile across his chubby face.

"You think they're here because of the missile attack?" Terra questioned.

Billy shook his head and shrugged.

"No, those are American planes, they shouldn't be here at all. Anyway, Professor Marcos called the hotel. It looks like we're sleeping here tonight."

Though Terra asked the question she only half listened to the answer. She kept looking out of the window at the two fighter jets. Her gaze switched when she noticed more military vehicles on the runway. She recognised the design from one of her father's old war movies as a Black Hawk helicopter. In total, three helicopters occupied the runway, they didn't have any nation's markings, instead just the letters 'S.O.O.'

"Hey, Billy?" frowned Terra with concern, still looking at the helicopters. "What do those markings mean?"

Billy took a long look, trying to decipher the letters. After the short, overweight American tried stringing together a few military-sounding words, he gave up. Billy shrugged and the pair decided it would be best to return to the rest of their class.

Fourteen students had all come to visit the new Kenya along with their teacher Professor Marcos. He was an ageing ex-Navy SEAL in his early fifties, and walked with a cane because of an injury from a bullet wound that had ended his career. Or at least that was what the students' current running theory was, as the teacher refused to let any information slip regarding his military career. He was yelling down a mobile phone at somebody whom the students assumed was from the same hotel they had been staying in over their trip.

Terra sat on the floor in front of one of the few classmates other than Billy that she could actually tolerate. Grace was skinnier and slightly taller than Terra with blonde hair and a sort of girl-next-door look about her that made Terra feel far larger than she actually was.

"Hope you like sleeping on the ground, cos we aren't getting our beds back," Grace moaned.

Terra didn't get a chance to answer as they were interrupted by one of the class jocks, an American football player named Bradley Morrison.

"If we have to start sharing beds, Grace, you and your chubby girlfriend can always bunk with me."

Grace smiled a little, while Terra rolled her eyes and looked away in disgust, though she subconsciously laid one hand on her stomach.

"Leave them alone, Brad," Billy called out as he stood up and approached the jock, who was a good foot taller than him. Brad simply laughed. He was taller, broader and could bench-press Billy any day of the week if he so chose.

"You feel like saying that to my face, pipsqueak?"

Billy squared up to Brad moving closer to the massive jock and doing his best to seem tough. Terra stood up and tried to get between the two but was pushed away by Billy.

A few feet away a soldier had been leaning against the glass window curiously watching the students' exchange. When the jock started squaring up to the chubby kid, he decided enough was enough. He called out in a well-spoken British accent.

"It's a bit cowardly to pick on someone half your size, don't you think?"

The soldier was dressed in his smart black uniform. He had no weapons or any of his usual military equipment. His smartness made him look out of place in this environment.

"Sorry to interrupt. I just don't particularly like seeing anyone get bullied, is all."

He made an effort to say the words clearly so his accent didn't confuse the American as he approached.

"What the fuck are you supposed to be?" Brad grunted. He turned to face the young man whom he didn't realise was a very well-trained soldier.

The soldier came to a halt a few metres from Brad, now satisfied he had pulled the bully's attention away from the students.

"I'm the guy who's going to make you look really stupid in front of those girls unless you apologise," he said with a cocky grin and a wink he gave to Terra.

Terra blushed slightly and tried to look away. But she was both too worried and too curious to see what would happen next to avert her gaze completely. She had an especially difficult time pulling her gaze away from the soldier's piercing eyes as they locked on to Brad.

"I think he's military," she whispered to Grace, who was too busy watching the exchange to pay her any attention.

Brad advanced on the soldier, muttering a curse under his breath. He took a swing at Sharpe who moved under the fist, barged his shoulder into the jock and used his momentum to throw Bradley Morrison over his shoulder and onto the ground with a loud thump that echoed through the terminal. As Brad tried to recover, the soldier dropped on top of the bully and slammed a knee under his chin, holding him in place.

"I'm still waiting for that apology," he growled as he started to add pressure.

The soldier's greying superior pushed through the crowd that had started to gather around the two men's exchange.

"Sharpe!" he bellowed.

Sharpe released his grip on Brad. The bully pulled himself back to his feet and moved to take another swing at Sharpe but stopped himself when he noticed the soldier didn't even flinch. The defeated bully skulked away to the back of the class. Professor Marcos cut his phone call short and came to see what was causing all the trouble. He met the gaze of the two men in black.

"Well, I didn't think I'd be seeing you here, Boss!"

Professor Marcos and Boss exchanged a hug and their greetings to each other. The students looked on in bewilderment as the two men excitedly shook each other's hands as they swapped compliments and questions about what they had been up to over the years. Sharpe stood a few feet away from the two men with his arms crossed. Terra found herself drawn to the young man. She moved over towards him but stopped in her tracks when the soldier looked at her. Terra did her best to stutter out her question as she felt her chest start to feel heavier.

"Uh… I… um, I was just wondering what you'd have done if your boss hadn't stepped in?"

Sharpe didn't give her a direct response; he just smiled and extended an open hand.

"Name's Sharpe, private military contractor."

Terra cocked her head but accepted his handshake, starting to feel more confident. He didn't seem so bad. His face now held a smile that she found rather enigmatic.

"Terra Kisaragie, student from Philadelphia."

She briefly looked into the soldier's eyes as she spoke. His gaze left her breathing ragged and unsteady; her body tensed up slightly as he spoke.

"Not with that accent you're not, Miss Kisaragie, you sound more like you're from my neck of the woods."

Terra went to say something but her attention was grabbed by Professor Marcos.

"Okay boys and girls, it looks like we've been saved. First off let me introduce an old friend of mine. This is Boss; we worked together back when we were in the military. He and his team are running a few security operations in the city following the attack and have some extra rooms at a local hotel for us to stay in. Some of you will have to share but you'll all have a bed for the next few nights at least. Grab your bags and meet me out the front at 6pm. Until then, do what you want, just don't cause any trouble."

The students split off into their various groups and headed in their own directions.

Professor Marcus stayed with Boss at the airport to meet a few of his soldiers. Terra turned back to Sharpe, while Billy waited nearby, trying to look like he wasn't keeping an eye on the soldier. Sharpe shot him a brief, curious glance.

"I'm from Luton," Terra said. Sharpe watched the others separate; he smiled at Terra.

"Do you normally lie when you're nervous, Miss Kisaragie, or is there more to it than that?"

Terra tensed up again.

"Sorry, people talking about my size unsettles me."

Sharpe cocked his head and ran his gaze up and down her. Terra was about average height for a woman; she wasn't the slimmest girl in the group but it would still have been a stretch to say she was overweight.

"I'm not sure why, you look better than the rest of your classmates to me."

Terra let out the tiniest of gasps as she felt her cheeks burn red. The soldier chuckled.

"Sorry, see you around, Miss Kisaragie."

Sharpe turned away and started walking back the way he came with his hands in his pockets. Terra let out a long sigh as Billy strolled over.

"Geez, do you want a tissue to wipe up that drool?"

◀▶

Terra and Billy made their way further into the terminal. It was still early, leaving them plenty of time to themselves. They found an empty bench at the far side of the building. Terra reached into her bag and pulled out a large notebook. She had customised the cover with doodles and drawings of various people, both real and fictional. A small portrait of Audrey Hepburn sat in the bottom left corner, the top right corner was occupied by *The Fellowship of the Ring* and a long serpent-like dragon slithered its way around her name. She opened the book and began working her way through the pages. She eventually reached a blank page with the title 'Heroes of Today.'

"Are you seriously working on that now?" Billy condescendingly asked.

Terra ignored him. She twiddled a cheap biro in her fingers. The project had been set for them by Professor Marcos just before the summer break. Terra had no clue of where to begin with this project. The idea was simple: each student had to produce a report on a hero of recent history. More importantly, they had to explain their reasoning for this person being a hero. While the rest of Terra's class turned to the media and their families to draw up half-arsed reports on why their parents were the real heroes for raising them, Terra wanted something grittier and more original, preferably something happening that not many people were aware of.

"Your old man's ex-military, right? Just write about him, get him to tell you some story of how he killed a bunch of guys and charged through fire like a real hero," Billy suggested with just a little too much excitement.

Terra shook her head.

“My dad doesn’t like to talk about his time in the military,” she murmured. “But I guess that’s what happens when you tour Afghanistan.”

She fell silent again, blocking out Billy’s voice and slipping back into her mind. He said something about going to find one of the others, to which Terra gave a short, half-hearted farewell.

Billy thought about trying for a hug but decided it was best not to. Terra waited until a few minutes after he left before she looked up from the page. The airport was beginning to quieten down as those who had places to go went to them, and those who were staying began to settle down. Terra looked over at the window opposite her, drawn to it by a loud, low rumbling noise. The two fighter jets had taxied onto the runway. She also noticed in the distance that there were far more security personnel patrolling the outskirts. Although she couldn’t properly see from this distance, it was very clear that they were armed. Something caught her attention in the corner of her eye. Sharpe was looking out of the window writing something into a small black notepad. He was now wearing an assault vest filled with large rifle magazines and even a few grenades. Sharpe carried his sniper rifle across his back. He also sported a pair of black sunglasses as well as his boonie hat.

Moi Airport was something truly spectacular. The new terminal was gleaming white with barely a speck of dust or dirt anywhere. The view outside was also stunning; just beyond the airport’s gates was a vast and beautifully inviting ocean. But Terra didn’t care much about any of that right now, she was far too invested in the soldier scanning the airfield. It was hard to tell for sure but he didn’t appear to look down as he wrote in his pad.

Sharpe removed the sunglasses and slid them into one of the pouches on his vest.

"I see you, quiet girl," Sharpe announced.

The soldier slid his notebook into one of his webbing pouches as he moved towards Terra, his presence making Terra's chest feel weighted.

"I'm sorry, I shouldn't have disturbed you," Terra apologised.

Sharpe held up a hand as he sat on the bench beside her, resting his weapon between his legs.

"That seems a little big for security work, doesn't it?" Terra asked.

Sharpe looked down at his rifle; he checked the safety catch and pulled back the weapons bolt, showing Terra the empty chamber above the magazine.

"My company has a pretty open contract with the local government," he said. "It helps in a way. One sword keeps another in the sheath."

Terra nodded slowly, still feeling intimidated by the size of the rifle.

"So, you're a samurai as well as a sniper?" she mocked playfully.

Sharpe chuckled. He moved the weapon over to his side leaning it up against the chair beside him so it was out of Terra's sight.

"So, what's a girl from Luton doing with a bunch of Americans in Africa?"

"Oxford," Terra replied. "My father told me not to trust mercenaries, especially the type trying to get into my pants."

Sharpe smirked; his smile widened revealing a set of perfect white teeth. Terra couldn't help but smile slightly herself.

"I've never been one for that kind of thing, Miss Kisaragie."

"Why? You gay or something?" Terra blushed slightly as she realised her words had come out more aggressively than she had intended. The soldier chuckled again.

"No, I'm not. Sorry, Miss Kisaragie, I'll leave you to your notes."

Sharpe stood up to leave but Terra grabbed his shirtsleeve to stop him.

"Wait, don't go!"

Terra blushed again. Her cheeks were beginning to hurt from all the extra blood flow. "I'm sorry, I'm really not very good at all this stuff…"

"What stuff, Miss Kisaragie?" Sharpe said with a wink and a smile.

Terra took the opening; in her mind she sighed with relief. She couldn't remember the last time she had felt so drawn to someone of the opposite sex.

"Do you mind if I draw you?"

"Draw me?"

"Well, your eyes specifically."

She could tell by the look Sharpe gave her that he wasn't expecting that question. The soldier shifted his body round to face her so that she could get a better view of him.

"That's perfect!"

Terra decided to use the same page. She swapped her pen for a thin pencil and began shaping the outline of Sharpe's eye.

"I'm really sorry about this, it's just… I don't mean to sound so forward but you have really beautiful eyes!"

Sharpe chuckled but still managed to keep his head steady for Terra to concentrate. She noted his level of control was incredible.

"I'm glad my eyes captivate you, Miss Kisaragie, but what is it about them you like so much?" Sharpe enquired.

"Terra, and it's a lot of things. They're piercing, like almost inhuman; you have such deep colour it looks almost unnatural. Oh gosh, sorry, I mean that in a good way. Looking at your eyes is like looking into those of a wolf… good match for a sniper."

Sharpe's smile dropped slightly. Terra continued swapping her gaze from his eyes to her pad. She was still finding it very difficult to look away for too long.

"You're very lucky to have eyes like that," Terra continued. "They're a lot more interesting than my muddy brown."

"I wouldn't say that. I find a lot of comfort in deep-brown eyes like yours. I can't help but relax a little more each time I look, it gives me a warm feeling. Safe, I guess would be the word."

Terra smiled again; she giggled bashfully and looked away from him.

"So, Mr Sharpe, when you're not in the field what do you do?"

"Sharpe isn't my real name, you know."

Terra paused for a moment as she felt a little silly for not catching the soldier's call sign.

"I spend a lot of my time training. I'm always trying to progress and get better at what I do and when I'm not doing that, I tend to bury my head in a book and forget the rest of the world exists."

"Would I be right in guessing there are a lot of military stories on your bookshelf?" Terra asked.

"You would, but honestly I'll read anything from Shakespeare to *Game of Thrones*."

Terra excitedly went to ask another question but Sharpe cut her off.

"I'm only on *A Storm of Swords* though, so no spoilers!"

Terra chuckled and flipped her notebook around to show Sharpe the perfect sketch of his left eye. Above that in cursive letters she had written, 'The eye of a warrior'.

"That's incredible! Though I'm not exactly a warrior, I'd just stick with soldier."

"You don't fancy yourself as a warrior?"

"No," Sharpe solemnly replied. "A warrior fights with honour and puts that honour before his life. He looks his enemy in the eye and gives him a chance to fight back. I've been blessed with the gift of being able to kill a man from far away with a single bullet. He'd never know I was there. There's no honour in that."

Sharpe looked down at her notebook page's title.

"Heroes project, huh?"

"Mm-hmm!" Terra replied excitedly as she noticed Sharpe's interest in the title.

"Extra credit project, give a short presentation of someone you consider a hero of today. I thought maybe 'The Private Military Contractor Sniper' would make for a good title."

Sharpe shrugged.

"I'm afraid I'll have to disappoint you a second time today. Like I said, there's not much honour in this line of work."

"You never hear much about PMCs on the news," Terra interrupted, "but my dad told me a little about them. Brave men sent into the most hostile environments where it would be too dangerous for regular soldiers to go. It all sounds like something out of a film!"

"That's a very romanticised version of it," Sharpe replied. "We spend most of our time running security details for oil workers or fighting off pirates looking to grab tourists for ransom money."

Terra sighed as she leant forward towards Sharpe, dropping her voice to a lower, more seductive tone, giving the sniper a clearer view of her cleavage. A trick she'd learnt from Grace but never had the guts to use herself.

"You mean you've never charged headfirst into the fire to save your comrades?"

Though Terra felt a little embarrassed, her move worked. Sharpe took a hold of his rifle. He tossed the weapon between his hands as the memories came back to him. He let out a long, sad sigh before he spoke.

"It was in my first year of fieldwork… a squad of US marines had ventured too far into hostile territory in Tajikistan and got themselves pinned down in a valley close to the Russian lines. My team and I were sent in to evacuate them."

CHAPTER 2

WAR STORIES

Sharpe kept tossing his rifle's barrel between his hands. He fidgeted uncomfortably as he spoke but powered through with a slight smile all the same.

"I'd only been on a few missions prior to this one. I'm not actually allowed to tell you how many. Anyway, at this time our armies didn't have a foothold in Tajikistan. There was a lot of suspicion that hostile groups were operating out of the country but it was hard to get any solid proof. Despite this there were a lot of patrols around the border and eventually some into the outskirts of the country. The marines had overextended their patrol and gone and found themselves out of their area of operations, pinned down by some angry farmers with a lot of guns. We happened to be stationed nearby. This incident could have caused a lot of trouble if certain other nations had caught on to there being American soldiers pushing up into turf that wasn't theirs. So, we got the job."

Terra was making notes in her notebook; she stopped as Sharpe paused and started murmuring some numbers to herself.

"Wait, Sharpe when did this happen?" Terra stopped herself as another thought struck her mind.

"How old are you?"

It was a question she wished she'd asked herself from the beginning. The soldier looked young but that may have only been because he was clean-shaven. In this light and without his smile, Sharpe looked older. The soldier nodded.

"This all happened in 2021, six years ago… I was eighteen, soon to be nineteen."

Terra steadily released a breath of relief. That made Sharpe twenty-four years old.

"My spotter Sam was sitting opposite me checking over her weapon," Sharpe continued. "We'd all been briefed before we took off so there wasn't much conversation. I'm telling you, the anticipation is worse than the fighting itself. When you're out there under fire, you know what to do. Your body runs on instinct. It's sitting in that helicopter with nothing but the beating sound of propeller blades to keep you company and the occasional nod from the guy next to you that gets you. The helicopter was winding and weaving as close to the ground as they could safely get to make us less of a target. The whole time we were sitting there twiddling our thumbs hoping someone with a rocket launcher wasn't paying attention. At that altitude, in those mountains, you have no chance of walking away if it goes down.

"The pilot called out 'Thirty seconds' and everyone's weapons started clicking; rounds got pushed into chambers and even the toughest sons of bitches held their breath as the chopper started slowing down. At ten seconds the helicopter reared up as it slowed to a halt; at five seconds it levelled out and we had just enough time to pull open the doors before Boss started screaming 'Go'. Before I had time to realise what was happening, I was on the ground, rifle raised, as the rest of the team dropped down around me. Someone tapped me on the shoulder and we started moving. The squad moved in a line at double pace. We approached the school. Sam and I went to the left, while Boss led the rest of the team down to the marines. There was a lot of fire coming from that school. We were a good seven hundred metres out, which is a little too far for me to just start taking shots. There are too many variables at that range."

Sharpe paused to catch his breath; his expression changed for a moment as he recalled something he didn't seem to like.

"There was one muzzle flash that was different from the others. I knew he was an enemy sniper; his shots were all aimed with terrifying precision. He dropped one of the marines with a round that ricocheted off the base of this guy's helmet. That was the last straw for me. I watched this soldier go down; he couldn't have been any older than me. I was wearing an earlier version of this exo-suit you see me in now; back then they were still in the field-testing stage but it still helped me clear the distance to the school pretty quickly. The hardest part of that run was stopping."

Sharpe ran a hand over his mouth as he took a moment to compose himself; his voice was more of a croak now.

"We can stop," Terra said. "You don't have to continue if you don't want to."

Sharpe forced a smile and waved his hand in an effort to reassure Terra he was all right.

"Breaching a door is the most dangerous thing a soldier can do. Especially when you're not familiar with the building. There are countless things that can go wrong. I grabbed one of the grenades from my belt, pulled the pin and started counting. The grenade should go off after five seconds. Five seconds is a long time for someone to get out of the way though so I waited until three seconds before I tossed the grenade through the door, which was now hanging off its hinges thanks to a kick from my suit.

"The explosion left my ears ringing and my head pounding, but I rushed into the doorway anyway. I fired at the silhouettes in the smoke, I didn't bother to count them. I headed straight for the stairs, leaving a couple of flash grenades to roll down the corridors on either side of me as I went."

Sharpe stopped and cleared his throat. He fiddled with his fingers nervously as he stuttered out the words.

"I-It was when I cleared the stairs… there was this boy, couldn't have been more than fourteen years old." The soldier looked a lot older to Terra all of a sudden as he sighed and composed himself. "He was holding a Kalashnikov AK-47 in his hands."

"What did you do?" Terra asked cautiously, making sure to hold back her excitement about the tale she was being told. Sharpe pulled down his boonie hat over his eyes to hide them from Terra. He forced a smile but the tone of his voice was enough for her to go on.

"I shook my head. Back then I didn't know much Arabic… I told him 'No'. But he didn't listen, and I did what I had to do. Not exactly heroic, though right?"

"Sharpe…" Terra started, "what you did saved the lives of those marines! All those men went back home to their families because of you!"

Sharpe lifted up his hat as he wiped his face with a firm hand.

"That's one way of looking at it. Of course, they were never meant to be there in the first place, I got the ever-loving shit kicked out of me by Boss because of what I did. But yeah, a bunch of men went back home to their families because of me. But because of me, a bunch of men who were just trying to protect their homes from the Western invaders didn't go home to theirs…"

Terra instinctively and suddenly placed a hand over Sharpe's as he fiddled with his weapon.

"My dad was a soldier too. But he doesn't talk about his time in the military much. I think he must have done some things too but he's still a hero to me, and that's all that matters."

Terra smiled. Sharpe responded with a low, warm chuckle.

"Yeah… maybe. Still, I hope that helps with your project, Miss… sorry, Terra."

"Well, well, what's all this then?"

Terra immediately withdrew her hand as Grace approached with a wide grin on her face and her arm through that of a soldier with silver hair. Sharpe flinched slightly when he noticed Zero with the student. Zero took a moment to introduce himself.

"Hi there, I'm Zero. Thanks for looking after Sharpe. I hope he didn't bore you too much."

Sharpe shot Zero an irritated glance.

"Not at all. He's been a big help and a joy to talk to," Terra replied.

Zero nodded a few times.

"Did he tell you about his really big…"

"Oi."

"What?" Zero replied with a wide grin. "I was only gonna say gun."

Zero motioned for Sharpe to follow him and the pair moved away from the girls to talk in private. Grace took Sharpe's seat beside Terra. She had a very excited look on her face.

"Oh, get you. The English girl finds the English soldier," she chirped.

Terra laughed, not taking Grace too seriously.

"I didn't realise you were a grey fox kind of girl," Terra teased.

Grace smiled, biting her lip and rolling her eyes playfully.

"He's only twenty-six, some kind of genetic thing; all the boys in his family have it. I was paying more attention to the rest of him if I'm being honest."

The two girls giggled quietly, keeping an eye on the soldiers to make sure they weren't watching.

"So how was Mr Tall, Dark and Handsome?" Grace said, now forcing Terra into the spotlight. "I've never seen you smile so much around a guy before."

Terra pondered the thought. She couldn't deny that Sharpe had an effect on her. Her heart had been racing during their conversation, leaving her feeling very heated up.

"It's been a really long time since I've let a boy into my life, I'm not sure if I'm ready for all that again."

Terra watched the soldiers talk for a moment. Zero was very emotive and animated with his movements but had a wide happy smile on his face, while Sharpe stood very still, listening with only a slight grin on his face.

"Honey, that there ain't no boy," Grace interjected. "That's a man!"

"Yeah, I guess I wouldn't mind seeing more of him," Terra concluded.

Terra kept watching the two soldiers. They were speaking too quietly from too far away for her to hear, but she did notice Zero push a finger to his ear. Probably to touch a microphone she couldn't see. The two soldiers' expressions changed and they made their way back over to the girls. Zero muttered something to Sharpe with a wide grin that made the sniper fall back half a step and shake his head. Zero stepped forward and bowed to the two girls. He spoke with a highly exaggerated British accent that made Sharpe cringe.

"I am sorry to be the bearer of bad news, fair maidens, but it would appear we are needed elsewhere. But fear not for we shall reunite later this afternoon to escort you to your chambers."

Zero moved off first; Sharpe watched him for a moment as he started to jog then shook his head at the two girls.

"Sorry, running joke," he said before turning and moving at a similar pace.

"He's a bit of a goofball," Terra mumbled.

"He can be as goofy as he wants with abs that hard," Grace responded.

The two girls laughed together as young women do. Grace revelled in the chance to talk to Terra about the opposite sex, since she'd never shown any interest in the guys from their classes. Terra felt her phone start to vibrate in her pocket. She pulled out the device and looked at Billy's face now appearing on the screen. Terra accepted the call and put the phone to her ear.

"Terra! Hey, you better get back to the boarding gate quick!"

"Billy, what's wrong?"

"Trust me," Billy said, completely unable to hold his composure. "You will really want to see this."

Terra and Grace made their way back to their boarding gate. Sharpe and Zero were already there. The two soldiers stood near the window Terra had been looking out of earlier. They were watching a man talking to Boss and, strangely, Professor Marcus. Billy emerged from the gathering crowd and rushed over to talk to the girls. Terra looked around as he approached; there were a number of other soldiers dotted around all wearing the same Sons of Odin uniform.

"Terra, are you blind? Look!" Billy forcefully whispered.

He pointed towards a third man speaking to her professor and Boss. Terra had been too focused on trying to pick out the soldiers to realise who her teacher had been talking to.

Terra looked into the warm face and crystal-blue eyes of Nathan Kebal. She held her hands over her mouth to muffle the excited sounds that followed.

"No wonder these guys are packing so much heat," Billy commented.

"What's he doing at an airport? With that much money I'd have my own private runway!" someone in the crowd murmured to another.

Terra's attention was grabbed as a soldier pushed past them through the crowd again dressed in the same uniform as Sharpe and Zero. Sharpe himself had also relocated and was now slowly patrolling up and down the long glass window, tapping his finger on the trigger guard of his rifle.

"I don't get it, is he a musician or something?" Grace asked. She spoke loudly enough to attract a few displeased looks from the people in the crowd around them.

"He's the man who turned clean-burning eco fuel into a reality. Nobody's too sure where he got the original investment or why he chose to set up his first factory here, but he changed the economy of the whole continent. They say in the next twenty years oil will be completely replaced within the First World because of him."

Terra stopped herself when she realised she was rambling. Grace shrugged, unimpressed.

"There are also a few rumours flying around that he's immortal," Billy added.

Grace gave him a confused look. Terra rolled her eyes.

"It means he'll live forever."

"I know what it means!" Grace shot back with indignation.

The students weren't the only ones who had taken notice. The press showed up. A pair of older soldiers moved to block the reporter and her cameraman, but were stopped by Kebal. The reporter was a powerful-looking dark-haired woman who held a wireless microphone in her hand.

"Mr Kebal, do you have anything to say regarding the terrorist attack?"

Kebal spoke with a low, booming voice that radiated with authority.

"I do not believe 'terrorist' is the correct term; this attack was clearly an act of aggression by another nation. I will be talking to the Minister of Defence and NATO officials to confirm the situation. Until then I'd suggest everyone stay calm and not jump to conclusions."

A low rumbling echoed through the building as a jet aircraft flew overhead. The soldiers changed positions again. This time they moved with more urgency; Zero directed a few men with hand signals. Terra meanwhile was too focused on Nathan Kebal as he continued to answer questions from the reporter.

"I thought he was a businessman; I didn't know he had a hand in the country's politics?" Billy questioned.

"He's had a hand in it since he saved the country's economy. He has more power here than the prime minister. I thought you knew that?" Terra answered.

"Guys!" Grace mumbled. Terra and Billy turned around to see Grace facing the long glass window as a sleek black military attack helicopter screeched past just a few feet off the runway.

"Wow, I didn't realise the local military had KA-52s in their arsenal," Billy proclaimed.

Without missing a beat, as Billy finished his point, a second helicopter descended from above and started hovering easily over the runway across from them. The machine was painted completely black except for a single red star on the side of its fuselage.

"Billy… I don't…" Terra started.

Two pods on opposing wings of the helicopter containing high-calibre machine guns burst into life. The helicopter swept from side to side spraying the terminal with glowing tracer shells. People screamed and ran for cover, but there was little that could protect them. Glass shattered, the concrete floor was torn up and bits of meat were forcefully removed from people in large bloody chunks as the bullets mercilessly tore the airport's visitors to pieces.

The helicopter pulled off as the soldiers that survived the attack returned fire. Rifle rounds bounced and sparked off the helicopter's thick armour forcing the pilot to leave. Despite the helicopter's departure, the screams and gunshots remained as people panicked, escaping the chaos.

Terra's legs gave out from under her; she dropped to her knees as her body became overwhelmed with shock. The right side of her face was hot from blood. She put a hand to her cheek to feel the wound but found only her bloodstained skin.

The blood wasn't hers. She looked down at her bloody hands as her senses began to return; her ears filled with the sounds of the carnage around the terminal. There was more shooting coming from further down the terminal, only it was more ragged and varied. There were two sides shooting at each other now.

Sharpe appeared from the chaos to kneel down in front of Terra.

He had to yell over the sounds of the gunfire; the soldiers were now shooting at something to her right. Terra tried to turn to see but was pulled back by Sharpe.

"Don't look, okay. Just run that way!"

He pointed to the exit on her left. Terra's gaze fell to her right as the thought set in that her friends had been standing beside her when the shooting started. Sharpe forced her head back around towards the exit.

"Listen to me, you run and you do not look back!" Sharpe screamed.

"Sharpe, get the fuck over here now!" a voice yelled from the right.

Terra got to her feet and started to run. As she stepped off she felt something slam into her lower leg. She fell to the ground and her head hit the blood-coated floor.

Terra's vision became a blur; her head ached from the impact and she felt a searing pain in her right leg just below the knee. The horrifying realisation began to set in: she had been shot. The frightened young woman ran her hands over the wound in an attempt to stop the bleeding but instead she felt only searing pain. When Terra saw what had happened to Grace, she forgot all about the pain. What had once been her best friend now lay limply on the ground. Her body was littered with shrapnel and blood oozed from multiple wounds.

Her chest had been torn open by a shell from the helicopter and the right side of her head was completely missing.

As Terra raised her hands to cover her mouth a small brass object landed beside Terra, and then another caught her in the face. Terra looked up. The soldiers had formed a staggered line and were firing at something down the terminal, each of them crouched on one knee.

A few wounded civilians tried to stagger between them but were being cut down by returning gunfire. Ahead of Terra and the Son's of Odin men was a new set of soldiers. They wore completely black uniforms with gas masks covering their faces and were firing small machine guns into the crowds, slaughtering anyone unfortunate enough to cross their sights. Terra felt a pair of hands reach in under her armpits; she leant her head back and caught sight of Billy. He too was covered in blood and was trying to pull her away from the fighting.

Sharpe knelt beside them, shuffling back every few seconds to stay closer to Terra and Billy. He adjusted his aim slightly as he moved between targets. His rifle was deafeningly loud, the weapon making a distinctive bass-like sound with every pull of the trigger.

Terra suddenly fell back. Her head didn't hit the floor, it hit something softer. Terra rolled over and saw that she had landed on Billy's lifeless body. She didn't scream; she wasn't sure if she could anymore. Her throat had closed up and her body refused to move. She tried to push herself up to a crawl but was met by another of the black uniform soldiers. This one was running in behind Sharpe and the others, raising his weapon to her. The soldier's mask cracked open along with his skull in a haze of red mist. Another hand hit Terra, this time pushing her back down. She managed to turn her head to see Sharpe firing his weapon in the direction of the mysterious soldiers. Several more soldiers ran through the exit to meet Sharpe's rifle as they tried to cut off the escape for anyone inside the terminal.

Terra's head felt heavy, her mouth tasted of iron and her body was slowly losing more and more feeling. When the helicopter returned Terra simply watched through her bloody and blurred vision. Sharpe turned back to the glass window in a futile effort to defend himself and Terra from the helicopter, but it was far too late now. A stream of rockets leapt from the helicopter's wings; they flew over the heads of Terra and Sharpe and exploded off the wall behind them. The last thing Terra remembered, before everything went black, was a wall of flame racing towards her.

CHAPTER 3

◂▸

THE PETRIFIED FOREST

Terra couldn't see anything after the blast, everything had turned black. It was a deep black, an almost comforting black. A black so thick no light could reach her now. There were no stars or moon, there were no shapes of any kind. Just an endless blackness. Terra's entire body felt numb. There was no pain. She tried to move her arms but couldn't detect the movement or even the slightest presence of her limbs. She didn't know if she even had any arms anymore, or legs. She wasn't sure if she'd just been blown into oblivion and there was nothing left of her.

After what felt like a few minutes of drifting through the darkness she began to regain a small amount of feeling in her body. Not a lot at first. It was just enough to let her know her limbs were all still attached.

Terra still didn't feel any pain, but soon she could feel her entire body and then the sensation of falling. The sensation became more and more apparent until eventually Terra could feel the wind blowing past her. She tried to scream, but her body refused. She opened her eyes.

Terra jumped to her feet, panting heavily. She was standing in the middle of a dead forest, surrounded on all sides by petrified trees. There was no green anywhere to be seen; the dirt around Terra's feet was a dull grey and so dry it was almost sand.

Terra looked up at the sky; it was dark here. Alarmingly there was no moon in the sky. Instead the space was occupied by thousands of thin purple lights that seemed to slowly slither their way through the abyss. There were no clouds and it was impossible to tell how far away the lights really were. It was beautiful in its own bizarre way. Had Terra been there under any other circumstances she would have taken the time to marvel at the sky. Instead she stepped back looking around frantically until she backed up against one of the petrified trees. The tree was dry and stripped of most of its bark. Terra spun around to take a closer look. She saw a variety of deep scratch marks in the tree that could have easily belonged to a bear or something of a similar size.

"Okay, okay, stay calm, just stay calm," she repeated out loud to herself.

Terra realised her satchel was still hanging over her shoulder. She dug her hands into the bag to find her phone, which was showing 100% battery. This was very odd as she hadn't charged the device anytime in the last twenty-four hours. Of course, there was no signal.

Terra cursed. She looked around at the trees again. There was no sign of any human presence, though there must have been someone there at some point. If not, then how had she arrived? Terra put her phone away and went about the process of rolling up her right jean leg as memories of her injury flooded her mind. There was no wound. The helicopter and the mysterious soldiers, the sight of her friends' lifeless bodies, and then the explosion. She remembered it all but her leg was fine. Was it all a dream, or was this the dream? Was she dead?

Terra snapped herself out of the thought. It tried hard to force its way to the front of her mind, but she had other things to be concerned about. She was alone in unfamiliar territory. Normally, the best course of action would be to wait for help, but Terra knew there probably wasn't going to be anyone coming to save her.

"Okay, so I'm probably dead but I don't see any flame so I guess this isn't hell," Terra whispered to herself in a calm voice in an effort to give herself some kind of reassurance.

"I don't see any bright lights though, so maybe the old vicar was onto something."

Terra decided her best course of action would be to move. She had no food or water and sitting in the middle of the forest wasn't going to get her anywhere. The young girl picked a random direction and set off. As she made her way through the woods, she didn't hear a sound besides her own footsteps. No birds, no bugs. Nothing at all.

After a few minutes Terra found a small structure. It was a single-storey wooden house with a small porch and a couple of windows. With no other options, Terra decided to investigate. She made her way to the door and knocked a few times.

"Hello? Is anyone in there?"

She received no answer.

Terra grabbed the doorknob and turned the brittle wooden object slowly. The door was unlocked, so she began to push the door open cautiously, peeking through the gap trying to see what was inside. Feeling something small and metallic pressing against the back of her head, Terra stopped and slowly raised her hands, realising it was the barrel of a gun.

"Do not move." The voice was muffled and had an accent Terra didn't recognise.

She was spun round and pressed against the door. A sub-machine gun was being held to her face by a large man in a black military uniform. His head and face were covered by a large gas mask with a tinted visor. Behind him stood another slightly larger man wearing the same uniform, and he too carried a sub-machine gun in his hands.

"Is the other one with you?" the soldier asked with a high sense of urgency.

"I just got here," gasped Terra, shaking her head. "Who are you? What is going on?"

Terra spoke with as much fragile composure as she could manage. The soldier pulled her bag from her shoulder and threw it to one side. He slung his weapon and thrust a hand low between her legs, taking a firm grasp.

"Don't you remember? You died."

Terra tried to scream but the soldier's other hand was thrown across her mouth, and his elbow pinned her arm against the wall. Though she struggled the soldier's strength was far beyond hers. The second larger soldier opened the door and Terra was violently thrown to the floor. She scrambled back in a desperate attempt to get away. She tried to scream again but a gun was raised to her head, forcing her to freeze in place.

"Hush now," demanded the first soldier. "We did not get paid for our last job, so you will pay us instead."

Terra's eyes streamed with tears as her body tensed up. She pleaded with the soldier in desperation. The second soldier stood in the doorway clutching his weapon, trying to distract himself from Terra's desperation.

As Terra looked around the damp and empty house to find something to defend herself with, the soldier standing in the doorway turned to the side. Though she couldn't see his face, she could sense the fear that overwhelmed him as he was ripped from the doorway. The muffled screams filled the ears of Terra, while her assailant turned back to the doorway, readying his weapon. The muffled screams continued. Blood sprayed against the outside of a window beside Terra and everything fell silent. The soldier levelled his machine gun at the wall and emptied the magazine. The bullets tore their way through the wooden walls sending splinters flying out at whatever had dragged the other man out of the building. Terra backed herself into a corner. Waiting a moment, the soldier heard a loud thud as something about man-sized fell to the ground. He moved towards the door slowly, keeping his weapon levelled. As he cleared the doorway and stepped outside, he screamed. Another man, this one taller, slammed an enormous gleaming bowie knife into his gut. The new figure tore the soldier's machine gun out of his hands. The two men tumbled to the ground, grunting loudly. The new figure quickly got the upper hand. In a desperate attempt to fend off his attacker, the soldier grabbed his wrists with both hands, but his oozing wound left him too weak. The new man took hold of the blade with both his own hands and started forcing it down slowly as the soldier struggled against him.

"Please! Please don't… I-I'm sorry!" cried the soldier as the knife moved closer.

Terra's body fell numb; she cried out in panic as the knife plunged down into the chest of the gas-mask-wearing soldier who had pushed her inside. He cried out again as the blade was raised and violently plunged down back into his chest. Though this time he stopped crying. As the new man rose from his victim, panting heavily, Terra got a better look at him. He was tall, clearly wearing black-and-white military camouflage, but his standout feature was a boonie hat pulled low over his eyes.

"Saw them grab you," panted the man in a low rasping voice. "Trust me, you don't want to be with them, Miss…?"

"T-Terra."

Trying desperately to focus, she stuttered out her name, not knowing how to feel, still crying. As the man moved into the light of the window, she realised it was Sharpe. He looked down his nose at her with a puzzled expression.

"What the fuck are you doing here?" growled Sharpe.

Terra heard another voice from outside the building as someone else approached the house. His footsteps were loud and his voice familiar. Terra almost screamed when Billy burst through the door.

"Hey, Sharpe, what's taking so long? Zero is…" Billy stopped mid-sentence, locking eyes with Terra. "Oh my God, Terra?"

Terra fell silent and still.

"Get her on her feet, I'll be outside," Sharpe snapped.

The sniper left the two students alone, closing the door behind him as he left. Billy rushed forward embracing Terra in a tight hug. Any other day, she would have pushed him straight off, but she needed this. Terra embraced him firmly as she let loose the rest of her tears. Sometimes it feels really good to cry.

◂▸

While Billy didn't look as bad as Sharpe, he did look tired. The young lad had also lost a considerable amount of weight. He helped Terra to her feet and escorted her out of the cabin. Billy led Terra into the trees, making sure he stayed close to her.

"We need to stay quiet," Billy whispered.

Sharpe's gloved hand closed over Terra's lips before she could respond. The shock of his sudden appearance combined with the deadly serious look in his eyes made Terra freeze. Sharpe gave her a stern, judgmental gaze for a few seconds, then left her as Zero appeared from the trees. Zero nodded and smiled to Terra; out of the three young men, Zero looked the healthiest. His presence was warming in a way and the air around her felt a little less cold, though it still greatly unsettled Terra that Sharpe and Zero had approached her so silently. She had not had the slightest idea that the two men had been so close.

Zero held up an open hand to Billy who nodded and proceeded after Sharpe taking Terra with him. Zero hung back with his rifle ready watching the small cabin they had discovered Terra in. His gaze briefly moved to the snaking lights in the sky before he followed the others.

The walk through the dead forest was agonising. There were no sounds except for the groups' footsteps. On the few occasions a sound did echo through the trees the line would stop, Sharpe's hand would be raised up and they would stand in total silence. Fear would hold Terra in place until the sniper waved them forward again.

For the best part of an hour Terra was alone to ponder, her mind racing with thoughts she couldn't hold back in her subconscious. The words of the soldier in black were echoing over and over.

"Don't you remember? You died."

Were they dead? If so then why were the soldiers carrying their weapons? And why did she have her bag? And what had happened to Sharpe? He was so different. He was so cold and serious now; were they in danger?

The more Terra watched him the more she felt that she wasn't watching the same man she'd met at the airport. Terra struggled to see Billy in the same light as before now as well. He had always been neat and tidy but now his clothes were torn and dirty. His face was normally smooth, now he badly needed a shave.

Something caught Terra's eye. It moved fast and was only there for a split second. Terra heard two metallic clicks, one in front of her and the other behind as two rifles suddenly levelled in the direction of what she had seen.

Everyone stopped. The two soldiers remained completely motionless. Sharpe slowly dropped to one knee, keeping his weapon raised in the direction of the movement. Billy tapped Terra on the shoulder as cautiously as he could but she still gasped in surprise. Billy nodded towards Sharpe and they slowly started moving toward the sniper. Sharpe's eyes worked back and forth between the trees. Zero joined them. He squatted down beside Sharpe and for a moment the two men seemed to share in a silent conversation before Zero gestured for Billy and Terra to follow him.

Sharpe stayed behind still watching the patch of trees until the group vanished into the darkness. Neither Terra nor Billy realised that Sharpe had caught up to them after another long bout of silent walking. The trees finally started to thin out revealing a string of valleys and hills stretching as far as the eye could see. They were made of the same dull, dry grey dirt as that of the forest floor, only here it was occupied by occasional shrubs spread scarcely amongst a low blanket of dry grass.

"It's not far from here. Just need you to hold on a little longer, okay?" Zero finally said.

He gave Terra a warming smile, which she unsuccessfully tried to return. Terra looked past the soldier at the ground ahead of them. The dirt rose up into a low hill just high enough to block the horizon. Zero looked up over her to Sharpe who was leaning against one of the few trees, facing to the rear.

"Ten-metre spread. You, then the kids in the middle, then me," he commanded to Sharpe.

Terra jumped slightly when she realised the sniper had once again sneaked up on her. Sharpe nodded to Zero. They moved out, beginning to crest the hill. Billy and Terra waited for a few seconds before following. Sharpe led them through the lower levels of the hills for ten minutes. The sniper's weapon was constantly shouldered, its barrel moving aim from the top of one hill to another. His eyes never left the scope. Terra looked back to Zero to see he was doing the same thing.

"We've got a base nearby," Billy croaked. "Once we're there we can answer any questions you have. Well, try to at least."

The low hills cleared into a mostly flat area. A small lonely petrol station with just four pumps sat at the base of a large hill. Vines had reached up from the ground and started wrapping themselves around the structure, working their way into the cracks and crevices within the walls. Terra looked at the station, perplexed, as she tried to piece together in her mind where the building had come from. Billy noted her gaze.

"Trust me," Billy whispered. "Best not to ask how or why. Just be thankful it's here."

Sam, a female soldier with dirty blonde hair tied into a neat bun, sat on top of the hill beside the station. She clutched a scoped rifle in her hands. She used the scope to watch the students advance with Sharpe and Zero flanking them. Sam paid especially close attention to the girl clutching onto Billy's arm.

"It's not actually that dark is it?" Terra whispered.

Billy slowed his pace slightly and started looking around for whatever Terra had seen.

"It's more like some of the colour is missing from the world," Terra continued, talking to no one in particular.

A quick but small flash of light drew Terra's attention. The light was only there for a moment in the corner of her eye but this time it was distinct enough for her to notice something. She stopped walking.

"What's wrong?" Billy asked.

Terra looked around her, trying to spot the moving light again, but it was gone. She shook her head and continued walking. Her gaze met Sharpe's for a moment. The sniper had stopped and was watching her. Sharpe's eyes followed Terra for a few seconds before he sniffed and continued towards the station.

It wasn't long before she could see the distinct orange glow of a small campfire coming from the station. Zero jogged up to the students from the rear.

"Wait here, don't worry, we've got eyes on ya'll," Zero said.

He headed up to the station at double pace. Sharpe on the other hand strolled up the hill towards Sam.

As Zero approached the station, a pair of soldiers emerged to greet him. Terra recognised the larger of the two men as Boss from the airport, looking as commanding as ever. Tall, broad and greying, he radiated authority and power with every step and gesture. The man standing next to him seemed far less impressive by comparison. He was smaller built, with a narrow face and white armbands just above his elbows on each arm, displaying a red cross. Boss called out to them in a deep bellowing voice that made Terra stand up a little straighter.

"All right. Come on over. It's okay, you're safe now."

Terra gripped Billy's arm as he urged her forward.

"Relax, Boss is actually a really cool guy," Billy reassured her.

She walked slowly, her gaze constantly darting around as she tried to survey her surroundings. Billy managed to take hold of one of her hands and squeeze to draw her attention back to him.

"It's okay, they've got this place covered. Nothing can get near us without them seeing it."

Terra thought about that for a second.

"Nothing?"

Billy smiled awkwardly; he released Terra as they reached the two waiting soldiers and moved off towards the station. Terra got a closer look at the soldier with the armbands.

Boss started speaking and drew her attention. His voice was calm, and he tried his best not to intimidate the student.

"Terra, I'm Boss. This is Sev, our team's medic. Now I understand that your time in this place hasn't been the most pleasant..."

"Am I really dead?" Terra interrupted.

Boss looked to Sev who returned a stern gaze. Boss sighed. His expression dropped as he tried to find a gentle way to break the news. Terra looked to Sev.

"I-If I'm dead, why do I need a medic?" she stuttered.

Boss jumped in before Sev could respond.

"Terra… you, me, all of these people are dead."

Terra's heart plummeted into her stomach. The feeling can only be described as if you've ever reached the top of a staircase and expected to find an extra step, only to feel your foot fall through the space the step should have occupied, as your mind tries to comprehend what just happened. Terra struggled to repeat her question again.

"S-So, why… why do I need a medic? How did Sharpe —?"

"Terra."

Sev jumped in, speaking with an instantly recognisable Russian accent though his English was perfect.

"The situation isn't as clear-cut as us… well… simply dying."

Terra lost her words; a few shocked and confused sounds left her mouth. She fell silent again as Boss elaborated.

"You, like the rest of us, woke up wearing the same clothes you had on when… The same thing goes for all of us. That's why we have all of our weapons. Our bodies are also the same in this place as they were before. Cut me, I bleed. A bullet still behaves like a bullet. We need to eat, sleep and breathe in this place just as we did back on Earth."

"And if we don't eat? Or sleep or breathe?" Terra asked.

As she finished her sentence her mind conjured images of the two men in black as they were cut down by Sharpe. She looked over at the top of the hill where Sharpe was now standing beside Sam.

"He killed those men, but that would mean…"

"We can still die here," Sev finished.

A tear ran down Terra's cheek; her throat felt dry and her legs didn't feel so strong anymore.

"Y-You can't be serious."

"Terra," Boss started, "you've seen it. Sharpe put down two men. I know this is a lot…"

In her panicked state Terra started listing off questions as she struggled to comprehend what she had just been told.

"What happens when we die here then? Do we transcend to the next level? What's the point in 'living' here? Why not just eat a bullet and be done with it all?"

"A number of reasons," Sev added, "the main one being we have no idea what will happen. For all we know it could just take us some place worse than this."

Terra shook her head as she tried to fight back tears. "So what, we just hole up here and wait to die?"

Boss and Sev looked at each other. Terra felt as if they didn't want to answer that question.

"We can't," Sev replied.

Terra's eyes shifted between them.

"Why not?"

"Because we're not alone out here," Boss replied. "Limbo seems to have some rather unfriendly inhabitants." Boss took a water canteen from his belt and started unscrewing the cap as he spoke. "There are these…" he struggled to find the right word, "… creatures here. They look human from a distance but up close they're a fucking nightmare."

Sev picked up the line of conversation.

"We've started calling them The Damned. They're not very smart, maybe as strong as an average human, almost as fast but definitely not as dangerous in a small group."

"Kind of sounds like zombies," Terra mocked.

"That's not far from the truth," Boss said. "But don't worry, if they bite you, you don't turn into one of them."

Terra stared at Boss in bewilderment.

"You've got to be fucking kidding me."

Boss smirked.

"I wish I was, kid, their bark's worse than their bite. Especially out here where we can see for a good mile or so around us, but you wouldn't want to face a bunch of them in those trees back there."

Terra was starting to feel faint.

"So, let me get this straight. I'm dead, but I can die again. I'm stuck in a nightmare with a bunch of rapists, murders and zombies, where it's night-time all the damn time and somehow I feel like there's still more bad news."

Boss handed Terra the canteen. Terra took a long gulp of something that definitely wasn't water judging by the way it burned and handed it back to Boss.

"Time gets a little hazy in some areas around here. In fact, depending on where you—" Sev went to continue but Boss interrupted him.

"But that isn't something you have to worry about," the old soldier said, more to Sev than to Terra.

"Got any good news?" Terra groaned sarcastically.

"Look up at the sky," Boss said. "What do you see?"

Terra looked up at the swirling purple lights. She realised she hadn't paid them as much attention as she probably should have.

"They're all moving in the same direction," she said.

"Yeah, Terra, this place isn't hell, we figure it's probably some kind of purgatory, limbo, if you will. Anyway, a little while ago we ran into someone," Boss smiled. "He claimed that the lights were a path to something. Specifically, he said there was a door. A door that leads to a better life than this one."

Terra laughed. She wasn't sure why but her body forced it out of her.

"So, what, you're on a mission to find a door that leads to heaven?"

Boss smiled again; this time it felt more sincere.

"I'm aware of how this sounds, kid. Nobody is going to force you to come with us. If you choose to stay with us, though, I can promise you a shot at a better life. Which is a lot more than you're going to get out here on your own. We can keep you safe, we have food, water and we can offer you protection."

Terra looked back over at the soldiers on top of the hill. Sharpe's boonie hat was pulled down over his eyes but he was still looking over in her direction.

"Sure," Terra said. "What do I have to lose?"

CHAPTER 4

◀▶

INTRODUCTIONS

Terra was escorted back towards the petrol station by Boss. Sev hung back to walk around the perimeter. Sharpe and Sam were now standing on the roof of the building. Zero had seemingly vanished from view. Terra's eye was initially caught by two men sitting around a small campfire. To the right, a man leant over a large pot radiating an alluring aroma. He seemed to be the oldest of the soldiers, probably somewhere in his early fifties. Though he was crouching over the pot, Terra still had a very good impression of his size. The man was practically a living tank. He towered over the pot with bulging muscles revealed by his lack of shirtsleeves. Terra wondered if he had removed the sleeves to show off or if it was just more comfortable that way.

The large man saw Boss and Terra approaching and rose to his feet. He smiled warmly and Terra instantly relaxed. The other soldier seemed much younger, probably somewhere in his early thirties. He had been lying on his back, adjacent to the big one. Suddenly, he bolted up to his feet when he caught a glimpse of Terra. He was around average height and would himself have seemed rather heavily built had he been standing next to someone else. His hair was cut into a short Mohawk and he could have used a shave. He swaggered his way over to Terra and Boss. As the younger man approached, Terra heard Boss sigh.

His accent was thick and unmistakably that of man who had grown up in New York City.

"Nice to meet yah, I'm Machine, team's handsome mechanic. How did you die?"

Terra fell back half a step, dumbstruck by the suddenness of this soldier's approach. The larger man's hand swiped up, connecting with the back of his head. The larger man spoke with an unmistakably Irish accent.

"What was that for? Poor young lass just got here, last thing she needs is to be putting up with you and your bloody shenanigans."

"What?" replied Machine. "Just asking the basic questions, Irish."

"You could have opened with anything! Literally. Anything else would have been better!"

As Machine and Irish kept bickering, Terra turned to Boss to see him shake his head disapprovingly.

"The big one is Irish and the loud one is Machine," Boss started. "They butt heads a lot, but they're practically inseparable."

Irish broke away from Machine to introduce himself properly. He extended a hand to Terra. His colossal fingers engulfed Terra's hand. His grip was firm but Terra didn't feel intimidated.

"Terribly sorry about all this. I'm Irish, as you can probably tell. If you ever need anything, anything at all, you can call on me."

Machine felt the need to butt in again.

"Yeah, yeah, nice to meet yah, doll. Now listen, Irish, explain to me again exactly what salvation God is going to offer me?"

"I never said salvation, I simply said…"

Boss pulled Terra away from the conversation and led her back around towards the petrol station. Terra struggled to take her eyes off Machine and Irish. Their argument was clearly beginning to heat up as arms began flailing into the air and the language being used became stronger. She couldn't help but chuckle at their exchange. Something caught her eye; she turned towards the petrol station and froze in place. A girl stood in front of her, about the same age as Terra. Make-up was smeared across her eyes, her hair was wild and untamed. She was thin, much thinner than she had been before.

"Grace?"

Boss turned around and shot Machine and Irish a glare; the two men quickly ceased their argument.

Terra stuttered as she tried to think of what to say. Grace rushed towards her. Throwing her hands around her friend, she burst into hysterical tears. Terra had never really been one for hugs, but she really needed this too.

"Bloody hell, Grace… in all the time I've known you, you've never had so much as a hair out of place. What's happened to you?"

"You… you have no idea what I would do for a shower right now…" Grace replied.

Terra and Grace shared a tear-filled chuckle. When they realised everyone around them was watching, they separated.

Terra looked up at the two soldiers on the roof of the petrol station who had come down from their perch to see what was happening.

"Terra, it's time for you to meet my sniper team," Boss started. "Sharpe, why don't you go first?"

"Actually, Boss, Sharpe and I already know each other."

Sam looked over at Sharpe and raised an eyebrow. Terra smiled, a little embarrassed, but Sharpe didn't answer. He looked down disapprovingly for a moment, tapping the trigger guard of his rifle. Terra's smile left her face when he turned and walked away. Sam motioned to stop him, but the sniper completely ignored her.

"I-I don't understand…" Terra mumbled.

Sam dropped down from the roof, catching Terra off guard. The two were the same height. Sam had wide blue eyes filled with life; her hair was a mix of brown and blonde tied back into a neat bun that complemented her exceptionally well-defined facial features. She was intimidatingly beautiful, so much so that Terra actually blushed a little when she shot her a smile and extended a hand.

"I'm Sam, spotter and sister to Captain Grouch up there…"

Terra took the handshake; she wasn't sure what surprised her more, the fact that Sam was so stunning, even compared to Grace, or the fact that she spoke with a perfect English accent.

"Well," Sam started again, "he is adopted."

Sam winked at Terra and chuckled slightly when she blushed again.

"It's going to be nice having another girl around; your friend Grace doesn't talk much."

"Settle down, Sam," Boss croaked. "Get up there and check on Sharpe, Terra still has one more member of the team left to meet."

"Oh!" Sam excitedly exclaimed. "Watch out, girl, he bites."

Terra looked to Boss for confirmation.

"Ignore that," Boss said with a hint of authority in his tone.

Sam took the hint and turned around to head back up the hill. Boss looked around. He walked Terra round to the side of the building in search of the last member of the team.

"Somewhere around here should be…"

From atop the hill a young Hispanic soldier leapt onto the roof of the petrol station. He squatted on all fours, ripped his head back revealing a hairy chest through an open shirt, and let out the most convincing attempt at a wolf howl Terra had ever heard.

"Wolfman!" barked Boss.

His voice radiated authority so much that even Terra stood up a little straighter.

"I told you to knock that shit off. Give me a perimeter check. I want a detailed report on those woodlands behind the hill."

Wolfman threw Boss a mock salute. He dropped from the petrol station with rifle in hand and jogged away towards the tree line. Boss sighed before he addressed Terra again.

"He's a good soldier but he still has…" Boss paused as he realised what he was saying. "Had a bit of growing up to do."

Terra smiled, despite everything that had happened. The antics of the team had lifted her spirits.

"You really do care about your men, don't you, Boss?"

Boss nodded a few times. He wasn't looking at her as he spoke; his gaze worked its way around the station.

"Thanks to them, I earned the title of 'The Boss'. It's more of a rank than a name; it's awarded to the leader of the best-performing team. They have their quirks and their demons, their faults and their shortcomings. But when it comes down to it, I couldn't name a better bunch to have your back in a fight. They all deserved better than this."

Boss paused again; he looked out at his men. He reminisced of better times and out of respect, Terra stood quietly and let him.

"Enough of that, though, go and see your friends and relax. I'll be sending out a fire team to scout the way ahead soon, and there's no telling when we're going to stop next when we head out."

Terra moved off towards the station but turned her gaze to the roof. She stood at the base of the steep hill that lead to the sniper's perch and the roof of the station. Taking a deep breath, she struggled her way to the top, stopping to catch her breath once more before she reached the roof of the station.

"How the hell am I going to keep up with a bunch of soldiers if I can barely get up a bloody hill?" she said to no one in particular.

Sam was back on the roof of the petrol station looking out at the soldiers' camp below. Sharpe was still sitting on the hill staring out at the woodlands they had come from. Terra watched him for a moment, trying to work up the courage she needed to approach him. It didn't help that Sharpe didn't move a muscle. The wind blew around them; the tips of Sharpe's hair shifted slightly but he still didn't move. Terra took a breath and walked towards him slowly.

"Hey, I'm sorry to interrupt you. I just wanted to say thanks," she chirped.

Sharpe didn't respond. He was staring at something out in the distance. Terra looked out in the same direction but couldn't see anything besides the trees and an endless supply of open fields.

"What are you looking at?"

"It's been following us," Sharpe spoke slowly, pausing again and again as he spoke, breaking the natural flow of his sentence and unsettling Terra.

"Keeping its distance but it's out there, it's always there. It hides. In the corner of your eye."

Terra looked again but she couldn't see anything. Sharpe seemed almost entranced by whatever it was he was watching. His body was present but his mind seemed distant. His eyes moved back and forth as he scanned the ground again and again.

"What are you talking about?" Terra asked cautiously, getting more and more nervous.

Sam noticed the two talking and strolled over to ease Terra's nerves.

"Ignore him, Terra."

Terra nearly jumped out of her skin; she hadn't heard Sam approach.

"He's in his own little world. He has been since we found him. Haven't you, little brother?"

Sharpe didn't reply. He stayed completely still. He didn't even blink as he scanned the horizon.

"See?" Sam started. "Don't worry about this thing. If there was something out there following us, it's had more than enough chances to strike. It's best just to forget about it."

"Well, anyway, thank you for saving me back there," Terra croaked, hoping for some response, but the sniper kept ignoring her. With a sigh of defeat Terra made her way down the hill as steadily as she could. Billy was waiting for her at the bottom. He held out a hand to help her with the last few steps.

"You okay, Terra?"

"I just went up there to thank him for saving me but he…" Terra cut herself off.

Billy looked up at the roof and shrugged.

"He's like that with everyone, don't take it personally."

Sam knelt down beside Sharpe. She placed a hand on his shoulder and shook him to get his attention.

"She's frightened," Sam snapped. "You could have said anything. Even just a 'You're welcome' would have been enough…"

Sam left Sharpe to his thoughts. He waited, motionless, until he was confident that Sam was out of earshot before he turned back to the station.

"Why are you here?"

CHAPTER 5

◆

WORSE THINGS THAN MEN

Three soldiers walked in a triangular formation. Sam led the troop with Sev behind her to the left and Sharpe slightly further behind him, covering the right. They were approximately four miles away from the petrol station having made their way through a maze of hills and small run-down buildings.

On their previous patrol, they had stumbled across what looked like a large town. Until this point the soldiers had only seen singular buildings or small villages at most. Searching the town was a job for a much larger team, but the soldiers couldn't risk the lives of the civilians so a small fire team would have to do. The soldiers moved in silence for the most part. Except for Sev who was singing to himself.

"And I would walk five hundred miles, and I would walk five hundred more!"

"Sev…" Sam hummed in a low tone. "Knock it off."

"All right, fine, you know I hate the silence. This place gives me the creeps."

Sam slowed her pace to shorten the gap between them.

"All right then. Fuck one, marry one and kill one. Hit me with your best."

Sev nodded slowly as he thought about it.

"I've got one… but it's bad."

"Go for it."

"Hitler, Stalin and Mao."

"Fucking hell, Sev!"

Sev and Sam laughed together. Sharpe meanwhile just continued following slowly, scanning the lands around them. Something caught Sam's eye. She flipped her rifle up to her shoulder. Sharpe and Sev moved into cover on her left raising their weapons.

"Contact front."

The soldiers locked onto their targets.

The town was in view now. A few tall apartment buildings stretched to the sky behind a wall of tightly compacted brick houses with shattered windows and bare driveways that had once held family cars. But it wasn't the town that the fire team were currently worried about. Five figures had crawled out of the shadows. They were human in shape, two legs, two arms and a human head. They wore small patches of clothing here and there, but mostly their clothes had been torn away. They only looked human from a distance; as they stepped out of the shadows it became much more apparent what they were. Their legs awkwardly shuffled their bodies forward. Their arms were stretched far longer than any human's, bent into awkward, painful shapes with long thick claws for slashing and stabbing. Their skin was black and thicker in places, sometimes so thick it jutted out like plates of armour.

Sam held up a hand as Sharpe and Sev raised their weapons, each of them picking targets. Sam spoke in a low, slow voice, with as little movement as possible.

"Wait… let's see if they move on."

The creatures stopped a few feet out of the town and stared at the soldiers who were roughly one hundred metres away. The largest of the creatures twitched its head up in a disturbingly unnatural manner. The thing suddenly raced forward towards the soldiers. The other four soon followed. Sam lowered her hand and the three rifles came to life. The skirmish ended in just a few seconds; despite their thick skin the creatures were put down by just a few high-powered bullets from the soldiers' rifles.

A sixth creature flanked around the side of the team. Sharpe spotted the creature as it charged towards Sev and quickly dispatched it with two perfectly aimed shots to the chest. Sev flinched as Sharpe's bullets whizzed past him into the attacking monster, which slid to a halt a few feet from him.

"Jesus Christ, I hate these fucking things," Sev spat. "When we get back everyone gets a mark check."

Once satisfied that the creatures had been dealt with, Sam waved Sharpe and Sev forward. The two soldiers advanced towards the bodies with their rifles shouldered. Sam moved to the creature that had tried to flank them; strips of torn clothing hung from the monster's body. Sam could tell from a look that it had once been a woman. A closer inspection revealed the creature had been wearing a doctor-style lab coat. Sam shook her head.

"A Damned doctor? Well whoever you were, you can rest now."

Sam closed the eyes of the monster before she rejoined the two men standing before the town. Sam slowed her pace as she approached the buildings, which seemed to stretch upward like a wall that screamed 'Danger'.

"Looks like it's just been torn right up out of the ground and dropped here, just like all the others," Sev noted to Sam as she approached.

"Yeah, but an entire town? What the hell happened here?" Sam asked.

She looked out at Sharpe who was further ahead, standing just before the tarmac of a road that abruptly ended just a few metres out of the town.

"All right," Sam stated. "Let's keep it nice and tight. Take it slow and if we run into another group of them, we bug out and lose them in the trees."

Sam gave a signal to move forward. As the soldiers moved closer, the street lights burst into life, illuminating the road around and ahead of them. The three soldiers instinctively dropped to one knee facing out to cover all directions.

"Well…" Sev commented. "That's creepy."

"Yep," Sam agreed. "Be careful and stay close, don't leave line of sight."

"We should leave," Sharpe croaked.

"We have a job to do. It's going to take a long time to go around this town and we could really use more supplies. Unless you feel like braving the bridge?"

Sharpe didn't respond. He checked his rifle's chamber and set off into the town without saying another word.

"He's getting worse," Sev said.

"I know…" Sam replied solemnly.

"He doesn't sleep, barely eats…" Sev continued.

"I know," Sam snapped. "Let's just get this over with and we can talk about it when we get back."

The soldiers moved forward down the street. Sev and Sam stayed relatively close to one another while Sharpe moved ahead of them scanning the buildings around them. Sharpe stopped when he reached a T-junction in the road. Sam nodded to the left and led the team forward. Sharpe said something to Sev that Sam wasn't able to hear and the two men dropped back slightly, opening the gap between them and Sam.

Sam felt like saying something about the loose formation but gave up; she was tired. The long walk was taking its toll and she knew it. She scanned the road ahead; at the end of the street was a tall gloomy house. The three-storey building didn't fit in with the others. It wasn't so much the style, it was the way the building seemed to sway unsteadily back and forth. Sam lowered her rifle as she approached.

Sam never understood if she noticed the change in that moment and ignored it or if she simply never realised what was happening. She heard a muffled voice from behind her and the sounds of children laughing and playing in front of her. Sam smiled as she passed the sign in front of the building. The air felt warmer, the glow of the sun lay across her cheeks, lifting her spirits. As Sam reached her hand out for the door a violent force tore her away from the building. Sam's head pounded, blood oozed from her nose and the air turned to ice. Her eyes strained against the darkness that washed over her again.

"Hey! Look at me, Sam!" said Sev forcefully as he checked over the frightened young woman. Sam had pulled her knees up into a foetal position. She lay on the ground shaking uncontrollably. Sharpe stayed close nearby.

"It's okay. You're safe, it's us," Sev said again, trying to reassure her.

"Fuck," Sam growled as she forced open her eyes. "How long was I out?"

"A while," croaked Sharpe. "An hour… maybe more."

Sam spat on the ground and was helped to her feet by the two men. She wiped the blood from her nose and allowed Sev to check her eyes.

"You're okay," Sev assured. "Let's finish this sweep and get out of here."

Sam turned her back on the building and started moving further down the street. Sev and Sharpe hung back for a moment looking at the building.

"Something from your past?" Sev asked once he was sure Sam was out of earshot.

Sharpe nodded slowly. His eyes were locked on one of the first-floor windows and his gaze wasn't shifting.

"But it isn't the same town, is it?" Sev started. "You'd have said something otherwise…What are the chances of finding it out here?"

Sharpe rubbed his eyes in an attempt to wipe away whatever it was he was seeing. Finally the sniper tore his gaze away and looked back at Sam.

"Not as low as you'd hope…"

◂▸

After a couple of hours of walking, Sam and her team neared the edge of the town. The formation walked down a long road flanked by expensive houses with long decorative front gardens… or at least what had once been decorative. Low brick walls separated bare areas of dirt that had once held patches of perfectly cut grass and neatly planted flowers.

"It's a shame we couldn't salvage anything, you'd have thought a big town like this would have had some supplies," Sev said, breaking the silence. "Someone probably came through before us."

Sam nodded in agreement while Sharpe ignored them. His gaze and rifle barrel flicked between windows as he scanned every building around them, checking for even the slightest movement.

"You okay, Sam?" Sev asked when he noticed her silence.

Sam shook her head, she couldn't put her finger on it but something here was wrong. At the end of the road one house stood taller than the others. It was older, its walls covered with vines and its windows shattered.

"Hey, it's okay," Sev said as he turned to comfort her.

As Sev made his turn a small glint of light reflected off his rifle and then bounced off something in the shattered window of the house at the end of the street. Sam caught a glimpse of the light and for a split second spotted a sudden and bright yellow flash that disappeared as quickly as it came. Something hot sprayed her face and the sound of the gunshot echoed through the town. Sev dropped to the ground clutching his stomach. Sam levelled her rifle at the window at the end of the street and let loose a volley of shots. Sharpe dropped down behind a low brick wall.

"Get him to safety!" Sharpe bellowed to Sam as he let loose a volley of bullets.

Sam grabbed Sev's collar and with one hand pulled him back across the street to Sharpe's wall.

"Running low here, Sam!" Sharpe growled.

Sam ducked down behind the wall and swapped out her rifle's magazine.

"I'll cover you, just get to that house!"

Sharpe replaced the empty magazine in his weapon and made himself ready. Sam jumped up and started firing her weapon. Sharpe vaulted over the low wall and raced forward as fast as he could. The sniper cleared the distance in seconds.

He slammed shoulder first into the door and fell into the empty room with his weapon loaded and ready. Sharpe stopped and listened; he didn't dare move. Sam's rifle had fallen silent. Sharpe kept his weapon pointed at the staircase opposite the now-empty doorway. He could hear the whimpers and murmurs of Sev coming from down the street.

Sharpe waited; he slowed his breathing and listened for any noise to tell him where the shooter was. Sharpe heard the floorboards above him creak slowly as something shifted its weight. Sharpe snapped his rifle to the spot above him and fired three shots through the floorboards. The last round connected with something, the echoing squelch of meat tearing rang through the soldier's ears. Sharpe moved towards the stairs, taking time to cover the openings to the rooms on either side of him with the barrel of his weapon. The stairs of the building moaned and sagged under the weight of the fully geared soldier. Sharpe advanced slowly; he kept his breathing slow and his steps as light as he could manage. The stairs led Sharpe to the body of the man that had attacked them. A large burly man lay slumped below an open window. Half of his face had been torn away by Sharpe's bullet. The man's lower jaw hung loosely from his head, held in place only by a stretched cheek. His blood had soaked the rest of his body and the ceiling above him was coated in a thick red mess. Sharpe advanced on the man slowly; he kicked away an unimpressive hunting rifle from the body and studied the man. The skin around his hands had discoloured and morphed into thick plates of black callouses. The veins around his neck leading to his face jutted out uncomfortably. Sharpe's rifle snapped up to the man's skull when his one remaining eye moved up towards him.

Sam waited until Sharpe stepped into the window of the house through her own weapon's scope before she moved to Sev, who was clutching his side with a blood-soaked bandage where the bullet had entered. He groaned as he shifted back and forth, convulsing from the pain as his blood left his body and pooled around him. The bullet had torn through him just below his armoured vest, which was now the only thing holding his intestines inside.

"Sam… are you… an angel?" Sev forced a smile.

Sam scrambled through her pouches trying to find a new bandage for Sev.

"Come on, don't get delirious on me now, it's not that bad."

Sam wasn't sure who she was trying to convince. Sharpe appeared beside them and handed Sam a clean bandage.

"Oh God, bring the angel back!" Sev tried to laugh but started to choke on the blood collecting in his mouth.

Sam looked to Sharpe with a serious look of concern.

"Hey…" Sev groaned. "I'm the medic here, I know how bad it is… Get out of here. Leave me my pistol and a couple magazines…"

"Not happening," Sam growled. "We'll get you back to the others and get you patched up."

"He won't make it back to your camp in that state."

Sharpe and Sam both spun on their heels with rifles raised as they heard the new voice.

Standing before them a good twenty feet away was a man. He wore a blue shirt with tan combat trousers over military boots. His head was covered by a thick mop of black hair and he desperately needed a shave. His face was harsh and strong, bags hung under his eyes from lack of sleep and a revolver hung from his belt. From his angle, Sharpe could see the protruding barrel of a Kalashnikov rifle slung over his back.

"Sorry," he said in a thick Australian accent. "This a bad time?"

CHAPTER 6

◀▶

THE BRIDGE

Terra took her turn on watch. Sam's patrol had been gone for hours, which was apparently normal for them. She wisely stopped herself from daydreaming about what it was they could be doing; it was either far too violent or she just didn't want to know. Billy and Grace had gone to sleep, Machine and Irish were still arguing about something while Boss stood at the edge of their perimeter. Terra looked down to see Zero clambering up the hill.

"Mind if I join you?"

Terra gestured for him to sit down beside her; she had been looking out over the horizon trying to see what Sharpe had supposedly been watching earlier.

"You won't find it," Zero croaked as he scanned the treeline. After a few seconds he shook his head in defeat.

"Ya'll are looking for the shimmer, but you won't find it."

"Why not?" Terra asked.

"Because it's not really there… we've all been here for a long time, the things we've done and seen in this place alone would be enough to break any man. And Sharpe has always been a little off; best just to give him a wide berth."

Zero shot her a smile.

"He's a killer. I see that," Terra mumbled.

"We're all killers, Terra," sighed Zero. "Every one of us that you've met has taken lives. Some more than others... Sharpe is no exception, and now he and all of us are probably here because of that. I don't know about you but to me, that's enough reason to be a little off, don't you think?"

Terra looked away from him; despite knowing he was right she still tried to find a counterargument.

"It begs the question though, don't it?" Zero suddenly asked, snapping her attention back to him. "Why are ya'll here, Terra?"

Terra met his gaze with a cold glance.

"Do you think I'm a killer as well, Zero?"

Zero smiled briefly; he looked out at the opening where Terra had been scanning.

"I'm not sure. But you must be here for a reason, right?"

"Is there a point to this?" Terra snapped.

Zero met her displeasured gaze and held his composure almost perfectly, just a little satisfaction crawling across his face. He decided it best to retreat rather than pry any further for now.

A pair of voices exchanged a few short words at the base of the hill. Terra felt more than a little surprised to see the Mohawk soldier Machine appear on the hill beside her.

"Did you come here to accuse me as well?" Terra solemnly asked.

Machine shook his head and grinned.

"Nah, I'm just here to take over the watch."

"Do you agree with him?" Terra asked without realising what she was saying.

Machine thought about it for a moment.

"We don't know you. You're a person, which means you're a complex mess of emotions, experiences and some other shit that hurts my brain to think about."

Machine paused as a new thought wormed into his mind.

"Zero forgets who he is sometimes, he hasn't been second-in-command long and to be fair, the only reason he got it was because his dad owns the company. I don't know what you did, Terra, I don't know if you did anything. What I do know is that you're yet to show me any reason to distrust you. So innocent until proven guilty, right?" Machine winked and Terra couldn't hold back the smile.

"Thank you."

"Go get some rest, kid, we'll be moving soon."

◂▸

"All right there, chaps, take it easy, let's not do anything we're going to regret."

As the man finished the sentence his words twisted from a cold attempt at humour to a sinister snarl. Sharpe took a few steps to the side, increasing the distance between himself and Sam just in case the man tried anything. The man looked to Sharpe as he opened his mouth again, choosing wisely to stop five metres away from the soldiers.

"Now, now, easy there, son, I ain't here to cause trouble. Who's your commander?"

Sam looked to the building directly to her left. Though it was faint and obscured by glass, the tells of uneasy movement were there.

Had they been there the entire time?

"I am," Sam called out.

Sam lowered her weapon; she made an effort not to break eye contact with the man. Sharpe kept his rifle raised and at the ready, his finger slowly caressing the trigger and its guard.

"Forgive my intrusion, heard the shots and, well, your mate looks like he needs a little help." The man looked over at Sharpe. "Your arm's not getting tired?"

The man's attempts to sound friendly left Sam's skin crawling. His eyes wandered far too much for her liking; they felt heavy as they stayed at Sam's chest for a painful few seconds.

"Name's Bruce. I know, typical Aussie name, ain't it?"

Sam rolled her eyes, not believing him for a moment.

"Pleasure," Sam snarled with a cold glare.

Bruce's grin crept back onto his face; the corners of his lips slithered back showing a set of pristine teeth, save a large silver filling near the corner of his smile.

"What's your name, gorgeous?" Bruce asked half mockingly.

Sam held her glare; she unenthusiastically waved her finger to the members of her team as she called their names.

"Sam, Sev and Sharpe."

"A name so perfect for the sniper he probably chose it himself," Bruce chuckled.

"I earned it," Sharpe growled.

Bruce winced. His smile left his face. He slid a disapproving glare in the direction of Sharpe. Their eyes locked with each other; they held that gaze for a long moment, silently battling for supremacy. Bruce turned back to Sam when Sharpe's ferocity proved a little too much.

Sev pulled himself up to his feet. He coughed and spat blood on the floor as his legs began to cave under his weight. Sam moved closer to support him.

"Look, your friend hasn't got long, I'd be surprised if he even makes it back to your camp." Bruce paused to make sure the soldiers were listening. "My associates and I happen to have some medical supplies; in exchange for some equipment, we might be able to help your friend."

Sam shook her head slowly; she began to back away with Sev. Bruce tutted loudly in disappointment.

"I wasn't really offering, ya know. So why don't we avoid the nasties and you guys just drop your gear? No one gets hurt and I'll even throw in a bit of morphine for the Russian."

Sev dropped two smoke grenades onto the ground making sure one rolled forward and the other behind, covering the soldiers. Sharpe kept his rifle fixed on Bruce until the smoke engulfed Sam and Sev; he listened closely for the sound of them leaving.

"You're going to be an issue, aren't you?" Bruce moaned.

"Only if you follow us," Sharpe warned.

Sharpe stood motionless. He didn't even blink until the smoke from the grenade engulfed him as well.

◀▶

Terra could feel a slight breeze in the air and it felt cool on her skin. She had found herself on the roof of the petrol station this time, sitting cross-legged with her notebook open across her legs, busy sketching the landscape in front of her. Terra made sure to leave a large space in the middle where she worked meticulously on the outlines of several people. There were ten figures in total huddled together as if posing for a photo.

"Not going to draw yourself?"

The words came from Billy. Terra jumped and gasped. Billy chuckled.

"Sorry, didn't mean to startle you. What's the inspiration for this one?"

"There isn't any… I just need something to concentrate on."

"Would you like to talk abou—"

"No Billy! I really, really don't want to talk about it," Terra snarled.

Images of the men in the cabin flashed before her eyes, followed by the screams of the people in Moi Airport. Terra rubbed a hand over her eyes as she recomposed herself.

"I'm sorry. This has been a lot to take in. The only reason I'm not crying is because I'm too dehydrated to generate tears."

"You know I cried for like a week straight after I got here. I'd say you're doing well," Billy smirked.

Terra couldn't help but smile slightly; she leant towards Billy and rested her head on his shoulder. She noticed he thought about putting an arm around her but stopped himself. Aware of his lack of confidence, Terra smiled inwardly at Billy's hesitation.

The soldiers around the camp snapped into action as Boss's voice called out to them. Terra and Billy looked up from her notebook to see Sam and Sev emerging from the hills. Sharpe was nowhere to be seen. Sam staggered forward; Wolfman rushed over to help Sev. Together they helped the injured man to the station and leant him against the outside wall as carefully as possible. This allowed Irish to get a better look at his wound. Boss jogged over; he beckoned Sam and Zero over to the side. Machine took up a position guarding the entrance.

"What happened?" Boss wasn't his usual warm, welcoming self.

"We found a survivor. He was held up in a house with a rifle. This guy let us walk halfway down the street before he fired. Sharpe took care of him pretty quick but then things got weird."

Sam recalled the events of their patrol, making sure to give a detailed description of Bruce and his men.

"And this guy in the house who ambushed you, was he with them?" Boss questioned.

"I don't think so," Sam explained. "My guess is this Bruce bloke was hunting the guy in the house, I wouldn't be surprised if he mistook us for some of Bruce's men."

"Guy goes crazy so they hang around waiting for him to drop himself or someone else so they can swoop in and grab the gear, that's kind of clever," Zero added.

"What about Sharpe?" Boss added.

Sam shook her head.

"He tried to draw them away from us. I don't know where he is now."

Zero jumped into the conversation.

"Boss, I can go back and get him, with Wolfman's tracking skills…"

"And leave us half the team down if they hit us?" Boss retorted.

"But Sharpe?" Zero questioned.

"Isn't worth risking more soldiers," Boss bellowed. He moved in close pushing his face to within an inch of Zero. "If he wants to get himself killed then let him. Protecting the kids is our priority," Boss growled.

Boss turned away, putting his hands behind his head trying to think of what to do.

"Boss!" Sev yelled.

Boss and the others all turned to face the wounded man.

Sev held an open bloody hand by his wound, his head tilted back against the wall with a forced smile across his bloody lips.

"Leave me my weapon and get out of here."

Terra and Billy came down from the petrol station's roof in time to hear Sev's last comment. Terra threw her hands over her mouth and Billy stayed very still beside her.

Zero moved towards them but Boss cut him off with a hand. Boss knelt down in front of Sev. Despite the immense pain, Sev managed to hold his conviction. Blood trickled from his mouth as he tried his best to say something to Boss.

"You need… to keep a better eye on him if she's here; he's becoming more unstable… you have to… stop…" Sev slouched forward, choking on the blood in his throat. Boss nodded in agreement. He rose back to his feet to meet Terra's frightened gaze.

Terra looked down at Sev who was panting heavily; he noticed she was looking at him as he tried his best to smile. Boss gave the order for the others to gather their things and move out. Terra sat down beside Sev; she recoiled slightly realising that she had put her hand down in a puddle of his blood.

"Whatever you're thinking, forget it," Sev whispered. He looked out as the other soldiers ran around frantically gathering their equipment and setting up landmines. Terra looked at him, confusion written across her face.

"I… I was going to ask why you're here. We all did something to get us here, right?"

"Ha, and you think what? If I get it off my chest I'll pass in peace? Why are you here then, Terra? Do you believe it is because you're too young to have lived a life?"

Terra didn't answer him; she stood back up and walked over to Billy and Grace who were waiting at the edge of the camp for her while the others finished packing their gear.

"You'll have to face it sooner or later, Terra. This place has a strange way of bringing the past back to haunt you."

With that, Sev fell very still; he managed to take a hold of his rifle before he finally lost consciousness.

Terra forced herself to turn away; the other soldiers had finished packing and were beginning to move out at a jogging pace into the hills beside the petrol station. The three students struggled to keep up as the soldiers ran. Periodically one of the PMCs would drop to a knee and cover the rear; they'd wait until the rest of the group had passed then turn and follow as the next covered them. Fatigue weighed in on the students, their movements slowing as their muscles ached and burned, until a bullet whizzed past them. A rifle-calibre round crashed into the dirt, kicking up a cloud of dust with a loud snap as it broke the sound barrier. Instinct forced the students into a full sprint. The soldiers at the rear of the formation stopped and began unhurriedly returning a few carefully aimed shots.

Pushing herself forward, Terra forced her burning legs to continue. Before she knew it, the hills closed in around her, forcing everyone into a single-file line through a very tight passageway that seemed to have been carved out of a wall of solid stone.

"Tight corners, stay close!" Zero yelled back.

Terra found herself in the middle of the group following Billy. The canyon seemed to be more like a maze, splitting into several different paths. Terra stayed close to Billy; she was being closely followed by Sam. Luckily for Terra the soldiers seemed to know the way. After a few minutes of light jogging through the canyon, the walls began to widen out leading into a small flat area. Terra and her student friends collapsed to the floor, heavily panting.

"Pfft... kids," Machine moaned to the side.

Boss barked something inaudible about a perimeter as Terra struggled to get her breath back.

Zero and Boss turned to the edge of the canyon. The ground gave way to an immense open drop. The canyon seemed to descend for miles. A thick layer of grey mist slithered its way steadily through the canyon. The air was uncomfortably warm around the edges of the ground; it licked at the faces of the soldiers, creating beads of sweat and a need to adjustment more private areas.

Across the open gorge the ground gave way to an open plain mostly devoid of cover save for a few large rocks that looked as if they would once have belonged on this side of the gorge. Way in the distance the clear silhouette of a large town could be seen, the buildings stretching high into the sky in tall apartment structures. The problem, however, continued in the form of a very precarious-looking rope bridge. The wooden planks mostly looked stable, except for the few that were hanging loosely from frayed stretches of rope.

"Age before beauty, right?" Zero joked.

Boss looked at him with a straight, unamused face. He smiled as Zero shrugged cockily and approached the bridge. The silver-haired soldier took a cautious step onto the first plank, gripping the ropes firmly for support. Boss turned his attention back to his other soldiers.

"Anything that comes down that path gets very dead, very quickly," Boss yelled.

"What about Sharpe?" Billy asked.

Boss had almost forgotten the students were there. Terra had managed to get to her feet.

"He's trying to lead some of them away. He's a smart kid, he'll throw them off his scent and come and find us when he's ready."

As Boss finished, the canyon through which they had entered exploded into a mess of rifle and machine-gun fire. The thuds, cracks and snaps of bullets hitting the stone walls filled the air, drowning out the sound of anything else. Terra stumbled to the ground, pushing her hands against her ears, trying to stop the noise. Closing her eyes in a futile attempt to block out the firefight, she felt the presence of someone touching her. A pair of hands reached around her, forcing her back to her feet, beckoning her to move. Terra followed. She didn't open her eyes; she felt the ground beneath her feet change from the firm dirt to the loose wooden planks of the wobbling bridge.

Feeling the pressure of the air change, her skin crawled as the thick, humid air engulfed her. It swayed past her then pulled back as though the canyon below was breathing.

A plank gave way from under her. Terra's foot slipped into the empty space. She cried out in blind panic, still refusing to open her eyes. Something beneath called to her, in a warm whisper of air that wrapped itself around her legs, clawing her down to the depths of the canyon.

"Come on!"

Terra was pulled back up onto the bridge by the arms of the man holding her.

Terra felt as if she were thrown at the last step as a new set of arms guided her across. She fell to the ground, once again feeling solid earth as she hit her head. Terra lay dazed on the ground; she opened her eyes.

Zero was standing beside the bridge with his weapon in hand watching the open ground on the other side as the soldiers one by one began to peel away. Billy was sitting leaning against one of the larger rocks panting heavily beside her.

"Th-thank you!" Terra stuttered.

Billy gave her a thumbs up.

Machine hastily but cautiously made his way across. Grace had fallen behind the other students, as she slowly began to make her way across the bridge after being screamed at by several soldiers. Grace made it halfway across the bridge before a bullet ricocheted off a nearby rock and took a lock of hair off her head. Grace fell to her knees, putting her hands to her head and praying out loud in a tear-soaked panic. Zero moved to cross the bridge to get to her, but Terra grabbed his ankle to stop him.

"Your suit is too heavy, you'll collapse the bridge!"

Zero looked up at the bridge and smiled. Wolfman was sprinting across the fragile planks as quickly as he could with Grace comically slung over his shoulder. Wolfman's foot cracked one of the boards, forcing him to one knee a few feet short of the safety of the ground ahead. He recovered quickly and handed Grace over to Zero with the smuggest smile Terra had ever seen. Sam crossed next leaving just Boss and Irish covering the canyon. Irish's machine-gun belt was down to its last twenty rounds; he wouldn't have time to reload.

"So, 'rock, paper, scissors' for it?" Irish mocked as he fired the last of his rounds.

Boss looked over from the other side of the canyon's opening and smiled. He nodded to his old friend.

"See you on the other side, brother," Boss barked.

Irish slung his weapon across his shoulder. As Boss stepped out firing his weapon down the canyon entrance,

Irish made a dash for the bridge, moving as quickly as he could. Boss emptied his magazine then started falling back to the bridge himself. As he turned, a bullet sliced through the bicep on his right arm. The bullet felt more like a hammer as it ricocheted off the bone. The impact almost threw Boss off balance. With his arm now rendered completely useless Boss switched to his sidearm and began firing at the canyon entrance. The attackers had begun pushing up the pass; some even climbed the walls to fire down at the soldiers on the opposite end of the bridge. Irish was slouched behind a large boulder as he struggled to feed a new belt of ammunition into his machine gun while the other soldiers did their best to suppress their attackers.

The team's fire was becoming more and more dispersed and ammunition wasn't infinite. Boss managed to make it halfway across the bridge before another stray round skimmed his leg. Boss grunted, shifting his weight to the rope railing of the bridge. Wolfman took a bullet to his chest, the force of the round causing him to lose his footing and fall back into the rocks behind him.

Wolfman made the mistake of standing up to cover the Boss. A bullet slammed into his chest plate; the impact knocked all of the air out of his lungs and forcefully pushed him back down behind the rock. Machine dashed out of cover to pull Wolfman away from the action. Zero moved to the end of the bridge to reach Boss. His fire took the face off an attacker who was either brave enough or stupid enough to leave the safety of the canyon's opening. But not before he was able to fire a burst of fire at Boss.

The rounds missed Boss but severed one of the lower ropes holding up the bridge, which drooped to one side. Boss gripped the remaining rope tightly while the rest of his body dangled above the bottomless canyon.

"Boss! Give me your hand quickly!"

Boss looked over to see Zero lying at the edge of the canyon reaching out to him. Bullets were flying back and forth between the PMCs and their attackers, most of whom were simply poking their weapons up above the ridgeline and firing blindly. Boss smiled. His exo-suit and gear were weighing him down too much, and only being able to hold on with one arm didn't help either. Maybe a few years ago he might have been able to pull himself up and use his legs to crawl the rest of the way, but not this time. Not with too many of his best years behind him.

"Zero!" Boss bellowed; he met Zero's horrified gaze with a smile. "Keep them safe."

Boss closed his eyes as the rope slipped through his fingers. The old warrior felt numb; the firefight around him seemed to fall silent. He opened his eyes again to see his second-in-command. Boss could tell by Zero's face that he was screaming, but he couldn't hear much as he fell. It was as if his body was being put to sleep; his vision, his hearing and all his other senses faded away.

As one final salute of respect to his men, and to maintain his fearsome reputation, Boss smiled as he dropped into the canyon.

CHAPTER 7

◂▸

TAKE A BREATH

It could have been an hour… or it could have been a day. Terra didn't know, nor did she really care. The soldiers weren't talking. How could anyone blame them? Their numbers had been almost halved. Sev and Boss were dead, Sharpe was missing and it seemed fairly impossible for him to find them now. Sam sat at the base of a dirt hill a few feet away from Terra. She was pushing shiny new bullets into an empty magazine with unsteady hands. No one looked at anyone else. Zero had his face in his knees, Machine was pacing back and forth rubbing his chin. Wolfman sat on top of the hill watching the canyon. He was well out of firing range and there was no way they could have been followed. Irish stepped into view from over the hill. He briefly placed a hand on Wolfman's shoulder to let him know he was there. Wolfman retreated back slightly until he realised who it was.

"All right," Irish croaked. "Now I get that nobody wants to talk about this, but we need to get moving."

Nobody moved at first. Zero looked up after a while with bloodshot eyes.

"Can't we give them a little more time to mourn?" he said, harsher than he had intended.

"You tell me," Irish answered. "You're in charge now."

Before Zero could form a response, Machine jumped in.

"I don't mean any disrespect, but given the circumstances I think someone with a little more experience should take the reins here."

"You don't think I can do it?" Zero snapped.

"Zero you're a smart kid but…"

"I'm twenty-six years old!" Zero interrupted. "And I've been with the company since I was eighteen! There have been people much younger and far less experienced than me lead fire teams!"

"But none of them were as hot-headed and reckless as you. I'm sorry, kid, but I'm worried if you take the lead then we'll all end up…"

"I'm not a fucking kid," Zero snarled. The young soldier closed the distance on Machine with his hands clenched into tight fists. Machine held his ground locking eyes with the younger soldier. Irish put his massive body in between the two men while Wolfman jumped up to his feet, ready to intervene.

"This isn't the time for this!" Irish asserted.

"Oh yeah, that's it!" Machine mocked. "Get the biggest guy in the team to fight your battles for you!"

Irish turned back to Machine and pointed a massive finger between his eyes.

"You need to calm down. There are two people here who are trained to lead a fire team and you're not one of them!" Irish growled. The big man turned back to face Zero. "If you're an adult then you need to start acting like one!"

"Irish, as soon as things start to get hairy, he's goanna break."

"Fuck you! I'm from a family of fucking warriors!"

Terra lifted her head slightly as Zero went on.

"I'm ready for this, Machine. We've got three kids here that need our help and with Boss gone, the chain of command says I'm in charge."

Machine laughed mockingly.

"The chain of command? The chain of command got blown up along with Moi! Out here it's all about survival; the strong live and the weak get left to the wolves."

Everyone stopped; they all locked eyes on Machine.

"What was that?" Irish asked after a painfully long silence.

Machine looked down across the faces of Terra, Billy and Grace. All of them looked tired and frail; tears had stained their faces and smudged make-up surrounded bloodshot eyes.

"It was Boss's idea to look after them. If you ask me they're all just dea—"

He never finished. Sam had got up and thrown a ferocious right hook into his face. The sound of the impact tore through everyone as Machine staggered back, falling to the ground. He threw up a hand to his mouth. Sam grabbed his webbing and hoisted the man back to his feet as if he was nothing. She glared at him with a rage that nobody had ever seen from her before.

"We're not leaving anyone," she hissed. "Stop waving your dick around and get your shit together." With that Sam released the stunned soldier and returned to her spot next to Terra, whose gaze followed her as she nonchalantly sat back down as though nothing had happened.

Well done, Sam.

Zero wiped a hand over his eyes to hide the tears.

Machine dusted himself off and stomped away from the group.

"I'll go scout ahead. Catch up whenever you feel like it."

"Just remember to follow the lights so we can find you," Irish yelled after him.

"Wolfman," Sam yelled. "Go make sure he doesn't get into too much trouble…"

Wolfman took a second to look to Zero and Irish for confirmation; after Zero nodded he briskly jogged off after Machine.

"Don't worry about him, he'll go kill or punch something and come back his old smiley self," Irish told Zero.

Zero nodded and mouthed the words 'thank you' before he went to find his own quiet place to sit and reflect.

"Sam, take ten and then get us a perimeter check," he ordered as he passed her. Sam gave him a brief thumbs up.

Terra had her notebook open and was scribbling down a few more lines of her group sketch in a futile attempt to take her mind off things. She was working on Boss and Sev, trying her best to focus on their faces. She drew them both smiling, feeling it suited them more. She noted that both men were, in their final moments, smiling at something. After a while Terra switched to the face of the other soldier who was no longer with the team, Sharpe. But Sharpe wasn't dead, he had run off to try and draw away some of the attackers, or so Sam claimed. Maybe he was dead too. Or maybe he had the common sense to hide and save himself. Terra wasn't sure. She didn't know him well enough to know the answer for sure but there seemed to be an endless canyon separating them, so he may as well be dead.

Sam was sitting beside Terra; she was wearing a black flat cap pulled down over her eyes. She disassembled her rifle and started cleaning the parts with an oil-soaked rag. On Terra's other side sat Grace, with her knees tucked up into her chest.

"We're all gonna die," Grace whispered. "If it's not those monsters trying to kill us, it's the other fucking people."

Terra shook her head; she didn't have the energy or the will to try and calm Grace down. She wouldn't even know where to begin. Terra ignored her and went about drawing some more details of her sketch.

"You belong here," Grace whispered again. "You're a fucking psycho just like the rest of them."

Terra winced. She knew that retaliating wouldn't do her any good so she decided to keep her mouth shut. She put away her notebook and strolled over to Zero.

"You okay?" she asked in the warmest tone she could manage.

"I don't really know, Terra. I just became the leader of half a fire team," Zero answered, trying his best to keep his composure, but ultimately failing.

"Well, the fact that you're on your feet is a testimony to your strength, isn't it?" Terra replied.

"Nah, just means I'm too stupid to go down. Besides just before you came along Boss gave us this whole big speech about saving the civvies. He said if you can just save one, get one of them to the end, then mission's done. Something worth fighting for, I guess."

Terra nodded in agreement.

"For what it's worth, thank you," she whispered.

As she had expected, Zero didn't answer. Terra briefly laid a hand on Zero's shoulder then walked over to Billy to sit by him. Billy extended an arm. Normally Terra wouldn't have accepted much physical contact but right now the company was what she needed.

◂▸

Machine and Wolfman walked in silence for a good hour before they stumbled across their first sign of shelter: a large town with a few tall apartment buildings and an extremely eerie-looking carnival wheel in the distance. The two soldiers moved in cautiously; the road signs were written in Russian making it difficult to ascertain what they had found or rather where they were. Machine moved in front while Wolfman trailed a few metres behind him.

"It's a shame Sev's not here, he would have loved to have filled us in on this place," Machine commented, trying to start some sort of conversation.

Though he immediately wished he hadn't. Wolfman stopped in front of a large sign; the large stone letters wouldn't have made much sense in English but the thing that stood out to him more than anything was the number below them. 1970.

"Something tells me we may not want to know what this place is," Wolfman said with shifty, unsettled eyes. "Let's just finish our sweep and get back quick."

"You're not getting superstitious on me now, are ya, kid?"

Machine looked back and gave Wolfman his trademark grin. Though he was only able to hold that face for a few seconds; after losing Boss even he was struggling to keep his spirits up. They cleared the sign and found themselves walking beside a tall apartment building. Something about the town seemed eerily familiar to both men.

"Hey, Machine, can I ask you something?" Wolfman inquired.

"Sure."

Wolfman paused for a long moment as he tried to find the words.

"Do you think that if we die here, we go to hell?"

"Don't think like that," snapped Machine.

Machine sighed. He felt Wolfman tense up behind him.

"When was the last time any of us did a mark check?"

Wolfman thought about it for a minute but never had the chance to answer. A noise from the building beside them demanded immediate attention. Somewhere inside, the clatter of pots and pans echoed down the halls and out of the door as something scurried between the rooms. Machine and Wolfman raised their weapons to the building's entrance with fingers on their triggers. An eerie silence followed and the wind blew past the two men. They both heard the faded, almost distorted sound of children laughing and looked at each other. Suddenly the apartment building seemed to loom much higher, towering over them. One of the double entrance doors swung slowly open and closed again, its peace disturbed by the intrusion of the men.

Machine signalled to Wolfman to hold his position by the entrance and slowly made his way inside. The floor of the building was littered with scraps of rubbish and mouldy wallpaper that had been stripped away from the building's interior. The thing that was getting to Machine more were the oceans of crusty dead leaves. There were none on the streets outside the buildings, but the floor on the inside was covered by them.

"Stay here and watch my back," Machine commanded.

"Machine!" Wolfman called. "I don't think this is a good idea."

"Kid... I really just need to shoot something right now, okay?"

Machine's attention was drawn to a shuffling sound coming from the floor above him. He slowly made his way to the staircase just beyond the entrance. Dead leaves crunched under foot and Machine felt sweat run down his brow. Sneaking up on whatever was upstairs wasn't going to be possible; it would know he was coming.

Why am I doing this?

Machine took the first step on the staircase and froze in place as cold air from outside engulfed the hallway. The leaves all picked up and shifted, temporarily blinding him as they swirled around him. Sharpe had once told him to beware of staircases. They had all laughed when he'd said it but suddenly the sniper's warning was resonating within him.

"You okay, bro?" Wolfman called.

Machine gritted his teeth and nodded slowly. He didn't bother checking to see if Wolfman had noticed his response. The soldier checked both sides as he cleared the staircase. Another noise came from the right as something shattered on the ground. One of the apartment doors hung open.

The number displayed was 237. Machine froze, shaking his head.

"Two hundred thirty-fucking-seven. Of course it is!"

A sound from the next room drew his attention and Machine let out a sigh of relief.

"Not today, Mr King..."

He advanced on the door slowly. Something was in the room. Machine heard the faint sounds of movement and shuffling. It could have just been a rat. Animals were uncommon but still roamed Limbo. Or it was one of the black-skinned creatures. They weren't a threat in small groups out in the open, but inside a small confined space they were a totally different story. Machine's train of thought was lost as the door he was approaching suddenly swung closed with considerable force. Animals don't close doors.

"Fuck it!"

Machine like all of the others was wearing a lower-body exoskeleton suit. He approached the door and slammed his boot into the timber. The entire door and frame tore from the walls and flew inside the room. Machine swung his rifle from side to side as he checked for any sign of the creature.

A small box-like television sat in front of a small mouldy sofa. The room stank of urine and rotting meat. Machine turned his attention to the next room and stepped forward slowly.

Outside, Wolfman stood in the entrance to the apartment building, leaning against the wall fiddling with his rifle waiting for Machine to exit the building. A long burst of rifle fire echoed from the building. Instinctively Wolfman dropped to his knee turning towards the staircase with his weapon shouldered.

"Machine!"

Wolfman's calls echoed through the street; he moved into the building checking the road behind him as he reached the stairs. His hands were shaking as he took the first step. The stairs creaked and a child laughed somewhere in the distance. Wolfman snapped his weapon to the corridor entrance. The taste of sweat slithered across his lips. He loosened his grip on his rifle, flexing his numbing fingers as he slowly made his way further up the stairs. Wolfman cleared the stairs and moved into the hallway. Machine was leaning up against the doorway to room 237. Wolfman loosened up a little bit and took a deep breath to relax.

"Everything okay?" Wolfman asked cautiously.

Machine's eyes looked wild, his breathing was staggered. Machine's smile had been wiped off his face and replaced with a blank expression. Wolfman moved towards the opening. Machine gestured with a hand for him to stop. He didn't speak for a few seconds then his smile returned and his face relaxed.

"It's okay, just a Damned. I cleared the room, we should probably just move through this town, though. There's too many ghosts here."

Machine pushed past Wolfman and headed for the exit; Wolfman moved to follow. Something pulled his attention back to the doorway.

"He said it's clear… he said…" Wolfman spat on the floor and rushed a quick prayer before he moved into the doorway.

The first room was clear yet in desperate need of a cleaner, though even then it wouldn't have done much good. Wolfman activated the torch on the side of his weapon, then moved to a closed door leading to another room. Wolfman turned the knob and slowly pushed open the door. He levelled his rifle, sweeping it from one side of the room to the other.

The walls were covered by peeling blue paint; a small television sat in the corner as well as a shelf filled with thin yet colourful books. A small red plastic stool held a mouldy teddy bear. But it was only when Wolfman looked down at the ground that he realised what Machine was upset about. A Damned, a very small Damned, no more than two feet tall, laying limply on the bloodstained carpet.

Wolfman fell back out of the room, his heart pounding and his eyes streaming. He rolled over, vomited, then dragged himself out of room 237. Machine was outside the building fumbling with a cigarette and a lighter as Wolfman staggered past him. Wolfman got a few paces past Machine before dropping to his knees.

"This is insane!" he yelled. "I can't do this, I can't go on in this place!"

Wolfman reached for his holster, pulling out his sidearm, releasing the safety in the process. Wolfman slowly moved the weapon to his chin as Machine took a long drag on his cigarette, watching Wolfman from a few feet away.

"It's been a long time since I had one of these," Machine croaked, trying not to choke on the smoke.

Even so, it felt good as the smoke filled his lungs. With a long, deep breath Machine felt the warmth of the cigarette wash over his body. He watched as Wolfman closed his eyes, moving his finger to the trigger.

"What do you think happens if we die here?" Machine said just before taking another drag. "Do you think if you pull that trigger that it all ends? You can be at peace? Honestly, I'm curious. I mean the way I see it, we've got to be here for a reason, right? Maybe for some kind of judgment? I wonder if you pulled that trigger, and blew your brains out all over the road, whether that would that defeat the purpose of you being here? Maybe you really would end up in hell. Being tortured for all eternity, all because you wouldn't see this through till the end."

Wolfman opened his eyes as he pondered Machine's words.

"Let's be honest here, brother; even if you go to heaven, Boss is going to kick the shit out of you for abandoning the mission," Machine added.

Machine moved closer to Wolfman, extending the cigarette.

"You can scream, you can beg and you can cry. No one will blame you. But if you take the easy way out and leave us another man down, we'll all resent you for it."

Wolfman put away his Glock and rubbed a hand over his eyes to wipe away the tears. He stood up and took the cigarette out of Machine's hand. Just before he could put it between his lips, Machine threw a hard punch into his gut. Wolfman lurched forward face first into Machine's knee and fell to the ground dazed. After letting the young man's head spin for a couple of minutes, Machine held out a hand and helped Wolfman to his feet.

"Feeling better now, kid?"

◂▸

The rest of the group caught up an hour later. Wolfman and Machine waited for them at the entrance to the town. Zero led the formation; he moved up to Machine as the rest of the team dispersed to cover the students.

"Well, this looks cosy," Zero greeted.

"Sure, if you like sleeping with a loaded gun in your lap," Machine retorted.

Zero looked at the apartment buildings behind them; something felt oddly familiar about this place.

"Where are we?" Zero asked.

Terra watched the exchange from a distance as she quietly eavesdropped.

"I'm not exactly sure…" Machine stated; he looked over the horizon at the Ferris wheel in the distance. "You know what, you're better off not knowing."

Terra looked over the two men at the Ferris wheel; there really was something unsettlingly familiar about this place.

"I'll give you a hint," came the voice of Sam in Terra's ear. Sam pointed down the road they'd approached from.

"You'd be forgiven for thinking that sign's written in Russian, but it's actually Ukrainian."

Terra gave her a confused look. Sam raised her eyebrows a couple of times.

"What is this place, Sam?"

"Ever heard of a ghost town?" Sam winked at Terra.

CHAPTER 8

◂▸

NO PROMISES

The group moved down the one of the main roads leading through the town. Rows of run-down houses flanked them, silently calling to the humans. Rifles were routinely raised to open windows and nobody felt like talking. Terra and her student friends were at the centre of the formation with Zero.

"I don't understand the need for this, why didn't we just go around?" Terra shyly asked Irish, if only to break the silence.

"The worst things we can run into here are the Damned," Irish replied. "And they're pretty easy to take down. But out there in the open, well, hopefully you'll never find out."

Terra nodded slowly; she slowed her pace so that she dropped back to the rear of the formation, where she found Sam.

"Hey, do you think Sharpe is okay?" Terra asked Sam.

Sam chuckled quietly and winked at her.

"He's far too stubborn to be taken out by a couple of mercenaries. Why did you ask, Terra?"

Terra noticed Sam had started to slow their pace, opening the gap between them and the others.

"Everyone was hit so hard by losing Sev and Boss, I mean you all wear it on your sleeves as much as you try to hide it, but nobody's said much about Sharpe since he disappeared. Shouldn't you be more worried about him?"

Sam shrugged.

"Nah, this isn't the first time he's gone and disappeared like that. One time he just vanished while the rest of us were sleeping, slipped right past Machine on guard. After what I assume was a couple of days, we ran into him just chilling on the side of the road waiting for us. Trust me, Terra, he'll be fine."

Sam shot her a sly look.

"Though I do think it's cute that you're so worried about him."

Terra blushed slightly; she opened her mouth to respond as they passed a narrow alley. Sam's hand suddenly pushed her back as her rifle levelled down the alley. Terra had never even heard the creature. But there it was, racing down the alley, extending its claws towards her.

Sam fired two shots into the creature. Further ahead of them, without missing a beat, one of the other soldiers screamed, "Contact!"

The rifles and machine guns of the soldiers burst into life as the creatures begun crawling out of every crevice and window around them. Before they knew it, the soldiers were surrounded by dozens of the things bearing down on them.

A clawed hand flew towards Terra; she fell back narrowly avoiding the swipe. The butt of Sam's rifle slammed into the creature, forcing it off balance long enough for a bullet to lodge itself in the creature's head. Sam stood over Terra. She pulled her back up, still using the rifle with her free hand. Sam pulled out her Glock, hit the safety catch and handed the weapon to Terra.

"Defend yourself!" Sam barked.

Sam held Terra's arm as she pulled her along with the rest of the soldiers.

Terra moved as fast as she could but still struggled to keep up. A clawed hand sliced into Sam's arm forcing her to release her grip on Terra. The creature pushed itself between the girls. Sam dealt with the creature but more were coming. Without fear the monsters rushed towards Sam, ignoring the bullets tearing into them.

"Run!" Sam screamed.

Overwhelmed by the Damned and with her magazine running low, Sam was forced to retreat to the other soldiers, leaving Terra to the mercy of the creatures. Terra darted into an alley. She ran as hard as her legs would allow. In her panic she narrowly avoided a swing from a clawed hand that reached for her face.

Terra moved until she stood in an empty street. She could hear gunshots and screams in the distance but couldn't pinpoint exactly where from. The city around her seemed to be covered with a low-hanging mist. Terra wasn't sure if she hadn't noticed it before because of the chaos or if it simply hadn't been there. Something hissed behind her. Terra spun on her heels and raised the gun. The silhouette of the creature twitched through the fog: a sickly, dark almost-human shape with stretched arms and claws on its hands. It advanced towards her slowly and awkwardly as if it wasn't entirely sure what to do.

"St-stay back!" Terra stuttered.

The creature paused. It inched forward enough for Terra to see its mangled face. Its twisted lips stretched into a smile. Terra shuddered. Its teeth were almost human, in fact some of its original human teeth remained. Most, however, had been replaced by jagged teeth shooting through its lips. Terra knew that if it was able to sink those teeth into her, she'd never escape the monster. She levelled the gun at the creature's chest with unsteady hands and pulled the trigger. A bullet slammed into the monster's shoulder. The creature howled in pain. Terra fired again, this time hitting the thing in the stomach. The creature held a clawed hand over the impact. Terra fired several more times until the monster finally fell to the ground. With shaking hands, she inspected the gun. The top of the weapon had slid back and locked itself in place. Terra looked into the magazine inside: it was empty.

Footsteps echoed through the street. Through the mist loomed the shadow of another creature. Terra silently cursed; it must had heard the gunshots. From somewhere behind her, she heard a loud snapping sound as something flew past her ear. The creature's head split open, accompanied by the sound of the gunshot that echoed through the street. Terra looked around her, she could see the faint outlines of more creatures advancing through the mist. Another shot came. This time, however, it landed beside her, tearing up the tarmac of the road. Terra froze for a moment. Was this person aiming at her? Another two shots landed in the same spot beside her. Terra looked back at the silhouettes of the creatures. One was cut down by another shot, one more ran straight past her towards the sound of the weapon. But once again a few bullets hit the ground beside Terra, only now she realised the bullet marks seemed to form an arrow. The arrow pointed towards the sound of the shots. Another shot hit something just a few inches from Terra as another creature charged out of the mist. Terra broke into a sprint, following the arrow in the ground.

Terra managed to run for twenty seconds at full sprint before, like a lion on its prey, a Damned leapt at her. Terra's gun slid from her hands and disappeared into the mist. She managed to roll away from a clawed hand and threw the creature off her. The monster swung out its arm, its claws scraping against Terra's leg, pulling her back to the ground as she tried to run.

"No, for fuck's sake!" she cried. "Help! Please someone, help me!"

The monster crawled back on top of her, Terra grabbed its hands and pushed with all her might. She managed to hold the creature just a few inches away from her body.

With a loud snap and a horrible crunch, the skull of the creature split open from another bullet fired from a much closer range. Terra threw the body of the creature off her. Her face was covered in foul thick blood and her leg ached just below the knee, but she forced herself back onto her feet. A hand grabbed hold of Terra. Someone she couldn't see through the blood and the mist ushered her through the open doors of a large building.

Through her blurred vision, Terra could make out the familiar sight of a soldier in a boonie hat, wielding a sniper rifle. Sharpe pushed Terra through the door and hurried in himself. The sniper shattered the ribcage of another creature with a heavy kick and fired a few more times at an unseen enemy. Even after Sharpe slammed the door shut and locked it, the stress took its toll on Terra. A black curtain descended over her vision; she slipped into unconsciousness.

◆

"Twelve dead."

The words seemed to linger around Bruce's head for far longer than they should have. He was standing at the edge of the canyon that his men had chased the soldiers across. A few of his troops stood on guard nearby, watching the canyon. Directly behind him was Bruce's second-in-command. A large, bold ex-Royal Marine. He was big, not so much in height but in a rugby-player build. Bruce and Paul were both in their late forties. Bruce figured that was why they got on so well, seeing as most of their followers were much younger.

"What about the wounded one and the sharpshooter?" Bruce groaned.

"Someone grabbed all the wounded soldiers' weapons, we couldn't salvage the exo-suit either. It seems they have some kind of fail-safe mechanism built in to them. As for the sharpshooter, we sent five men out to get him, and so far, none of them have returned."

"That fucking cunt!" Bruce growled. "All those men lost for nothing."

Bruce rubbed his chin as he looked back at his other men scattered around the canyon.

"We're almost out of ammunition; we can't afford to face them in a straight-up fight again."

"I could take a small team and..." Paul started.

"Not a chance," Bruce interrupted. "It's not worth risking any more of the men for just a few rifles; the larger the force we have the better. We only do what we do to survive, so there isn't much point in going out for revenge..." Bruce looked out over the canyon again.

"Knowing this place. We'll get our chance for revenge later."

◀▶

When Terra came to, she felt something warm beside her. She soon found herself blinded by the fierce light of a fire. As Terra recoiled and her eyes began to adjust to the sudden light, she realised that she was inside an old church. The large doors were blocked by the majority of the benches and the stained-glass windows were mostly covered by wooden boards or dirty clothes. Sharpe sat opposite Terra putting the fire between himself and her. His unassembled rifle lay on a large mat before him. Sharpe was taking his time to clean each individual part of his beloved weapon.

After trying unsuccessfully to catch Sharpe's eye, Terra looked to the fire. She noticed a lot of the kindling seemed to be burnt paper. It didn't take her long to realise where that paper had come from.

"That's a little ironic really, isn't it?" she joked.

Sharpe didn't respond; he held the barrel towards the fire for a moment, checking it was clean. Satisfied, he went about reassembling the weapon. Sharpe had laid out all his weapon magazines in front of him. There were seven in total but only three were loaded; a few loose rounds sat beside one of the magazines.

"How many bullets do each of those hold?" Terra asked.

"Twenty," Sharpe replied.

His eyes never connected with hers, his words were barely even a whisper.

"So that's sixty shots and some spare? That sounds good," she said, trying her best to instigate conversation.

"No. I only load eighteen. Stops the magazine from jamming."

Sharpe finished reassembling his rifle. The sniper leant around behind him and grabbed something. He tossed Terra's bag over to her; her notebook and phone fell out in front of her.

"You dropped this outside."

"Oh, thank you!" Terra politely chirped, trying to lighten the mood.

Something hissed outside and Sharpe raised a finger to his lips. He slowly moved to one of the windows. He peered through the corner and studied the grounds outside.

"There's still a few out there. We'll wait them out, they'll get bored before long," Sharpe concluded.

He moved back to his magazines on the ground and started putting them away. Terra looked at the state of the building. A small toolbox sat beside the barricaded doors, an empty cardboard nail box sat next to a dull, rusted hammer.

"What are those things?" Terra asked. "Are they those Damned things everyone keeps talking about? They look human."

Sharpe looked up, finally locking eyes with Terra for just a moment.

"Yep."

He moved to the other side of the church and checked the other windows there.

"What happened to you?" Terra finally asked.

Sharpe ignored her; he sat back down and started putting his magazines back into their pouches across his vest.

"Have you just been hiding here while…?" Terra stopped herself short.

Sharpe shot her a glare; he pointed to a bloody bandage wrapped around his upper right arm.

"I've been busy."

"Boss and Sev are gone," Terra croaked; she studied his gaze looking for some kind of reaction.

"I know," was all Sharpe gave her in response.

"You know?" Terra snarled. "They died. While you were… what? Hiding safely in here?"

Sharpe pulled his bowie knife from his belt. Terra froze. The soldier held the blade out in front of them and put a finger to his lips. Something scratched against the wall outside; after a moment they heard faint footsteps moving away.

"I wasn't hiding," Sharpe whispered. "I was leading a few of them away. By the time I got back, the bridge had been cut and they were gone."

Terra stood up and advanced on the sniper.

"I never took you for a coward, but I guess I was wrong."

Sharpe was on his feet in an instant; he stood just a few inches from Terra's face. Rage tore across his face but Terra held her ground.

"Listen, kid," he snarled. "Don't you fucking dare. You don't know me, you don't know what I've done or what I've seen. Sev bled to death in my arms while Boss died trying to protect you and your fucking friends."

"You're lying," Terra grimaced. "There's no way you could have got there in time for that."

Sharpe moved to the side, sitting on an empty bench was the short AR-15 rifle that Sev had been carrying. A pair of dog tags, soaked in blood, hung from a chain wrapped around the barrel. Terra's composure dropped as she realised what she had just done.

"The worst thing is…" Sharpe growled into her ear, "the rest of my friends are all going to die trying to protect you. Just like Sev… or worse. But that's not what's really bugging me about all of this. What really gets to me is that they're all going to die protecting someone who did something so bad she ended up in this fucking nightmare."

"Fuck you! You don't know me either!" Terra screamed.

In a fit of rage, she punched Sharpe in the chest; her fist struck his armoured vest and split her knuckles. Terra recoiled in pain. From behind them the roof caved in. A single Damned dropped into the room. As the creature rose from the pile of rubble, Sharpe advanced with his bowie knife in hand.

"Wait, please don't!" Terra cried.

Sharpe leant back narrowly avoiding the swing of a clawed hand. He slammed his boot into the chest of the Damned. His exo-suit propelled the creature into the wall of the church and Sharpe rushed forward. With its chest cavity now completely collapsed, Sharpe pinned the struggling Damned to the wall with one of his legs.

"You wanna know about these things?" growled the Sniper. "This, Terra… is a Damned. Once upon a time it was human just like you and me, but the person it was spent too long in this place…"

"S-Stop… please!" Terra stuttered through an ocean of tears.

Sharpe continued.

"It stayed here for so long that it lost everything that made it human: its soul. And what was left morphed into this thing and this is what will happen to any of us who are lucky enough to stay alive in this place."

Sharpe locked eyes with Terra; she was a quivering mess kneeling on the floor in front of him. His cold eyes suddenly turned soft. He turned back to the Damned and with one heavy swing of his blade, stabbed the creature clean through the top of its head.

"I shouldn't be allowed to talk," Sharpe groaned. "The things I've done… I have no right to judge you."

He turned back to Terra, his neck bleeding from a wound he didn't have before the Damned had entered the church.

"Nobody deserves this… I'll get you to the end, Terra."

Terra shook her head as tears ran down her face.

"Why though? Why am I worth risking it?"

"Because I made a promise… and I intend to keep it."

CHAPTER 9

◆

IN THE HOUSE

Crawling through the fog-filled city proved more nerve-racking than Terra could have possibly imagined. Since they had been inside the church the fog had grown much thicker. She walked just a few paces behind Sharpe at a snail's pace as they slowly crept through the Damned-filled streets. Sharpe took care to steer them between the twisted humanoid shadows and figures. The sniper was now wearing a pair of what appeared to be sunglasses. Terra of course knew there had to be a lot more to those glasses than it seemed, but either way they looked very out of place in the darkness. It became immediately clear they had reached the end of the town when the fog simply stopped.

Terra stepped out onto what remained of the street ahead of her and was greeted with a wide-open field stretching out into the distance; on the other side a thick treeline loomed. Sharpe held out a hand as she neared the abrupt end of the tarmac. The road simply stopped a few feet from the fog. Sharpe scanned the treeline, slowly moving his head from side to side.

"What is it?" Terra asked cautiously.

The field was made of dark dirt, devoid of any of the usual trees and shrubs that covered the rest of Limbo.

"The others are at the end of that field," Sharpe croaked. "This is where it gets interesting."

Terra raised an eyebrow. Sharpe took a knee and pointed to the opposite side of the field.

"The second you set foot on that ground you need to run. Run faster than you've ever run in your life, do not stop, do not look back. Whatever happens, you have to get to the other side. I'll stay here and cover you. If we go together, we both die."

"What's out there?" Terra croaked.

Sharpe just shook his head. He pressed a button on the side of his rifle, which made a loud thud as a spring was released.

"Get ready. Do not look back. No matter what you hear, no matter what you see. Do not look back."

Terra nodded; she made sure her bag was secure and readied herself for the sprint. She guessed the distance was about five hundred metres to the trees. There were no Damned in the field, so this shouldn't be too difficult.

"Go."

Terra sprang off her heels and ran; she didn't look back, she trusted Sharpe's word and just kept running. She panted frantically but moved as if her life depended on it. There was something unnatural about this place, even by Limbo's standards. The ground was hard beneath her feet and the dirt didn't shift as she kicked off. As Terra ran, she felt good, she could make the distance. She felt this right up until she heard it. A sudden rush of air pushing down on her body accompanied by the low thumping of colossal wings beating the air.

She didn't dare look back; she shifted her limbs harder, faster, pushing them beyond their limits, but the flying creature came closer. She could feel the air pounding down as her legs started to burn; her eyes watered as her lungs started to tighten up, straining to pull in fresh air. When Terra was just one hundred metres from the end, two men wearing SOO uniforms stepped out of the trees and aimed their rifles in her direction.

No matter what happens, keep moving.

The two men opened fire and bullets whizzed past Terra's head. The snapping sounds Terra heard were a combination of the bullets breaking the sound barrier and then shattering off the hide of the thing bearing down on her. The flapping began to lose intensity as the creature pulled away. Terra collapsed just before the end of the field. She rolled onto her back, desperate for air. The two soldiers slid down the slight embankment and begun to pull Terra back up.

Terra watched as Sam slid down as well, levelling her rifle as Sharpe approached. Sam grabbed Sharpe's webbing with ferocious strength. Sharpe was a big guy but with just her right hand Sam almost ripped him off his feet. Terra didn't know what was more terrifying, Sam or Sharpe's ability not to show any fear while being manhandled by his sister. She stood there shaking with rage for a few seconds before her head dropped into his chest and the siblings embraced each other. Terra felt very guilty all of a sudden that she hadn't called her brother since she'd left for the States. A quick stabbing pain shot up her right thigh. The siblings pushed away from each other pointing their rifles to the sky and started blasting again.

Terra tried to spot the winged thing but her view was blocked by the trees. The soldiers pulled her through the gaps in the trees where she was able to catch a glimpse of a pair of thick black feathered wings that were holding up a body made of pure dark muscle. The creature seemed to be bipedal in nature with long claws at the ends of its feet, but she never did manage to get a good look at it.

Terra was helped to her feet by Machine and Wolfman. Sam and Sharpe returned to the group. Machine and Sharpe exchanged a quick nod. Irish patted him once on the shoulder and Wolfman stood very excitedly next to Sharpe for a second. He almost flinched when Sharpe raised a hand to his head and ruffled his hair affectionately. Sam threw Terra's arm over her shoulders for support.

"Told yah!" Sam chirped. She sniffed as she wiped a single tear from her eye. "It's good to have you back."

Terra tried to laugh but just ended up choking as she struggled for air. She caught a quick glimpse of Sharpe; he was barely winded.

If I had one of those exo-suits I wouldn't even need the gym, she thought to herself, not that she'd been to the gym for a while.

Terra was escorted to what had once been a farmhouse. She could tell this by the large barn that stood not too far past it in a clearing. Zero, Wolfman, Billy and Grace waited patiently on the porch of the house as the others approached. Billy rushed over to greet Terra.

Terra questioned if the group would be safe to hole up there but was assured by Irish that it was. Irish and Wolfman went about setting up a fire while Machine moved into the house. Zero ordered Sam to join him but she stayed close by as Zero confronted Sharpe. Billy ushered Terra towards the house but she stopped him to watch the exchange.

"What happened to leading them away?" Zero asked.

Sharpe met his cold glare; he pointed to his bloody bandage. "There were more than I expected; I got a couple though."

"Yeah. And the rest of them got Sev and Boss." Zero moved in close to Sharpe, who held his stance. All eyes were drawn to the two soldiers. "Not exactly a fair trade, you know," Zero hissed.

Terra headed towards the two men; she didn't know or care what pulled her forward and she definitely didn't care for Billy's half-hearted attempt to hold her back.

"He saved me. I'm only alive because of him," Terra interjected.

"Two men are dead."

"And they probably would have died anyway even if Sharpe had been with us… the only difference is, I would be too."

Zero shot her a glance before turning his attention back to Sharpe.

"Next time ya'll pull this shit, don't bother coming back," Zero spat.

The silver-haired soldier retreated back towards the farmhouse, defeated. Sam headed over to Sharpe. The sniper motioned to walk away but Sam got in the way. Terra never found out what exactly she did or said to him but suddenly Sharpe spun around and looked back at her.

"Thanks," Sharpe offered.

Sharpe moved off towards the treeline followed closely by Sam who gave Terra a brief thumbs up when she was sure Sharpe wasn't looking.

I guess that's as much as I can hope for from you. I'll take it.

◀▶

Austin Spencer sat at the desk in his office. A long, large window behind him showed the majesty of the SOO base. Dozens of operators ran their daily routines as helicopters took off and landed carrying various personnel with various different jobs and duties to attend to. All of which was accompanied by the beaming light of a summer's day in Texas. Austin himself was a tall, broad man in his late sixties. His hair had completely left his head long ago. All that remained was a thick grey beard that hung a few inches past his chin, stopping just shy of his shirt. He looked across his desk; it was occupied by an expensive-looking laptop complete with a fashionable light-up keyboard that glowed green in the office. To the right sat a picture of Austin, his late wife and two sons. Zach's head was locked in the arm of his older brother. Austin's youngest son was the spitting image of his younger self. Tall, silver-haired and pale. His brother took after the boy's mother more. Jacob was slightly shorter with a kinder face and warm smile. The picture had been taken just after Jacob took control of his own squad and earned the name 'Akira'. Austin didn't understand that reference but apparently it was from some Japanese movie and that told him all he needed to know.

Once upon a time these two men had just been young boys playing in his yard. Now the eldest was thirty, leading one of the best teams in the company, and his brother was looking like he was going to follow very soon. Beside that picture sat another image, this one of Zach again in his smart dress uniform grinning like an idiot next to his best friend from training. A tall, dark-haired young man who went by the name of Sharpe.

"Good thing you're keeping him safe, who knows what kind of trouble Zach would get into without you around."

The door to Austin's office opened and a large burly man in a clean suit stepped forward holding some files under his arm. The large ginger-haired man didn't looked much younger than Austin despite the colour of his hair. His expression was cold, his eyes open wide, as if he'd just seen a ghost.

"What's the matter, Mac? You keep looking at me like that, I'm gonna start getting Desert Storm flashes."

Austin chuckled to himself for a moment then slowly lost his smile when he saw the expression on Mac's face hold firm. Mac's Scottish voice growled through the air like fingernails down a chalkboard.

"Moi airport was just attacked. The whole building is on fire and nobody can get in touch with Boss's team. Akira is en route to reinforce but the situation isn't looking good. Kenyan military forces are moving to secure the area as well. Several attack helicopters have been intercepted and shot down."

Austin leant back in his chair; his heart sank deep into his stomach.

"I want everyone in the country on that location right now. Have them secure and aid in the rescue effort as best they can."

Mac looked Austin dead in the eyes, taking a long pause before speaking the next few words.

"Sir. The whole building is on fire. There's no way anyone survived."

◂▸

Terra and Billy walked slowly towards the barn. Sam had called them over to go through something she had described as important. The other soldiers were gathering up equipment and picking up some of the few mines and traps they had set around the farmhouse, though Terra couldn't see Wolfman or Sharpe anywhere. She shrugged, figuring they must have been inside the house. As they walked, Terra lifted her head and looked up at the sky. Thick clouds hung overhead; between them Terra could see those purple lights slithering between the openings.

Do they really lead anywhere? Or are we just clinging to them for comfort?

Sam was leaning against the open barn doors with a blank expression as she watched the treeline.

"Hey Sam," Billy greeted. "What's going on?"

Sam's head snapped to the two students, her face changing as her mind drifted back from whatever it was she had been thinking about, and a warm smile crossed her face.

"Something you're really gonna like, Billy."

Billy excitedly hurried inside the barn leaving Terra and Sam behind. Terra gave Sam a concerned look.

"He's in a surprisingly good mood," Terra said.

Sam's expression changed slightly; for just a second, she looked sad. She was probably thinking about Boss and Sev, Terra reasoned.

"Yeah…" Sam murmured. Her warm smile came back to her face along with the twinkle of excitement in her eyes. "Come on in, class is in session."

Terra followed Sam into the barn. A small fire had been set in the centre of the open floor. Several bales of hay had been pushed out to the far sides of the room and the small fire was surrounded by rocks and stones to contain the flame.

Sharpe stood opposite the fire. Billy and Grace sat opposite him. Terra felt something move around in her bag. Sam produced the handgun she had given Terra in the city and checked the chamber. She shot Terra a quick wink before stepping around the fire and handing the weapon to Sharpe.

He checked the weapon over a few times, his large hands dwarfing the compact pistol. He spun the weapon around before he handed it back to Sam.

Sharpe walked briefly to the back of the barn out of the light and walked back holding Sev's rifle.

"We had a talk while you guys were resting in the house. We've decided that each of you should be carrying a weapon, and know how to use it," Sharpe said with about as much energy as Terra had heard from him since she had arrived in Limbo.

Sharpe tossed the rifle around in his hands a few times and held the weapon up to the students.

"I won't bore you with too much detail but this is an AR-15. With the exception of myself and Irish, it is the weapon carried by everyone in the team. Although they vary in size and shape they all operate in the same way."

Sharpe pointed to a small switch on the right side of the weapon just above the trigger. The small arrow was surrounded by three icons in the shape of bullets. The one it was set to showed a white outline with a line through it.

"Safety catch. This stays on until you have the sight on target and really want to kill something." Sharpe switched the lever to the second setting, a single red bullet icon. "Semi-automatic. For every pull of the trigger you get one bullet out of the barrel. The final switch is fully automatic. Which means it turns into a machine gun. This is almost never used in combat and if you have to use a rifle like this, just pretend it doesn't exist. This weapon will empty its thirty-round magazine in about two seconds and everything after the first three shots is going to miss."

Sharpe pulled a short sling from his belt, attached it to the weapons stock and handed the rifle to Billy. Billy's eyes expanded so wide, he looked as if they might pop out of his head.

"It's fitted with a red dot sight; just put the dot on target and pull the trigger. You've got one magazine. Thirty shots, but this is only ever to be used in an emergency. Only if you have no other choice."

Sam appeared beside Terra and whispered into her ear.

"That's probably a little bigger than what he's used to playing with."

Terra had to bite her tongue to stop herself from laughing. She snorted once as she wrenched forward. Sharpe glared at Sam who just shrugged nonchalantly.

"And what exactly would class as an emergency?" Grace barked as her frustrations got the better of her. "What's the point in us learning this? We're not soldiers! If we get attacked by more people or those things then we're just going to hide behind you guys!"

"Grace!" Terra snarled. "I don't like guns either but this could keep us alive out here…"

"Shut it, freak!" Grace snapped. "You only care about this so you can get closer to Captain Psycho there!"

Terra gritted her teeth as she locked eyes with Grace; she grabbed Grace's shirt and pulled her in close.

"Sorry, but while you were busy hiding behind Zero, I was out there nearly getting eaten alive by those fucking monsters!" Terra's tone dropped to a cold, almost primal growl. "Why don't you try getting this close to one of those things and tell me you'd still rather not learn to defend yourself."

Sharpe's cold, flat, empty tone cut through the tense teen girls.

"Hiding from something is a perfectly natural response to a dangerous situation, as is seeking the help of someone stronger, but what exactly are you going to do when there's none of us left to hide behind?"

The hearts of all three students suddenly fell into their stomachs. Terra understood now why they were all so calm. The soldiers had already accepted the fact that none of them were going to survive this journey.

Terra looked to Sharpe. The sniper's eyes met with hers for a moment. Thick bags hung from those cold blue circles, his whites were bloodshot and even his breathing was a little ragged. After a few seconds Grace stood up and left the barn; she hissed a curse in the direction of Terra as she left. Sam walked over to Billy; she tapped him on the shoulder and motioned for him to follow her.

"Hey, I'd rather stay here. With Terra," Billy said.

"No..." Terra mumbled. She took a deep breath and wiped the tears from her eyes. "It's okay, really."

Billy reluctantly followed Sam out of the barn. Sharpe's gaze followed them until they were outside.

"Back in the town," Sharpe started, catching Terra off guard. She couldn't believe he was speaking so much. "When you fired at that Damned, that pistol didn't feel right in your hands, did it?"

Terra motioned to her bag, but realised Sam had already taken the pistol back.

"Well, I've never shot a real gun before so I don't really know what I'm looking for..."

Sharpe cut her off.

"Your little finger was under the grip; it didn't look comfortable in your hand."

Terra tried to respond but still didn't fully understand the question. She stuttered out a few incoherent words before Sharpe reached down for his own holster and produced his Glock handgun. He checked the safety and spun the gun around and handed Terra his pistol, grip first.

"That's a 34; it's been heavily customised to fit my hand. Sam's got tiny hands so she uses a smaller model."

As he spoke Terra took the weapon and practised taking aim. Unlike Sam's weapon, Sharpe's Glock had a small red dot sight at the rear. It was much sportier, too, though a little larger.

"I have to admit this is a lot nicer." Terra placed the red dot over one of the barn's support beams.

"I grabbed a spare on my travels so you can take that one. Safety catch is the lever just above your thumb; just put the dot on the target and away you go."

Terra looked over the weapon; it truly was a better fit and it even felt oddly comfortable in her hands.

"Won't you need it?" she asked honestly, though silently hoping Sharpe would say no.

"No. Soldiers don't tend to use their pistols in combat; if they do it means the situation is bad and they're probably not going to survive anyway."

"Thank you for this," Terra said. She couldn't help but smile, even though she knew the sniper would never accept her gratitude.

"You're welcome, kid."

Terra almost gasped. Sharpe tensed up a little. "Truth be told I wanted you to carry the rifle, but Zero disagreed and that's that. If… when you need to use that, try aiming for the chest and if you can, the head, and it should do the trick."

With that he kicked out the fire and walked out of the barn. Terra followed only to find Sam leaning against the barn door. Terra waited until Sharpe had made it a few feet away.

"I didn't think he was capable of talking so much!" Terra said a little too excitedly.

Sam winked.

"Smart guys have hobbies. All you have to do is get them talking about those hobbies, and then your only problem will be shutting them up. Though when they're done talking, they'll start listening."

"Hey, Sam. Back at the petrol station, I overheard something between Boss and Sev. It sounded like they were talking abou—"

Sam cut her off very abruptly.

"Forget whatever you heard," Sam sighed. "It won't be a problem so long as the rest of us are around."

Terra looked at her confused.

"Then why did you leave us in there all…"

Wolfman came jogging out of the trees before Terra could finish. His face told the women something was very wrong.

"Hey Sam, you and Sharpe are going to want to see this."

Wolfman was speaking so quietly Terra struggled to hear him. His eyes fluttered about from side to side; he almost screamed when Sharpe appeared beside him.

"All right then," Sam whispered.

The three soldiers followed Wolfman towards the trees; after a few paces Sam motioned for Terra to follow. Terra wearily followed the soldiers and Sam fell back to join her. Worryingly, though, Sam's eyes seemed locked on the trees to their right as they walked.

Is she looking at the same spot from earlier?

As they walked Terra looked up at the swirling purple lights above. She'd forgotten all about them during the chaos. The lights continued on their journey towards wherever it was they were going, the same place she and the soldiers were going. In the pit of her stomach, though, Terra felt wrong. Something was different in the air now.

The overhead lights disappeared beneath the canopy of petrified trees. It was dark here, darker than the first set of woods Terra had found herself in. Her eyes strained against the new-found darkness as she ran through her satchel trying to find her phone. Sam's gloved hand fell on Terra's arm with a gentle touch.

"I know that seems like a good idea but all it's going to do is blind you," Sam croaked. "You don't realise just how dark it is because you've spent so much time in it; if we turn on our flashlights or you your phone, it's going to blind you for at least a minute, and even after your eyes adjust to the light you'll be completely blind if you look anywhere other than within that circle of light…" Sam peered over her shoulder into the darkness. "And whatever is stalking us will do anything and everything in its power to avoid that light."

Terra froze.

"St-St…" She took a deep, shaky breath. "Stalking us?"

Sam nodded slowly; she indicated to a tree just ahead of them. Terra could faintly make out the white of the uniforms belonging to Sharpe and Wolfman. The two soldiers were crouched down running their fingers through the dirt. Sam and Terra approached cautiously.

"Any ideas?" Wolfman asked.

Terra looked down at the ground. She could barely see anything until she knelt down beside the soldiers. Wolfman held up a hand to the girl. Terra followed as he pointed down at the shape of the dirt. He traced the outline of a shape planted into the ground.

"A footprint?" Terra whispered.

Wolfman nodded slowly.

Terra studied the shape. The enormous print dwarfed her own feet.

"Is this some kind of bear print?" she asked cautiously.

Wolfman rubbed a hand over his face.

"Yeah, see that's what I thought. But this shape is more reminiscent of a wolf."

"Too deep for a wolf," Sharpe added. "Matches the shape, but it would have to be about the size of a grizzly bear to sink its feet that deep into the ground."

Terra looked over at Sam. She was standing with her legs spread out uncomfortably wide. Any wider and she would have dropped into a split. Sam slung her rifle across her back and dropped down to all fours, splaying her limbs out as wide as she could.

"Ah… this thing…" she grunted as she stretched her body out. "It must be a bear, definitely stalking something." Terra carefully moved up beside Sam.

"Wow, I didn't realise you were so flexible, Sam!" Wolfman giggled. He stopped and looked away when he realised Sharpe was glaring at him.

Terra traced the four prints Sam was using; something was wrong with this image.

"Sam… look at the front prints, they don't match the rear ones."

Sam righted herself as the two male soldiers came to join them. Sharpe knelt down at Terra's feet.

"She's right. The way the digits sink in…" He paused for a long moment.

"It's walking on its knuckles?"

"Like a gorilla?" Terra asked.

Sharpe stared down at the mysterious print, anticipating Terra's follow-up question.

"Why would it walk on its knuckles?"

Sharpe extended his hand into the dirt; he curled his fingers around, mimicking the motion of the creature. It moved with its hands held slightly open, so its fingers could be pointed away from the palm of its hand.

"Oh no…" Terra murmured.

"It's keeping its claws out of the dirt." Sharpe paused for a moment as he thought about it. "Big claws."

"Okay then," Wolfman interjected, "so we have a wolf–gorilla hybrid that's the size of a grizzly bear stalking the camp?"

Wolfman's eyes lit up with childlike excitement.

"It's a werewolf!" he exclaimed.

"Wolfman," Sam hissed. "Don't be ridiculous, it's not a bloody werewolf."

"No…" Sharpe croaked; something in his tone drew the attention of everyone else. "It's not just one…"

The sniper reached out for the light at the end of his rifle; he turned a dial at the rear of the device and the faintest, weakest beam fell on the ground by Terra's feet. They all followed as the beam scanned across the ground revealing the monster's tracks.

One set, two sets… five sets… ten… twenty…

"Oh my God!" Wolfman croaked.

A twig snapped somewhere close by. Terra was immediately surrounded by all three soldiers. Rifles scanned from side to side, searching for any sign of movement.

"We're thinking giant wolves, right?" Sam panted. "They'll try to split us up and take the stragglers first; keep Terra close and move slowly."

Rifles scanned the darkness, flashing from one tiny noise to the next. The barrels of the weapons moved methodically as they traced invisible targets hiding in the darkness. The soldiers managed to keep their cool right up until they cleared the trees and made it back to the farmhouse compound. Sharpe and Wolfman instantly dropped to one knee pointing their weapons back towards the tree line while Sam and Terra made a dash for the rest of the team. Zero watched from the open door of the farmhouse as the two girls approached. Irish and Machine took up their weapons when they noticed the commotion.

"Give me the good news," Zero moaned.

Sam looked around them, scanning the trees. Zero studied her expression; Sam leant in and whispered into his ear.

"We're surrounded… they're in the trees. We need to go."

Zero tensed slightly at the next part.

"Not Damned, something worse."

The silver-haired soldier nodded slowly; he turned to Machine and Irish.

"You two, go round up the rest of the kids. We're moving."

Machine and Irish shared a look.

"Don't you want to pick up the traps?" Machine said in a slightly louder tone than usual. "We got a lot of mines around this area, we wouldn't want anyone stepping on one by mistake."

Zero smirked.

"No, it's okay, we left the front entrance clear. I doubt they'll come out of the trees." Zero lifted three fingers to Machine. The soldier nodded.

Within a minute everyone was gathered at the rear of the clearing behind the farmhouse. Billy, Grace and Terra found themselves at the centre of a tight formation with soldiers on all sides. With a deep, heavy breath Zero nodded to his group, and led them into the trees.

CHAPTER 10

◆

IN A HEARTBEAT

The ground was littered with dead leaves that crunched loudly with every step. Terra and the other students tried their best to move quietly but the soldiers were hurrying them along. Terra and Grace had to break into a jog a few times to keep up.

"Will someone please tell me what's going on?" said a disgruntled Grace. She'd been part way through washing her hair; the air around them stunk of cheap soap as they moved through the trees.

"Grace..." Terra panted, "shut up and keep moving."

"Why?" Grace complained. "It's not like we're running on dead crunchy leaves that are making plenty of fucking noise anyway!"

Zero suddenly raised a hand and the formation came to a halt. The students almost rammed into the soldiers leading the group. Something disturbed the dirt ahead of them, dead leaves rustled to the right while something scratched one of the trees to the rear. The squad leader turned back to his troops.

"Glasses on."

The soldiers all reached into their webbing and took out a set of the same black sunglasses that Terra had seen Sharpe wearing back in the town.

"Oh my God!" Machine croaked.

"Aye," replied Irish. "They're everywhere."

Terra felt another hand take hold of hers. Grace's eyes were darting around the formation, trying to see the creatures.

"What the hell is going on!" she cried.

"Stay calm and keep quiet," Zero ordered.

"Jesus Christ, they're fucking huge!" Wolfman moaned.

Terra was far more focused on Grace. She was shivering; she darted around the tight space in the middle of the soldiers, her chest rising and falling in rapid breaths. Terra gently took hold of Grace's shoulders.

"Hey, Grace… you need to relax a little, okay?"

Something growled. It was a hideous low rumbling sound that echoed through the trees, cutting right through the girls. Somewhere else another wolf howled.

"What the fuck was that?" Grace yelled.

"Keep it down," Sharpe hissed over his shoulder.

"Hey, it was probably just a wolf," Billy reasoned. Though it was clear from a single glance at his expression he didn't really believe that. A large tree branch snapped from the rear of the formation.

"Zero," croaked Machine. "We need to make a move, brother."

"No, we stand our ground and stay together!" Zero snapped.

"Aye, he's right," Irish agreed. "They'll go for the stragglers first."

"What will?" Grace's voice had raised to a high-pitched squeal.

"We're being hunted," Sharpe croaked, his rifle moved slowly to the right as he tracked his target.

"Well, do something then!" Grace yelped.

"Grace, shu…" Sam turned back to her target.

"Back off!" she snarled.

The three students all glanced over as something reared up onto its hind legs, and it really was as tall as a bear. Its arms were longer, its fingers were flexed, catching a sliver of light from above, revealing a set of six-inch claws at the tips of almost-human fingers.

"No, no, no, please no!"

"Everyone stay calm!" Zero ordered.

The beast's lips pulled back revealing sharp white teeth and a thick red tongue. Another silhouette appeared beside the monster, this one moving on all four limbs. The second creature reared up onto its hind legs and let out an enormous howl.

And now the hunt begins.

"No, I don't want to die!" Grace screamed; she pushed through the formation, rushing between Machine and Irish. The two soldiers were too focused on the creatures surrounding them. Terra, fuelled by pure instinct, raced through the split between the men to follow her terrified friend.

"Grace, stop!"

"Damn it, kid," hissed Sharpe. The sniper tried following, but the moment he cleared the formation a wolf-like creature leapt out of the darkness in front of him, while a second carved its way into the gap between him and the other soldiers.

"Fuck! Open fi—"

Nobody waited for the order; the soldier's rifles burst into life as the monsters came pouring out of the trees.

Either Terra was getting fitter or she was just full of adrenaline. Either way she easily managed to keep up with Grace. She firmly grasped Sharpe's handgun taking care to keep it pointed away from herself and Grace as they ran. Terra stopped when she realised Grace was slowing down; she ducked behind a nearby tree as Grace staggered over, falling to the ground beside her. Terra reached out, pulling Grace round behind the tree. Grace was skinny but in her limp state Terra still strained to get her into cover quietly.

"Grace, what the fuck was that? What were you thinking?" Terra whispered.

Grace struggled against her aching lungs. Terra peeked around the base of the tree as she heard more gunfire. The trees were echoing the sound, throwing off the shooter's position. The only upside she could see was that at least whatever they were running from would be thrown off as well… Hopefully.

"The monsters are coming…" Grace murmured. "We're all going to die."

"We'll be fine," Terra whispered. "If we can't see them then they can't see us!" She didn't believe the words she was saying but panicking wouldn't help their situation.

She knew if they didn't find the soldiers soon they would be in trouble, though if they did then by the sounds of things they may be in even more danger. Something disturbed the leaves just beyond the tree. Terra readied her weapon as Grace's breathing became more and more frantic behind her; she was mumbling some sort of prayer but Terra suspected nobody was listening.

Terra's suspicion was only confirmed when a set of long clawed fingers reached around the base of the tree just above her head. The two girls froze; Terra held her breath. The fingers looked similar to those of a Damned. Or rather, they would have if they had been half the size. This was no Damned, they were twisted, once-human things whose bodies had been bent and moulded into awkward shapes. This hand belonged to something designed to kill. With just the slightest effort its claws sank deep into the bark of the tree.

"Grace…" Terra mouthed, too frightened to form words. "G-Get… back."

The snout of the monster soon followed around the tree. It was shorter than that of most dogs and bore a clear resemblance to the furry animals Terra once loved. The beast growled with a tone so deep and low, Terra felt her very bones resonating the sound. It was huge. Before its eye could come into view its sickly black lips peeled back, showing rows of thick, strong white teeth, perfect for crushing bone. Slowly its mouth opened; the smell of rotting meat slammed the two frightened girls like a fist. Terra's stomach turned inside out but she was too scared to vomit. She was frozen in place. A huge black eye followed the snout around the tree; though it held no pupil, Terra could feel the monster's gaze on her face. A thick red tongue slithered across its teeth, flicking droplets of bloody saliva over Terra.

Terra's shaking hands gripped the handgun; if she was fast, she had a chance. Yes, she'd put the gun to the monster's eye and blow its fucking brains out. She wasn't going to die here. A sudden force pushed Terra forward; her face planted into the dead leaves and dirt. She felt the force of a foot on her back as Grace stepped over her screaming, "Take her and leave me alone!"

Terra managed to right herself in time to see Grace's legs being pulled out from under her by a long-clawed arm attached to another of the wolf-like creatures. Grace screamed as she fell to the ground. The monster must have stood at least ten feet tall; its forearms were unnaturally long, with short, stocky hind legs that made the creature move more like a gorilla than a wolf. A clawed finger slipped into Grace's lower leg like a hot knife into butter. Grace was dragged back towards the monster kicking and screaming, pleading for her life.

"Please! No, don't! I don't wanna die, take her! Take Terra and leave me alone!"

Terra could have sworn the monster smiled. Its jaws opened. Grace screamed a desperate primal scream of pure fear as the bloody jaws closed around her left arm. It wasn't a fast snap, more of a slow build-up of pressure.

With the slightest effort, the monster took Grace's arm clean off with a hideous squelching sound. Terra's gun was up; she placed the red dot on her sight over the monster's face as it crushed Grace's severed arm in its mouth, splattering blood and fragments of bone over the floor, the screaming girl still pinned under its claw.

Grace's scream tore through Terra's ears like a thousand nails down a chalkboard. It was a horrible, desperate sound. Terra moved the gun down to Grace's head and started to squeeze the trigger.

"Shoot it! Shoot it, you stupid fucking bitch!" Grace cried. Her mouth starting to fill with blood.

Terra never noticed the original monster approach from behind, but she felt it. A long-clawed hand reached over, gently resting on her pistol and pushing her arm down, its open snout extending into view. Terra sobbed; she had nothing left. Too scared to fight and not fast enough to run away, she was going to die, but first she was going to watch her friend be torn to pieces in front of her. With a swipe, the monster pinning Grace down flipped her onto her back and sliced open her belly, spilling thick red guts onto the floor in a cloud of crimson chaos. Terra closed her eyes, preparing herself for the end. At least if the monster grabbed her head, she'd die quickly.

Terra's eyes suddenly opened as the high-speed rattling of an assault rifle tore through the trees. The hound on top of Grace fell back, violently convulsing under the long burst of fire. Zero stepped into the light as he put the remainder of his magazine into the wolf's face. The creature holding Terra grabbed her, forcing her in front of itself to be used as a human shield. Zero drew his handgun and took aim. Terra could feel the fear running through the creature, or it could have been excitement. Its mouth was making a low, unsteady growling sound. Zero's gaze darted to the trees beside him; when he looked back at Terra his expression had changed. The thing holding Terra stopped as it realised what Zero was about to do.

"Just shoot the fucking thing!" Terra yelled.

Zero looked down at his gun, then back at Terra. He shook his head slowly.

"I'm sorry, kid…" Zero, along with all of Terra's hopes of survival, disappeared into the trees.

A series of low thumps of a high-powered rifle echoed past Terra. The creature looked around trying to find the source of the sound. Terra remembered she was still holding Sharpe's handgun. If no one was going to save her, she'd have to save herself. Her body moved on instinct; before she knew it, she'd taken aim at the wolf creature's knee joint and fired. Stunned, the wolf dropped Terra to clutch its shattered knee. Terra hit the ground, rolled over, kicked the wolf creature's snout, knocking out a few teeth and finally fired five shots into its ugly muzzle.

The wolf cried out briefly as the bullets tore into its face. After the fifth shot it fell onto its back. Terra lay still on the ground panting heavily as the effects of the adrenalin started to fade. Her muscles ached, her wrists in particular from the recoil of the gun.

"T-Terra…" spluttered Grace.

Terra rolled over and managed to make it up to her feet. Grace's last remaining hand was reaching out, her chin covered in thick blood.

"I-I'm s… sorr…" she started to cough violently, fresh blood spluttered from her mouth, covering her face. Terra looked down at the gun in her hands; she knew what she had to do. First Grace, then herself. It would be a far better fate than what they'd receive at the hands of these beasts.

A twig snapped behind her. She spun around, squeezing the trigger as she moved. A gloved hand caught the gun just as it went off, barely a millilitre away from Sharpe's face. Terra froze. A thin cut was now carved across his right cheek. Sharpe held up his free hand.

"Sorry, I should have called out first," he croaked, completely unfazed by the fact that Terra had just shot him.

Terra tried to apologise but was completely unable to form words. Sharpe paid her no attention. He moved slowly towards Grace; with a blank expression, he knelt down beside the dying girl.

"I-I couldn't… I couldn't…" Terra sobbed.

Sharpe shook his head. He produced a small syringe that he slid into Grace's remaining arm. Grace tried to say something but Sharpe stopped her.

"Relax… this will help with the pain."

The morphine entered Grace's body, and after a few seconds her eyes closed and she lay very still.

"You don't ever come back from that..." Sharpe croaked. "Whatever the reason. When you kill another human being, even out of mercy, you never get back that little piece of yourself. It dies along with them." Sharpe stayed beside Grace for a few seconds. "I hope you never go through that."

He reached into one of his pouches and pulled out a pair of the black sunglasses he had been wearing earlier. He held them out towards Terra.

"Put these on and head back to the others... you don't need to see this."

"N-No..." Terra sobbed. "You'll just leave again."

The sniper shook his head.

"I'll be right behind you," Sharpe croaked in a tone that was almost as human as the voice Terra had heard from him at the airport. His cold blue eyes relaxed ever so slightly. "I promise."

Terra took the glasses and pushed them over her eyes. She instantly realised how Sharpe had been able to shoot all those Damned through the fog. The seemingly normal, if slightly oversized, sunglasses were, in fact, high-powered night-vision goggles. Terra could see ten times further through the trees. Sharpe's name and a rough image of his sniper rifle hung above his head. As Terra looked around her, she spotted a compass at the top of her vision. Then she caught a glimpse of the names of the other soldiers. They were all grouped together to the north.

How can there be a north?

Terra looked up at the sky and got her answer. The lights were all flowing in that same direction.

Terra turned from the sniper and ran towards the other soldiers. She slipped past a few more of the wolf creatures, doing her best to give them a wide berth, and soon reached the edge of the forest. Terra found herself in the middle of a war zone.

Before Terra stood a twenty-foot stone wall that shot up out of the ground and stretched as far as the eye could see. The remaining soldiers were clumped together at the edge of the wall firing their weapons relentlessly as the wolves charged towards them. Machine and Irish stood at the front of a V-formation blasting anything that dared to move. Sam's rifle must have run dry as she was now fending off the wolves with her sidearm. Wolfman stood at the other side trying to put down a large creature that was barrelling towards him, holding up its arms to shield its face. His rifle clicked empty. Terra watched in bewilderment as he dropped the rifle, drew his combat knife and flung it straight into the wolf's stomach. The monster looked down at the blade now sticking out of its gut and then slowly raised its head to Wolfman, who laughed nervously.

The wolf creature took a hold of the blade's handle with its sickly long fingers and tore it free. Somehow the inhuman beast had found a way to look even more terrifying. With a gunshot that was far more comparable to a lightning strike the right side of the wolf's face exploded. Irish was now wielding his machine gun in one hand and in his other he held the largest revolver that Terra had ever seen. The gleaming silver weapon was a piece of destructive art that dwarfed Terra's handgun. After Irish had fired, the weapon had kicked up so high it was practically pointing at the sky.

That thing would make Clint Eastwood green with envy.

"Terra, down!" Sam barked.

She dropped to the ground as Sam fired over her head into the beast behind her. Before she could get back up to her feet,

Sharpe ran out of the treeline and scooped her up under his arm. He cleared the distance to the others in a second, dropping Terra to the ground behind the formation. Terra looked back at the wall to see Zero and Billy trying desperately to pull out a series of smaller rocks that seemed to be covering the opening to a cave. Zero stopped as his gaze met Terra's. The shame that washed over him was so intense that Billy seemed to feel it as well.

"Time and a place, guys!" Billy grunted as he pulled out a particularly large rock. The remaining rocks crashed down, almost crushing Billy and Zero before they could move aside. The cave entrance was narrow, barely large enough for one person.

"Hey, most of us aren't going to fit through there!" Machine yelled as he moved behind Irish to reload.

"We send the kids through here and we'll go around!" barked Zero. "Sam, Wolfman, you guys are small enough to fit so you go with them. Everyone else with me."

Zero didn't make eye contact as he pushed past Terra. He was too fixated on blasting a wolf that had got within swinging distance of Sharpe. The sniper had to have seen the monster coming but chose to completely ignore the creature to cover his left flank. The two men moved together as one; they fired their weapons with expert precision and trust in each other. Even though she wasn't a soldier, Terra found their coordination impressive.

Wolfman and Sam threw on their glasses. Sam moved into the cave first followed by Terra and then Billy. Wolfman stayed at the entrance to cover them. The cave was incredibly dark; even with the glasses on, Terra could barely see Sam in front of her. The gunshots echoed down the cave. A deep scream followed as the creatures got to someone.

"Ignore that, they'll be fine, just keep moving," Sam yelled back. The cave seemed to split into a series of smaller tunnels. Sam led the trio down the largest opening; she moved slowly, swinging her rifle towards every opening and crevice. She froze. Billy bumped into Terra as she stopped as well. Sam held up one hand.

"Against the walls now!" she whispered.

The two students followed the command. They each slid up against one side of the cavern making themselves as flat to the wall as they could manage. Sam did the same across the opposing wall. Terra could see about two feet in either direction with the glasses, figuring they must have had some sort of built-in infrared light. Terra was once again ripped away from her thoughts by the ruthlessness of Limbo. One of the wolf creatures was strolling slowly down the cave. The creature was a little smaller than the ones Terra had seen outside; it moved slowly on all fours. Its nostrils flared as it caught an alluring smell. A thin line of text appeared over Terra's eyes: "Shift left slow."

Terra looked up at Sam, who was slowly moving to the side, trying to slip past the creature without it noticing. The beast turned its head towards Terra, stopping just a few inches away from her face. Terra held her breath instinctively, turning her head away, trying to get away from that repulsive smell of rot emitting from the wolf's hideous snout. She felt its hot breath as its jaws opened slowly.

A small stone rolled down the cavern. Terra could see Wolfman's arrow in the same direction. The wolf's attention shifted to the stone and then up towards Wolfman, moving towards him. As the beast moved towards what it hoped was prey, Terra and the others slipped carefully past. The passageway split into two directions ahead.

Sam looked back at the students, though with her glasses on they couldn't see her eyes, but Terra just knew it wasn't a look of pleasure. Sam's body tensed; she had seen something the students hadn't. She mimed a curse through gritted teeth. The lines of text appeared over Terra's vision again.

"Billy."

Terra turned around slowly. Billy was just a few feet behind, clumsily reaching out to find her. Hovering there above his head was the long bloody snout of a wolf. Its nostrils flared as it took a long slow breath inwards, smelling the air. Billy must have felt the change in the wind as he fell very still. Sweat dripped from his forehead; his eyes slammed closed as he silently prayed for help. Sam's rifle raised as she took aim at the creature. A second snout appeared, followed by a third. Text appeared over Terra's vision once more.

"Get going Terra."

Terra turned back to Sam. The soldier had relaxed her stance a little; she was looking at Terra with a slight smile creeping across her face.

"Take Billy and go."

Terra shook her head; she mimed her objection but Sam had already made up her mind.

"Goodbye my friend."

Sam dropped an empty bullet casing onto the ground by her feet. The three snouts all locked on to her. Terra grabbed Billy on instinct and turned for the first passageway. She had just made it through the opening before another line of text appeared over her eyes for the final time.

"Keep bro safe."

If Sam screamed, Terra never knew. Sam's rifle lit up like a jackhammer in one long burst that echoed through the cave, leaving a ringing in the ears of the frightened students as they ran with all the strength they could muster.

◂▸

When Terra and Billy reached the cave's exit, they found the other soldiers already there. Irish was crouched in front of the cave's exit keeping his machine gun raised at the opening in case any of them were followed. Terra and Billy fell out of the cave into an open field. Zero was facing out away from them scanning across the open space. Sharpe was crouching down with Machine, whose left arm had been sliced open. Sharpe was busy applying a bandage. Machine looked over at the students lying exhausted on the ground.

"Oh, fancy meeting you guys here," he greeted excitedly.

His expression suddenly dropped when he realised it was just the two of them. Sharpe's gaze fell on Terra.

"Hey, we seem to be missing some sex appeal, where's the rest of the girls?" Machine asked.

Terra's ears were still ringing but she could just about make out his words. She looked to Sharpe, dropping her glasses to the floor as she tried to find the words.

"Contact rear!" barked Irish.

Every gun the group had was suddenly pointed at the cave exit. Wolfman stumbled into the light with his hands raised. He was soaked in sweat, his right eye bruised; new cuts and scratches covered his face and exposed lower arms but of more concern, he was missing his ring finger on his left hand. The others all relaxed.

"There were so many of them…" Wolfman panted.

"Go take a rest, kid, I'll take a look at that hand in a second," Irish said softly.

"Where's Sam?" Sharpe asked.

Wolfman shook his head.

"I didn't see her, man, couldn't find Grace either, I think those things got…"

"Grace is gone," Sharpe growled; the others all turned to face him. "I found her with Terra; one of those things got hold of her."

The heads of the others all bowed in a moment of silent mourning. Billy put his hands over his mouth, shaking his head violently. Sharpe looked down at Terra. Her hearing was back but the ringing still hadn't stopped, and it was going to be a while before it did.

"Where's Sam?" Sharpe croaked.

Terra looked away from him.

"Terra!" Sharpe barked.

"Easy!" Machine growled. "The kids have been through a lot. Look, if Wolfman got out then Sam can't be too far behind."

"She's not coming," Billy yelled, grabbing the attention of everyone else.

"Billy," Sharpe said firmly. "What happened?"

The frightened young man shook his head; his expression told the others everything they needed to know. Everyone fell quiet; the wind whistled past them into the trees.

"Oh no…" Irish murmured.

Machine was on his feet; he kicked a rock and cursed in frustration. Wolfman dropped to his knees with a blank expression and Terra found herself watching Sharpe. The sniper's cold eyes fell on the cave exit. Terra knew what was coming.

"All right then," said Sharpe with an eerily calm tone. "Take the kids and I'll go get Sam. We'll catch up…"

“Not a chance.” The words came from Zero’s mouth as he re-joined the group. Sharpe looked back over his shoulder not making eye contact.

“Boss gave us a mission. We all need to see it through. I can’t risk the lives of anyone else.”

Terra had managed to pull herself up to her feet; she wasn’t sure why but she had subconsciously moved very close to Sharpe.

“Do you honestly think you can stop me?” Sharpe challenged, moving back towards the edge of the cave.

“Oh yeah sure, you go and then we’ll see who gets killed next because of you!” Zero retorted.

Something in Sharpe snapped. He turned back to Zero with fury in his eyes.

“The fuck did you just say to me?”

The two soldiers advanced towards each other ready to fight. Irish and Machine were up and between them in a second, each holding the two young soldiers back from each other.

“All right, that’s enough!” growled Irish with a voice even more commanding than Boss’s. “Tensions are really fucking high right now and I think we could all use a break, but we need to get out of here before those fucking things show up to tear what’s left of us apart.”

“And just leave Sam back there to die?” Sharpe barked. He tried to push past Irish but the old soldier was ready for him.

Irish kicked Sharpe’s legs out from under him and dropped him to the ground.

“You need to calm down!”

“He’s right,” Machine added. “Sharpe, listen to me. If anyone has a chance of making it out of there alive and getting back to us in one piece, it's Sam. But we are almost out of ammo and those things are out there looking for us. We need to fall back and regroup and I'm willing to bet that Sam will catch up to us when she can. But going back into those caves now is just going to get you killed, brother. And we've lost enough friends already."

Sharpe threw his hands up over his eyes, gritting his teeth and hissing as he washed down his emotions with a heavy breath of air.

"Fuck it."

◂▸

It had to be around here somewhere.

The alpha lifted his muzzle, flaring his nostrils as he tried to find the scent. He was sure one of his pack mates had brought down the human female that had fled the herd. The chaos of the battle with the strange humans had his pack fractured and dispersed. The rest of the humans had fled into the tunnels or fought their way around the great cliff. He'd sent his younger members to hunt them but it seemed they had not been successful. The smell of their blood was thick in the air here, but behind him, he could taste the sweet smell of fresh human entrails.

He found the human female in a small clearing in the trees. One of his brothers had sliced open her belly and spilled her across the ground, giving him clear access to the best parts within. The body of said brother was also nearby along with one of the older females that had accompanied him on the hunt. The alpha realised he had dramatically underestimated these humans and paid the price for it. Mourning his fallen would have to wait; he had sustained an injury from the blue-eyed human. He needed to consume food to convert into energy in order to heal. He held his head low as he advanced on the human female. He wasn't sure why he moved with such caution, but his instincts were demanding it.

He stopped as something caught his eye; there was another creature here. The creature's size was almost impossible to gauge; it looked as if it wasn't there, a tall, broad, shimmering object in the darkness that morphed and bent the limited light around it. The alpha raised up onto his hind legs; he was big for his kind but this strange being easily rivalled his size. The alpha growled; he folded his ears back and bared his impressive teeth. The creature charged at him. The alpha was lifted and tossed back to the ground with unstoppable strength. He yelped in pain as something slammed into his chest. He felt an unimaginable pain as the new creature grasped something inside of his chest. He couldn't breathe; his limbs refused to respond to his commands. Finally, he fell very still as the hand tore free. In his final seconds his limply hanging eyes bore witness to his own headless body.

CHAPTER 11

◆

PAYBACK

It was time for another walk in the woods. Just as before, everyone fell silent. Sharpe had moved well ahead of the main group; the others all decided it would probably be best to keep their distance. Zero didn't seem to be doing too well either. Billy fell back to join Terra. The two students were being trailed by Wolfman, who dropped back when he saw Billy approach to give them a little more privacy.

"You saw what happened to Grace, didn't you?" Billy whispered.

Terra nodded slowly; her gaze fell on Zero at the head of the formation. Billy followed her line of sight. Confused, and perhaps tired, Billy failed to manage his volume. His shock pushed the words out of his mouth far louder than he intended.

"Did something happen with Zero?"

The silver-haired soldier looked back over his shoulder at the students. He grumbled something under his breath briefly before Terra let out her challenge.

"Yeah, our glorious leader left us to get eaten by those werewolf things."

Every set of eyes in the group fell on Zero. Machine and Irish briefly shared a look of concern. Somewhere a voice mumbled, "Told you so."

Zero pushed through the two older soldiers, stopping an inch away from Terra's face. To her credit, Terra didn't even flinch as he closed the distance. Billy wisely chose to take a step back.

"I did what I had to do," Zero snarled. "My primary was dry and for all I knew there were more of those things closing in. Boss would have done the same thing."

"Right, 'cos Boss always said the best way to defend your objective is to feed them to the monsters, didn't he?"

Terra hadn't noticed Sharpe standing so close. Silence filled the woods as the two young men locked onto each other. Wolfman gently ushered Terra to take a few steps back, giving the men some room. Sharpe's rifle was in the hands of Machine. Zero handed his weapon to Irish as he accepted the sniper's challenge.

"You carry a sidearm for a reason, Zero; Grace was beyond saving but there was no need to lose Terra as well," Sharpe said with the now usual cold tone.

"Well, it's a good thing you showed up to save your girlfriend then, isn't it?"

Terra made a bizarre gasping sound that was nowhere near as subtle as she hoped; luckily if any of the others did notice they at least had the courtesy not to comment.

Was it always this hot here?

Sharpe shook his head slowly, apparently not as affected by that last comment as Terra was.

"I didn't expect Austin Spencer to raise such a coward."

"This isn't some fucking Eastwood movie," Zero snapped. "I couldn't draw my secondary and headshot that fucking thing in the dark! I'm sorry Terra, I really am, but I had a bunch of my brothers scattered around the woods that needed pulling together."

"And I have a sister," Sharpe snarled, "who's missing now because you sent her and the kids into the caves. So much for pulling everyone together."

"We barely made it out of there alive!" Zero hissed. "There's no way we could have protected the kids as well as ourselves!" Zero took a moment to recompose himself. "I get why you're upset, but we all lost Sam, not just you."

"You can't even begin to imagine what I'm going through." The sniper took a step closer. "You have a family. You've never lost anyone. The only family I ever knew was Sam's, and they were ripped away from us when we were just kids. So, I bounced around homes and foster families for years, and the only certainty I had was Sam being there with me through it all… But she's gone now. Because of you!"

What happened next was too fast for Terra to keep up. It was clear though that the sniper initiated it. Sharpe and Zero collided into a frighteningly violent exchange with a crunch. Seconds later Zero had Sharpe pinned to the ground holding his combat knife to the sniper's throat. Sharpe glared at Zero, silently challenging him.

"Zero!" Machine growled. "That's enough!"

Zero paid Machine no attention.

"Get your shit together. I'm in charge here, I made the call. Get back in line and follow my orders."

"All right, Zach… point proven." Irish stepped forward with his hands raised. "Let him go now."

Zero pulled his knife away from the sniper, leaving a faint red line across his neck from the pressure. The silver-haired soldier stomped away to the edge of the clearing, muttering something to Machine and Irish about a perimeter. The two older men shared a look for a moment.

"Didn't feel like stepping in?" Terra growled at them.

Sharpe pulled himself to his feet. Machine patted him on the shoulder as he took back his rifle. Sharpe didn't make eye contact but nodded subtly to him.

"Out here it's better to let your feelings out," Irish answered.

Terra felt like saying something to challenge that but didn't have the energy for the argument. She looked to Wolfman as if to say "Anything to add?" but the youngest soldier just shrugged.

"They'll be okay, this is just how men work out issues with each other."

"I swear there is way too much testosterone floating around you guys," Terra muttered.

Wolfman smirked.

"Give him some time and get some rest while you can; it looks like we're going to be here for a minute."

Terra welcomed the chance to relax; her feet ached and her muscles were tense. She sat herself down by a tree beside an unusually quiet Billy, who was staring aimlessly at the ground, twisting Sev's rifle around in his hands. He didn't look sad or shocked though, and hadn't said a word during the Sharpe and Zero confrontation.

Something's off with you, Billy. I guess you're just tired. I know you, though, you'll talk when you're ready.

Terra looked around, trying to distract herself. Sharpe was making every effort he could to avoid eye contact. He was facing outwards scanning the trees to the rear. Terra had seen him do this so many times but still hadn't quite figured out exactly what he was looking for. His eyes would drift slowly between a group of trees, then dart back to the centre of those trees before moving onto the next set of trees, then instead of returning to those trees, he would instead look back at the original set of trees and repeat the process. The muttering of hushed voices drew Terra's attention back to Machine and Irish who were now sitting back to back chuckling about something in Terra's direction. Rather than challenge the men Terra shook off the anxiety that had started to creep over her and scanned the rest of her surroundings instead. Zero was up ahead of the others moping silently, and Wolfman had seemingly disappeared into the trees.

Can just the five of them really protect us? Can they even protect themselves?

Terra took her notebook out of her bag in an attempt to shake these intrusive thoughts. She went to the only page she could think of, her group sketch. Her pen hovered over the outline of what would become Sam, but she wasn't the only person missing this time. Instead, Terra's hand moved to the edge of the portrait where she was supposed to draw herself, Billy and Grace.

I always wondered why you were here, but I guess I understand now.

Terra started on just a pair of outlines. One for herself and the other for Billy.

"I can't believe she's really gone," Billy croaked, breaking the silence.

"You mean Grace?" Terra said in a harsher tone than she'd intended.

"No, Sam, she always seemed like such a badass... a smoking hot badass soldier chick." Billy whistled.

Terra managed a slight chuckle.

"We didn't actually see what happened to her."

Terra checked the spacing of the soldiers again. Sharpe was still relatively far back, while Machine and Irish were stuck in a conversation of their own.

"Sharpe's managed to stay alive out there on his own, I don't see why Sam can't..."

"Do you actually believe that or is that just what you want to believe?"

Billy's words were cold; his new tone didn't suit him at all.

"If we don't even have hope then what do we have, Billy?" Terra mumbled. Something caught her eye. Terra hadn't noticed until now but the skin around Billy's upper arm seemed to be discoloured, covered in something dark.

"Oh my God, Billy! Did you get hurt?" Terra said a little louder than she should have.

Billy didn't respond. Sharpe appeared beside the pair; he crouched down beside the students. His tired eyes fell on Billy's shoulder. Billy pulled his arm away from the sniper.

"Hey, get away from me!" Billy protested.

"Billy!" Terra snapped.

"He's fine..." croaked Sharpe. "Though I would keep an eye on that mark—"

"Yeah, that's rich coming from you," Billy interrupted.

Sharpe considered him for a moment; he was chewing slowly on some kind of gum as he thought about what to do. Terra held her breath, half expecting him to lash out, until he dismissed Billy to talk to her.

"How is your mark by the way?" Billy's words now just felt flat-out condescending.

"It takes its toll," Sharpe told Terra, making an effort not to even look at Billy. "The more it spreads, the more of yourself you lose."

"Hey, Sharpe, you okay, brother?" Machine called out, drawing their attention.

Sharpe nodded slowly; he rose back to his feet and walked into some of the nearby trees. Terra looked down and away from Billy. She wasn't nearly as surprised as she should have been, she'd heard the men talk about the marks in the past.

"Did you not wonder why he kept pushing you away like that?"

"Billy!" growled Irish. The student glanced over his shoulder briefly at the old soldier. "Time and a place."

"She needs to know!" Billy retorted in frustration.

Terra's eyes stayed on the ground.

"What are you saying, Billy?"

"What he's saying isn't anything you need to be concerned about," Machine added.

"Are you kidding me? He's been like this for weeks. If Terra's going to insist on being so close to him then she should understand the risk."

"He's no more affected than the rest of us," Irish growled.

"Fuck you he isn't!" Billy argued. "He's been getting quieter and quieter, talking nonsense about a shimmering light and running off into the dark on his own. Even Sam was worried about—"

Terra finally snapped.

"Would you all just shut the fuck up a second!"

They were all silent.

"I know I might be the youngest one here, but I am still an adult and I have the right to make my own decisions…" She turned her attention to Zero.

"Zero… I know you and me aren't exactly on the best of terms right now. And I know your relationship with Sharpe is a little ropey right now…"

"A little?" Billy said.

Terra shot him a death glare. Billy backed down.

"But he was your best friend, wasn't he? So, I'm asking you. With everything that's happened, with Sam now gone… am I in more danger by being close to him?"

Zero wiped a hand over his face as he thought about the answer that he never gave. Wolfman and Sharpe came jogging out of the treeline and the squad leader's priorities changed. Without making eye contact with Terra, he pushed past her. She was getting really tired of that.

"It's them! The people from the gas station," Wolfman panted.

Machine smiled widely, raising his rifle to the air, as he pushed in a fresh magazine.

"Sounds like it's time for a rematch," he excitedly exclaimed.

Irish butted in, in agreement. "Aye, it's time they paid for what they did to Boss."

"That ain't very Christian, brother," Machine added.

"I'm Catholic. I'll make sure I go to confession the next time we hit a town."

Zero sighed; he reluctantly looked to Sharpe.

"We don't have much ammo," Zero whispered. "How many?"

Sharpe shrugged before he spoke. "About thirty, they look pretty beaten up. Not many weapons between them, and they're all bunched up nice and tight." A slight smile crept across Sharpe's lips.

"Right then." Zero turned to his men as he swapped his rifle's magazine. "This'll be a snap ambush like we've done before. Irish, get up on the right side, Sharpe, see if you can get up one of those trees and pick out the guys with the big guns. Wolfman and Machine, ready any grenades we have left. Billy, Terra, get down behind those trees and cover your ears, this is going to get loud."

Everyone was grinning from ear to ear except Terra and, to her surprise, Wolfman, whose sad eyes followed the others as they moved into position. He himself took cover further back near Terra and Billy. Terra watched his eyes fall on Sharpe as the sniper climbed to one of the low-hanging branches of a thick tree. The youngest soldier was mumbling something to himself. Terra spun around as she heard the clicking of another rifle. Billy was setting up his own weapon and preparing to fire. Wolfman watched him as well.

Terra mimed her concern to the soldier.

"Are you okay?"

Wolfman nodded slowly.

"There's been enough bloodshed…"

"Oh, man up and do your job," growled Billy.

Wolfman shrugged, paying the student no attention. Terra looked back at Billy.

What changed?

◀▶

Bruce knew he couldn't send scouts ahead like he usually would as they moved through the trees. The creatures his men had irritatingly dubbed 'Lycans' were far too much of a threat.

Instead, his twenty-eight remaining men moved together in an uncomfortably tight formation. The men were at most only a foot apart as they moved in one large clump through the trees. It was a soldier's worst nightmare, though Bruce did still have a few men he could trust. Paul was leading the formation at a good pace. Bruce himself was at the centre of the group so that he could better coordinate the men.

"Oi, gov," whispered the man to his left. "Bootlace is untied; you trip up here, we all go over."

Bruce nodded. He dropped down to one knee to tie his laces; the soldier had a point after all. He struggled against his shaking hands as the rest of his men pushed past him. He had never been a fan of crowds of people.

The trees ahead of him ignited into a blaze of gunfire. Blood splattered his face as his men fell under the sudden hail of bullets. The sounds of detonating grenades masked his men's screams. Someone grabbed Bruce's shoulder strap on his webbing and tugged him back away from the chaos. Bruce managed to let out a long burst from his Kalashnikov rifle as he screamed so loudly he felt his throat begin to tear.

"That was for Boss, you fucking vultures!" screamed a southern American voice.

Bruce tore out the empty magazine of his weapon and yelled back as he struggled to put a new one into the weapon.

"Oh yeah, thirty of my men for one of yours, that sounds real fair!"

"Hey!" groaned a voice from the tree beside Bruce. "We need to get out of here!"

Bruce peered round the base of the tree. A bullet slammed into the bark just above his head, sending splinters and dust into his face.

"Fuck," Bruce hissed.

"Bruce!" the man said again. "We need to go."

"But Paul?"

"He's dead, mate… I'm sorry."

Bruce sighed; he nodded to his remaining men and they all stood up and emptied their magazines as they escaped back into the trees.

◂▸

The gunshots fell silent. Terra was curled up into a tight foetal position, quivering.

"Hey, it's over," Billy whispered. "It's over now, come on let's get out of here."

Terra didn't move; she kept her feet pulled up into her chest.

"She's in shock," Sharpe croaked. Billy jumped to his feet spinning the gun around. Sharpe caught the smoking barrel in a gloved hand. His eyebrows scrunched together as he inspected the weapon.

"I thought we agreed this was only for emergencies?"

"And this wasn't?" Billy argued.

Sharpe snorted. He gently bent down and hoisted Terra up into his arms.

"Hey, maybe… um, I should be the one to… I'm her friend after all," Billy struggled.

"I'm stronger and I have the exoskeleton to help me take the weight. Go and help the others scavenge up some ammunition from the bodies."

Sharpe turned away but Billy called out to him, stopping the sniper before he made it more than a few steps.

"Look man, I just think that she'd feel safer with me!"

Sharpe turned back towards him. Terra had stopped quivering and fallen very still. She'd instinctively moved her face into Sharpe's chest in search of the warmth.

"There are bigger things at stake here than your crush, kid. A word of advice though…"

Billy tensed up as he waited for the soldier's response, bracing himself for an argument.

"Stop trying to be the tough guy; you're surrounded by trained killers, you're never going to match up to them. She hangs around with you because you're kind to her and you listen to what she says. Stop trying to compete with these guys and start acting like the person she knows. Maybe then you'll have a little more success."

Billy looked away from him.

"Nah… it's pretty clear she likes someone else."

Sharpe stopped chewing.

"Regardless. What she needs right now is a friend, and if you stop being that for her, you'll lose her altogether."

Billy shook his head.

"Why should I take advice from you? I've seen the way you look at her, how do I know your advice is good?"

Sharpe looked down at Terra briefly.

"My mission is to keep the students alive, that includes you, Billy."

Sharpe left Billy to his thoughts. Terra kept her eyes closed. She thought about saying something but she was too comfortable and warm. She felt safe in the hands of Sharpe, despite everything that had been said just minutes ago.

If they won't give me a straight answer then I'll make the choice for myself.

CHAPTER 12

◂▸

THE LAST CAMPFIRE

Terra always knew she was dreaming. In every one of her dreams since the day she was born it was snowing. The scenes tended to change a lot but it was always snowing heavily. So heavily in fact that she couldn't see the horizon, or the sky, or even the end of the tip of the spire of the old English church that she found herself below. Though she couldn't see his face, the young man standing ten feet away facing away from her was also a common theme of her dreams.

"I never thought I'd be so happy to see you, Eddie."

Eddie was a stocky blonde-haired English lad. His skin was pale and he was wearing a black blazer over black school trousers, though peculiarly enough his feet were completely bare. When Eddie didn't answer, Terra spoke again as she advanced towards him slowly.

"What happened to your shoes, Eddie?"

Eddie's head raised slowly to the sky. As he spoke his words didn't come from him but from all around Terra, as if played through hidden speakers. His voice broke as would be expected of a young boy halfway through puberty.

"It's all wrong… it's all so wrong…"

"What's wrong, Eddie?"

Something flashed in the sky above. The white sky faded away as streaks of purple thunder tore away the clouds, leaving a black, moonless sky.

"Well, this is new," Terra noted.

The lightning continued to tear through the clouds in the distance; everywhere it touched turned black. There were no stars or moon, and the only light seemed to be emitting from the church.

"This… is how it's supposed to be…" Eddie said.

"I don't understand, Eddie. What do you mean?" Terra questioned. She held her ground firmly as her eyes wandered the blackness above. "What are you trying to tell me, Eddie?"

Before Eddie could answer Terra was blinded by a brilliant flash of white light that engulfed the church. The light began to fade and fall back, granting Terra her vision once again.

This doesn't feel like my normal dreams. Would I even know if it was though? It is a dream after all.

The light fell back into a single beam that shot down from the sky. The fantastic white light was difficult to look at, but fell from a hidden point like an avalanche of fresh white snow.

"It isn't supposed to be like this…" Eddie muttered.

Purple thunder erupted from above, this time it seemed to spew from the white light and tear across the black sky like the claws of an angry beast. Eddie raised a hand to the sky. He screamed with inhuman rage.

"It's not supposed to be like this!"

The sound was deafening. Terra threw her hands over her ears as instinct took over her. Everything was brighter, though seemingly bathed in a faint purple glow. Cautiously, Terra looked up at the sky.

"Oh no…" she whimpered.

Thick purple lights slithered across the black sky. Terra looked up at the alluring purple lights of Limbo.

"Eddie. What does this mean?"

Eddie dropped to his knees grunting loudly as he clutched his chest tightly. Terra tried to step forward but something was holding her in place.

"No… t-time…" Eddie struggled.

"Eddie please! I don't understand, what are you trying to tell me?" Terra pleaded.

"Terra!" A female voice echoed through the scene. "Get away from him!"

"Sam?" Terra called out. "Where are you?"

"Forget about me! Get away from here! Run!" Sam replied, her voice still too difficult to locate.

An inhuman voice called to Terra, a deep, horrible sound as something struggled to form words.

"Terra."

Terra looked back at Eddie as the young man turned around to face her. His hair fell from his head; thick black lines tore across his face, moulding him into something inhuman. His eyes bulged impossibly large in their sockets, his arms and legs stretched outwards before her eyes. A clawed hand reached towards Terra as an insidiously wide grin ripped across the monster's face. It called to Terra again.

"You…" Its voice was a hideous deep gurgling sound. "Did… this." Every movement of its lips looked painful, like it was straining to form the words. "To me!"

Terra fell back to the snowy ground, crying.

"I'm sorry! Eddie please, I didn't know, I'm sorry!"

A hand grabbed Terra's shoulder from behind; a force ripped her, throwing her back away from the creature. It was Sam.

"You have to move, Terra! It's coming!" Sam barked.

Before Terra could respond, Sam fired a burst from her rifle into the creature, which seemed to agitate it even more. The monster swiped Sam to one side, effortlessly throwing her into the snow, leaving a cloud of blood floating where Sam had once been.

"Eddie, stop!" Terra cried as the creature advanced on her.

A clawed hand reached towards her, but just before its fingers reached her face, a volley of gunfire tore into the creature from behind. The monster turned back to a bloody Sam. The soldier was sitting upright, deep gouges running across her chest leaking fresh blood.

"Leave her alone!" Sam roared.

The giant Damned rushed towards her.

Terra shot upright as her eyes opened. She clawed desperately at the air to get back her breath. As she sat there panting, her eyes wandered around their new surroundings; she wasn't in the forest anymore. She was lying on a clean, fresh bed. The room was small, but cosy. A lit candle sat on a small chest of drawers beside her, along with a small china cup filled with something dark, warm and very alluring. Beside the cup was a small note which read:

Downstairs with the guys, we thought you should have the bed.

Billy.

Terra checked herself over; she was still dressed and didn't have any new injuries. Other than a splitting headache and a ringing sound in her ears, she was fine. Terra's bag sat at the end of the bed, along with a new set of clothes. The clothes weren't anything special, a fresh set of jeans and a red checked shirt that was a little too big for her, but a fresh change was all too alluring to deny.

Terra's attention was drawn to the small china cup. It was clearly from a larger set, small, white and covered with decorative flower paintings. She pressed the cup to her lips and almost choked from pure surprise when she realised it was tea. Terra couldn't even remember the last time she'd had a hot cup of tea. Her American student friends always used to tease her about her obsession with the stuff and her need to import 'proper' tea from back home, as the American stuff simply wouldn't do.

Once she'd changed, Terra checked over her satchel, and to her surprise her notebook was missing.

"Fuck! I was sure I secured it. Damn it."

Terra begrudgingly left the room and made her way down the stairs, with her now much lighter satchel slung over her shoulder. She wasn't expecting to find the four heavily armed men, all sitting comfortably in Victorian furniture, with fancy china mugs that paled in size in the hands holding them. She chuckled at the sight.

"Oh, hey, look who's up!" Machine greeted.

Irish actually stood up and offered Terra his seat, even though there probably would have been enough room for her to squeeze in. Wolfman and Zero were both present too, though the latter was fast asleep.

"It's good to see you up, Miss Kisaragie," Irish welcomed. "I've got a pot brewing over a fire outside. There's a real nice lake here too. Go get yourself washed up and once we've all had a bit of food, we're going to have a little meeting."

"Where's Billy and Sharpe?" Terra asked.

"Sharpe's outside on watch and Billy went out back to... do his business," Wolfman replied.

Terra nodded politely before she headed out of the front door to find this lake. Wolfman stretched out his arms before he went upstairs to get some rest himself.

"Hey Irish," Machine said. "Mind if I ask you something?"

Irish raised an eyebrow.

"Sure."

"After all of this, after what we've seen out there, do you really still believe in God?"

Irish pondered the thought for a moment, trying to work out how Machine was going to twist this around into an insult.

"Yeah, I do, why?" Irish answered cautiously.

"Throughout my life I've gone back and forth on the idea. Before SOO, I was training to join the air force as a mechanic. I was pretty good, too. Studied engineering at college and almost ended up as an officer... right up until the last month of my training when a couple of idiot kids, who'd stolen their dad's car, ran me off the road. I lost everything... Spencer literally picked me up off the street. I mean, I was stealing candy bars out of gas stations to stay alive before he gave me this job. See, back then I was pretty sure God wasn't real. If he was, he wouldn't have let any of those things happen. It wasn't just me. There were others. It's amazing what people will do to stay alive even when they have nothing. But then when Spencer picked me up it felt like I had hope, I met you guys and I thought maybe God is real. Then back on that patrol, there was this kid. He or she, fuck I don't know. They were one of them, and now I'm not sure I can believe in a god who is willing to let things like that happen to such innocent people. How do you do it, brother?"

Irish looked at Machine for a long moment waiting for the punchline. Machine just smiled and looked away.

"Yeah, I'm sorry. I've got nothing left but honest questions."

Irish let out a long, tired sigh.

"I've always held faith that the life we lived was never our final resting place. That we were meant to live the best life we could and when we died, we would pay for our sins and eventually move on to the place we were meant to be. I do not believe in true evil and by extension I do not believe in hell, but I do believe that everything happens for a reason, Machine, and there's always two sides to every story."

Machine nodded slightly.

"I guess so, brother."

"And besides," Irish started, "might not have been a kid, it could have been a midget."

The two men laughed so loud that Terra could hear them even from outside. She turned back to study the house. Terra was really starting to wonder why there were so many of these single buildings scattered around Limbo in the middle of dense woodlands. Though this one would probably have been someone's secret holiday home back in the real world. It was a big timber house, probably constructed from the wood of the very trees that had once surrounded it. The house sat in a wide clearing a few acres in size. The thick tree line circled the building. Terra found the lake that the others had mentioned pretty quickly; it was about a hundred yards from the house. A wide, beautiful thing connected to a small stream that ran through the woodlands. Sharpe was kneeling down at the edge of the lake.

The sky overhead was clear and Terra had a grand view of the purple lights. Just as before, there were dozens of the things all snaking slowly through the air. But it was only when Terra caught their reflection in the lake that she noticed the change. It was subtle, and damn near impossible to spot unless you were looking from the right angle, but the lights were beginning to worm into each other.

They're converging. I guess they really might lead somewhere after all.

Sharpe's movements clawed at her attention again; after a moment of watching him, Terra realised he was drawing something.

Is that my notebook?

Approaching as quietly as she could manage, she saw the pencil in his hand. The sniper was sketching his missing sister onto the page.

"I was wondering where that ended up," Terra greeted.

Sharpe finished his mark. The resemblance to Sam was remarkable. She was smiling, with a flat cap worn backwards on her head.

"It fell open on this page… I didn't look at anything else."

"That's okay, there's nothing bad in there anyway," Terra lied. The truth was that there were some seriously provocative and thought-provoking things sketched and written throughout that book. She didn't realise, as her thoughts drifted, that she had started staring at Sharpe's broad shoulders.

"You okay?" he asked suddenly.

"Huh?" Terra's cheeks turned red as she realised. "Oh yeah! Sorry, I'm still waking up. Thanks for carrying me by the way."

Sharpe frowned.

"How did you know it was me?"

Terra shrugged. "Lucky guess." Which wasn't a complete lie.

The sniper accepted her answer all the same. "All right, here's your book back. I'll be back at the house, water's safe."

"You're not going to peek on me with that scope, are you?" Terra joked.

Sharpe groaned disapprovingly.

"No," he said flatly.

Terra sighed, too exhausted to try again.

"Congratulations, Sharpe, I give up!" Terra sarcastically cheered. "Yay you!"

The sniper considered Terra for a moment. Terra glared at him, waiting for some kind of response, but of course the soldier remained stoic.

"You act like it's a crime to show any emotion, Sharpe; you just lost Sam!"

"Stop," Sharpe croaked. The girl ignored him.

"You've lost so many people for this. Now you can try and hide it all you want, but you're falling apart."

"Terra..." Sharpe croaked again. But the girl still refused to have any of it.

"No, you listen to me! You can't be okay. If you don't stop and..."

The soldier raised his rifle. Terra instantly froze. Fear washed over her like a bucket of ice; she was staring straight down the barrel. At this distance he wouldn't even need to aim. Sharpe's eye locked onto his target through the scope. He pulled the trigger.

The flash of the muzzle was far smaller than Terra had expected. She felt the air rush past her but all she could hear was a ringing in her ears. Terra dropped down to her knees. Sharpe lowered his rifle slowly. Terra looked down at her body; not a speck of blood in sight. Sharpe's rifle was still aimed at something just past her. The sniper advanced slowly, then walked straight past Terra; he was saying something but Terra couldn't work out exactly what. Her eyes followed him as he passed her and fell on the body of a Damned that had fallen just at the edge of the lake. The creature twitched slightly as Sharpe approached, so he fired another round into its skull, spreading black brains all over the ground.

Terra didn't realise it, but she was shivering violently. Sharpe placed his rifle down on the ground beside the Damned, then he dropped his assault vest. Terra's hearing was starting to return as the soldier struggled against his equipment. Terra stared at the ground, once again falling into that state of shock. Sharpe gently laid something soft over her shoulders and sat down beside her.

Sharpe sat there for a moment, looking around awkwardly. Finally, he sighed and gently wrapped one arm over her shoulders. Terra grabbed the soldier in a firm and tight embrace as she sobbed.

"I'm sorry…" Sharpe whispered. "They react to sudden movements…" Sharpe looked around himself again as if he were literally trying to find the words.

"P-Please…" Terra whimpered. "Please j-just stay here for a bit."

Sharpe sighed.

"Yeah, all right, Terra."

They stayed there like that for about twenty minutes and to her credit Terra stopped shaking after about ten. Sharpe took breaks occasionally from scanning the treelines to look down and make sure she was all right.

"You good?" Sharpe asked.

Terra released her grip on the young man. She pulled away from him slowly but didn't move too far away. Sharpe had been wearing a black vest beneath his shirt, which is just as well as his body was extremely distracting.

"Hey, Kisaragie?" the sniper croaked.

"Huh? Oh sorry!" Terra blushed. "Look, I'm sorry I snapped like that, I'll leave you alone from now on, I promise." Terra rose to her feet and started to walk away defeated.

Sharpe watched her walk for a few seconds, repeating her words in his head, dissecting her flat, depleted tone, as a new emotion washed over him. The sniper sighed.

"Come back," he called out.

Terra turned around slowly. She waddled back towards the sniper, and Sharpe patted the ground beside him. Terra looked at him for a moment, just to be sure he was serious, then sat herself down beside him.

"I've never really been that good at the whole 'expressing my feelings' thing. Even before Limbo." The words didn't come out in Sharpe's usual slow, steady croak. Instead he sounded more like a human being. There was energy and emotion; he sounded as if this was very difficult for him to say.

"I don't have a family, not a blood family anyway. Sam was the closest thing to that. We've been together for almost as long as I can remember. Boss and Sev, well, I already expressed my feelings about them…"

Sharpe pushed that thought to the back of his mind. He wiped the sadness away from his face with his hand, but his eyes still showed his true feelings.

"There were others here before you. Grace and Billy were picked up not long before we found you. The team picked me up a couple of months ago but I was out here for a long time before that."

Sharpe looked out at the lake as if the memories were coming to life before him.

"Six months ago, or at least somewhere around that number, I met someone here. She was a little older than you, a little taller too."

"Sounds like the perfect woman," Terra moaned.

"Nah, she was French," Sharpe replied.

Terra snorted, she almost bit her tongue from the sudden shock.

Did Sharpe just make a joke?

"We survived together. I taught her how to fight and survive and she taught me about the Damned and watched my back. We were together for about three months. Just the two of us."

"What happened to her?" Terra asked, even though she already knew the answer.

"The Damned got her. We'd stopped by what we thought was a shallow river; the fucker came straight out of the water just like that one did. I called out but she couldn't react fast enough."

"I'm so sorry," Terra answered.

Sharpe shook his head.

"You remind me of her. You're strong, stronger than you realise, and smart too. A little training and you'd be formidable."

Terra couldn't help but smile just a little. But the sniper wasn't quite done yet.

"I'm sorry for the way I've been acting. This has been hard for all of us, and you need a wall to lean on or just hide behind and that's supposed to be me."

Terra looked away from him as her expression dropped.

"I'm sorry," she croaked.

"Don't be." Sharpe nudged her in the ribs to get her attention. "I'm glad you chose me."

He managed a slight smile. Terra wasn't sure if he was just putting this on as an act or if he was being truthful with his feelings, but she didn't really care either way.

"For what it's worth, you make a good wall, Sharpe."

Sharpe managed a slight chuckle at that strange compliment. A new thought struck him; the soldier got back up to his feet and reached into one of his pouches. He pulled out a long red cylinder, removed the cap and struck the top. The flare lit up the area in a thick red glow. The sniper reached back and tossed the flare into the water. The red light dimmed slightly but kept burning even below the surface of the water. The sniper watched the flare burn for a few seconds.

"They hate bright lights. If there were any more in the lake, they won't come near this side for at least an hour, even after the flare burns out."

Terra studied the flare.

"Why haven't we been using them this entire time then?"

"That was the last one. Get in there and wash up so it doesn't go to waste."

Terra glared at Sharpe in total bewilderment.

That's either the most romantic or stupidest thing anyone's ever done for me.

Terra blushed again when she realised she was staring at the soldier.

"I'll leave you in peace; the flare will go out in a couple of minutes but, like I said, you'll be safe," the sniper said.

He collected his things and faced away as he started reattaching his assault vest.

◀▶

The water probably should have been a lot colder than it was, but Terra didn't mind. She'd scrubbed up vigorously and been escorted back to the house. All of the curtains had been pulled closed, probably so that the soldiers wouldn't be tempted to sneak a peek.

Even so, I'm glad Sharpe is the only one with a scope... at least I don't think the others had any.

Terra pushed that thought to the back of her mind; she was upstairs in the same room she had awoken in. Lying in front of her were the contents of every wardrobe and chest of drawers she had found on the second floor of the cabin. Clearly, whoever had once lived here liked to keep things simple and left her choices a little more limited than she'd have liked, but Terra was nothing if not resourceful. She was the last woman standing, surrounded by a bunch of big military men, and she knew exactly what to do to give herself a little edge over them.

The soldiers and Billy were all sitting around in the main living room. Machine was standing at the centre of the circle. They were all waiting for Terra to join them before they started the meeting.

"She really is a woman, ain't she?" Machine croaked.

"It's not like her to take this long," Billy added. "Maybe one of us should go check on her."

Sharpe surprised everyone by speaking up next. He was sitting on one the of the chairs with his hat pulled down over his eyes.

"Never walk in on a woman while she's changing, kid."

"I thought I told you to get some sleep!" Irish said.

Sharpe didn't respond.

"Steady, big guy," Machine said. "Terra's only just got him out of that shell; let's not let him slip back into it so soon."

They all chuckled. Wolfman and Irish suddenly shot up to their feet as Terra stepped into the room. Billy's mouth hung open and Machine just froze.

"How do I look?"

Terra was wearing the flannel shirt open over an Iron Maiden vest she had found in one of the rooms, along with a pair of slim-fitting blue jeans over her old gothic boots. Her hair was tied back into a neat ponytail that suited her perfectly. She looked awake with just the right amount on dark eyeliner and shadow.

"Holy shit!" Billy exclaimed.

"Looking good," Zero croaked.

"If I were five years younger…" Machine mumbled to himself.

Sharpe lifted his hat to check what all the commotion was about. His piercing blue eyes made their way slowly up Terra's body. When they met her warm brown gaze, he couldn't help but smile just a little.

"Looking good, Kisaragie!"

Machine stood up; he raised his cup to the celling.

"To Terra Kiser-kiasie…"

"Kisaragie," Sharpe interrupted.

"Right!" Machine nodded. "To Terra Kisaragie, for putting smiles on all of our faces!"

The others all raised their cups and chanted together, "To Terra!"

Terra smiled at the men.

"How about one for those we've lost?"

The soldiers looked around at each other; they shared a few nods and quiet murmurs. Machine lifted his cup again.

"To Sev, to Sam, to Grace and, of course, Boss! Without them we wouldn't have made it nearly this far and when this is over, we will all drink to their memories. Hurrah!"

"Hurrah!" they all chanted, Terra included.

Terra couldn't help but watch Sharpe during Machine's toast; he was still holding that slight smile on his face even during the mournful toast.

He's either taking Sam's death really well… or he knows something the rest of us don't.

"All right, time to get down to business," Machine started. "As some of you have noticed, the lights up above are starting to converge. Now I know we've all suffered and lost along the way… but we really might have a chance at reaching the end. By our best guess, we're looking at a day's hike at most. Now what we need to discuss is what happens when we get there."

"How can we discuss it if we don't know what it is?" Wolfman asked.

"We have to plan for every scenario," Irish added. "We don't know where it leads, or if there is anything there. Now I believe that if it is a case of nothing being there…"

"We hole up somewhere," Sharpe interjected. "Once we're safe and sheltered, we'll all decide what we want to do individually."

"Yeah," Irish agreed.

"What if it leads somewhere else?" Billy added. "What if it just drops us right back at the beginning?"

"Then we go with the same plan as if there's nothing," Machine answered.

"And if it is a doorway to somewhere else, then we go in," Zero said. "No ifs, no buts, we go in, guns up ready to deal with whatever's there."

Terra listened intently; the men were all remarkably calm, they even showed just a tiny bit of excitement. Except for Wolfman.

The young soldier had gone very quiet since his question. He was holding his glasses in his shaking hands staring at Sharpe trying to get his attention with a look of desperation on his face. Terra subtly nudged the sniper, and with his attention grabbed, she nodded to Wolfman.

He watched the young soldier intently for a few seconds as the others continued their conversation. Wolfman was tapping the lenses repeatedly. Sharpe pulled out his own glasses and slid them over his eyes. Then he too went very still.

Terra's eyes drifted past Wolfman to the kitchen entrance. It took her a second to realise, but something was wrong. The light was distorted, almost bending around the outline of something occupying the space. Something very big was standing in the doorway to the kitchen. It swayed there slowly from side to side. A chill ran down Terra's spine.

The shimmer, the thing that Sharpe had been watching, the thing I saw in the corner of my eye…

"Hey, Terra, Billy," Machine said, snatching their attention towards himself. "Why don't you guys head outside and check on Irish's pot."

Machine's eyes were wild. He'd seen it too. His hand rested on the handle of his assault rifle, and the safety was off.

"Aye," Irish agreed. "If we leave it there too long it'll be ruined."

Billy was completely oblivious to what was happening. He started looking around the soldiers, trying to figure out why they had all gone so quiet.

"Yeah… sure," Terra croaked. "Come on, Billy, let's head outside."

Billy shrugged and followed Terra out of the door, leaving the soldiers alone with the creature.

Back in the house, the soldiers all sat very still. Nobody was sure what to do. Sharpe was wearing his sunglasses to conceal his eyes, which were firmly locked onto the shimmering shape.

"Hey Sharpe, guess I owe you an apology, huh?" Zero said with only the slightest hint of fear in his voice.

"Let's talk about that later." Sharpe's words concealed the sound of Machine gently pulling the pin from a hand grenade.

"We doing this?" Wolfman asked.

"Yeah…" Zero croaked. "Now!"

CHAPTER 13

◂▸

THE SHIMMER

The house exploded into a mess of gunfire. Armour-piercing bullets tore through the walls as a stream of soldiers poured out of the door. They all hurried out safely except for Wolfman. Terra never found out exactly what happened; she didn't know if he decided to jump or if the shimmering thing threw him. Whatever the case, Wolfman smashed through the window and rolled across the ground just before a cloud of dust and debris followed him. To his credit the soldier exited the roll with rifle in hand and ran towards Terra with the rest of the men like nothing had happened.

"Go, go, go!" Zero shouted.

Terra sprinted full throttle into the trees followed closely by the soldiers. She was getting pretty good at maintaining this pace. She was also getting pretty good at dodging the trees and low-hanging branches as she moved at full speed.

Once again, the forest ended abruptly. And to the horror of everyone in the group, there stood a tall stone wall that seemed to have shot out from the ground just like before.

"Oh, you gotta be kidding me," Machine growled as he slid to a halt beside Terra.

"Why are there so many fucking cliffs here?" Wolfman questioned between ragged breaths.

"Some say there are seven layers of hell," Irish answered. Everyone took a moment to glare at him.

Billy, Zero and Sharpe were the last to make it out of the trees. The two soldiers instantly turned back to the trees, raising their weapons.

"Find us a way through it, guys!" Zero called out.

The others all started cursing, eyes and guns raced around the perimeter looking for any unnatural change in the light. Terra studied the wall. It was almost a perfect ninety-degree angle, though unlike the previous wall it wasn't a smooth face. It was jagged and eroded. There were dozens of small cracks and protrusions.

"We can climb it!" Terra shouted back to Zero.

"Seriously!" Billy cried. "It's a fucking vertical wall, if we fall, we die!"

"And if we stay here, we die, kid!" Sharpe yelled back. "Terra, Billy get up that wall, we'll peel off and follow."

Terra was no stranger to rock-climbing. When she was younger it had been one of her favourite hobbies. That was before she discovered boys and Netflix. She was six feet off the ground before Billy found the courage to follow. Sharpe and Zero started moving back slowly as Zero reeled off the names of Machine, Irish and Wolfman to follow in thirty-second intervals.

"You next, Zero," Sharpe croaked.

"Nah, you go. Call it an apology for not believing you about this thing."

Sharpe nodded. He peeled off and jumped up onto the rocks. Zero followed soon after. The two young men were very adept at climbing; they took to the wall with ease, though alarmingly there was no sign of the shimmer anywhere.

Terra was hanging from a slight ledge watching the soldiers while she waited for Billy to catch up.

"Come on Billy, you can do this!" she cheered.

"I don't think I…" Billy's foot slipped out from under him.

He screamed as he fell a good fifteen feet to the ground, rolling to spread the impact, though his rifle had slammed into his gut, knocking the wind from his lungs.

"Billy!"

Terra started making her way down to him; ten feet off the ground Sharpe called out to stop her but it was too late, Terra had already jumped.

"Damn it, get out of there!" Machine roared.

"Hey Billy, are you okay?" Terra said, as she rolled him over onto his back and tried to pull him back up to his feet. Then she saw it. Standing there at the edge of the treeline was that same shimmering shape. The shimmering lights faded as the creature deactivated its camouflage. It was a Damned, an impossibly huge Damned that stood on two very muscular but very human legs. Its torso was far wider than should have been possible. Its long arms almost reached the floor, but most alarmingly of all, the thing had three twisted human heads.

"Oh my God!" Terra exclaimed.

Terra's eyes fixed on the three faces; one was clearly female, the centre one was unfamiliar, but the third face…

"E-Eddie?" Terra murmured.

She reached into her bag for Sharpe's pistol, but the Damned charged her before she could take aim. A clawed hand swung down towards her but didn't connect. Sharpe tackled the creature with all his might, pushing it back away from the students. He jammed his bowie knife into its gut as the monster cried out with an orchestra of inhuman screams. The Damned wrapped one colossal hand around Sharpe's torso and tossed him to the side as if he was weightless. Sharpe flew eight feet, bounced off the ground and rolled back up to his feet, rifle ready. He squeezed off several rounds that all slammed into the Damned.

Terra had seen that rifle practically decapitate other Damned in the past but this time the bullets barely broke the skin.

The creature advanced towards Terra and Billy again. Sharpe charged the beast still firing his rifle. One of the creature's heads turned and up came another clawed hand. Sharpe slid under the swing, landing at the monster's feet. He jammed the barrel of his rifle into the stab wound his blade had left earlier and pulled the trigger. Nothing happened.

"Sharpe!" Terra cried desperately.

A clawed hand slammed down into Sharpe's chest. Terra struggled against her shaking hands to aim the pistol. She couldn't get a clear shot; the monster was holding Sharpe up as a shield. The sniper cried out as he was lifted up. Sharpe struggled against the colossal mass as it pulled him towards its three faces.

"I'm wearing body armour! Or did you forget that, Maria?"

Sharpe pressed his spare handgun to one of the faces and pulled the trigger. The Damned dropped him and fell back in agony. It swung an arm out striking Sharpe's face, sending him flying into the cliff face in a cloud of blood.

"Sharpe, no!" Terra screamed.

Billy was back on his feet raising his AR-15. He hit the

fire selector to full auto and emptied his magazine into the Damned as Terra ran to Sharpe. Sharpe was holding a bloody hand to his face as he rolled around moaning.

"Let me see!" Terra ordered.

Sharpe removed his hand. A claw had torn a thick cut down his face, and destroyed his left eye. Billy's rifle clicked empty and the Damned gave the frightened boy its full attention. Terra pulled Sharpe's handgun and fired three times. The bullets simply bounced off.

"Billy, run!" she screamed.

The Damned raised its clawed hands; Billy was frozen with fear, unable to move.

"Oi, ugly!" called a voice from the cliff.

Irish was easily the largest of the soldiers, which made it all the more impressive that he was dangling from the cliff face with just one hand. The other held his Smith & Wesson hand cannon.

"You got something on your face!"

Irish pulled the trigger. Terra didn't know exactly what was in those bullets but whatever it was, it worked. His first shot struck the monster in the shoulder, tearing its right arm clean off. The creature fell back in pain only to have its right head ripped off by Irish's second bullet. The Damned decided it had other places to be and disappeared back into the tree line as the other soldiers all slid down the cliff face to the aid of their friends. Machine reached Sharpe first.

"Guess I owe you an apology, brother," Machine croaked. "Man, I know chicks love scars but that one is gonna be nasty," he joked.

Sharpe managed a slight smile, and raised his middle finger. Machine pulled Sharpe's free hand away from his now completely blood-soaked face. The smell and sight combined with the prior engagement and pure terror was all that the young girl needed. First her vision went fuzzy, then she lost consciousness.

◀▶

Terra had been sitting beside Sharpe under a tree near the edge of the cliff. Exhaustion had taken its toll on the soldier and thanks to a heavy dose of morphine, he had been able to fall asleep. His head lay in Terra's lap with a bloody bandage wrapped around his ruined eye. Billy stayed close as well while the others all made a perimeter. Irish and Zero stood at the edge of the cliff looking down.

"You think it can climb?" Zero asked solemnly.

Irish shook his head.

"If this is the thing that Sharpe has been talking about, then it's been following us this whole time. Damn it, why did it wait until now to attack?"

"There's fewer of us than before. It's been waiting for an opening." Zero sighed. "Just like he said."

Wolfman jogged out of some of the trees towards the two men.

"Tree line carries on for a mile or so, and then it's hills and open ground… But there's something you guys really need to see."

The two men turned towards him, then their gaze moved up over his head.

"How did we not see that?" Zero asked.

"Too busy with Sharpe, mate," Irish replied.

They were all staring up at the purple lights, or rather the point they converged. A thin beam of white light fell from the sky just over the horizon. At the source of the light, the purple lines all converged, slithering into a lone brilliant white star where they vanished from view.

"We might actually make it," Zero croaked.

Irish grinned beside him.

"Yeah, looks like it, buddy."

"Not with that thing on our asses, we won't."

Sharpe was back on his feet. Billy looked on as the wounded soldier approached his friends.

"I've tried to lose that thing so many times… Even after I found my way across the canyon it managed to follow."

"That's why you really left, isn't it?" Zero asked.

Sharpe nodded.

"When we ran into Bruce and his men in that town, I saw it there… I figured it was the perfect chance to lead the thing away."

Machine wandered over to join the men.

"And of course, we didn't believe you…"

"If I'd been in your shoes, I wouldn't either."

Zero looked up at the light, then back over the side of the cliff.

"Ya'll are leaving again, aren't you?" asked the silver-haired soldier.

Sharpe nodded.

"No!" Wolfman interrupted. "Please, there has to be another way. Irish, your gun hurt it! We could set a trap, another ambush! Hit it with some explosives."

"Carl," Sharpe interrupted, he spoke in a slow, calm voice barely louder than a whisper. "This thing has been on my tail for weeks… it's beyond anything we've seen. It's practically bulletproof, it can camouflage and I took one of its arms off the last time I faced it. Yet there it was with a new one. We can't fight it."

"Then you're just going to let it take you?" Wolfman cried out.

"Not if I can help it. I need to lure it away from you guys, give you a chance to get to the light. Then I'll follow you guys through."

Wolfman turned back to the other soldiers.

"And you're okay with this?"

Machine and Irish looked away. Zero sighed.

"Of course not. But this thing… it's like those wolf creatures…"

"No," Sharpe interrupted. "More like the one with the wings. A creature like that could never have existed in our world… I'm sorry, Wolfman."

Wolfman looked to Sharpe with tear-filled eyes.

"What should we tell Terra?" Machine asked.

Sharpe shrugged. "Whatever you want."

"Come on, son. Drop the act already, it's obvious how you feel," Irish added.

Sharpe looked back at Terra. She looked so peaceful there against that tree, he knew she wouldn't be happy about his departure. But it wasn't safe for her to come with him.

"She's young and strong." Sharpe's expression dropped. "She'll get over me."

"No, she won't," Billy added. He limped over to the group of soldiers.

"She's head over heels for you, dude; after all of this loss, you would push her over the edge."

"Well, it's a good thing she's got you to watch out for her then." Sharpe forced a smile.

Terra woke up very suddenly. She was still sitting under that same tree, with Billy by her side. She looked around as she slowly drifted back to reality. Machine and Irish were both close, trying to get a fire going using a couple of rocks and a stick. They weren't having a lot of luck. Zero was standing by the edge of the cliff and Wolfman was lazily walking around the perimeter. But of course, Sharpe was nowhere to be seen.

"Oh, hey you're awake," Billy greeted.

Terra was on her feet a second later, locking her gaze of fury on the two soldiers in front of her.

"Where is he?" she growled.

"Terra…" Irish started.

"I asked you a question," Terra snarled. "Where is Sharpe?"

"He left to draw that monster away," Billy said.

Spotting the commotion, Zero and Wolfman approached the group as well.

"And you all just let him go?" she shouted rhetorically. "In his condition?"

"He's pretty tough, kid," Machine added, though his tone seemed a little too forced for Terra's liking. "He can handle himself."

"He's missing a fucking eye!" Terra snapped. She felt a little unsteady as the memory of his blood-soaked face drifted back. "There's no way any of you could be okay with that."

"I made the call," Zero croaked. "I need to consider the mission…"

"Fuck your mission!"

"Terra!" Billy said. "Calm down."

Terra looked to Wolfman this time.

"Which way?"

Wolfman froze. Terra asked the question again, this time a little more firmly.

"Wolfman… which way did Sharpe go?"

"Terra, stop this!" Billy cried. "You'll get yourself killed if you go out there alone!"

"Well, unlike the rest of you, I actually care about him!"

"That's enough!" Billy roared.

Terra fell silent.

"All you do is go on about him. Sharpe this, Sharpe that… I get it, you love him because he's strong and handsome and British, but let me tell you something. He doesn't care about you! You're just some stupid little girl who can't tell when to quit. If you go out there, you'll just wind up dead over what? A stupid childish crush!"

Billy expected a slap for what he said. But he didn't expect a full-power right hook from the little Asian girl. He fell into the tree clutching his face, tasting blood in his mouth. Terra looked back across the faces of the soldiers, expecting a rebuttal.

"All right," Machine said calmly. "I say we let her go."

"Let me go?" Terra questioned.

"Yeah," Machine answered. "You're not our prisoner. Boss did say you could leave at any time, didn't he?"

"Absolutely not," Zero chimed in before she had a chance to answer. "All our wishful thinking and prayers put aside, Sharpe is walking to his death. If Terra goes after him, she's just going to end up dead too. Our job is to protect them!"

"And your job as a squad leader is to protect everyone!" Terra snarled. "What's one more casualty to you at this point?"

Zero glared at Terra; he opened his mouth to say something but Irish cut him short.

"I agree with Machine." Zero and Terra both turned to him, and the old soldier smiled softly. "Boss said it: you have the right to leave us at any time, Terra. Not to mention we still don't know what we're walking into. There could be an army of Damned between here and the light, or that thing may have cut us off. Maybe it's in the trees right now we don't know and we'd never know. Terra is an adult, and she can make her own mistakes if she chooses."

"Let's make it a vote then, shall we?" Machine said. "Irish and I vote you can go, Billy and Zero vote stay, that makes Wolfman the tiebreaker." Machine grinned at the youngest soldier. Wolfman tensed up, suddenly hit with the weight of the choice. He looked to Zero for confirmation, only to have Zero shrug reluctantly. Wolfman's watering eyes fell on Terra.

"I-I don't feel right about sending you out there alone… if I could go with you I would but…"

"They need you here," Terra said easily. "They're your family, I don't expect any of you to leave the rest of the group for one suicidal idiot."

Wolfman nodded a few times; he wiped his bloodshot eyes. Before he gave his answer, Wolfman handed Terra his sunglasses.

"I have set a marker for his last known location, if you follow that and keep your mind focused on finding him, maybe Limbo will show you the way."

Terra took the glasses but looked to Wolfman, confused.

"Did you not find it a little too coincidental that you found him in that town?" Wolfman said.

"Or how about the time we all found Machine and Wolfman outside that same town despite never setting a rendezvous point," Irish added. "I can't explain how it works but if you want to find someone in this place, Limbo will take you to them."

Terra didn't completely understand but nodded all the same.

"So, this is goodbye then?" she sniffed.

The two older soldiers smiled. Machine reached around and pulled out a small pistol magazine and his combat knife and handed them to Terra.

"Take these, find our man and bring him back."

"You say that like you're recruiting her!" Wolfman joked.

"Well, call it an initiation," Machine answered. "If she succeeds, she's one of us."

"I'm not sure I'd make a good soldier to be honest," Terra mumbled nervously.

"No," Zero said. "You're slow, small and you cry way too much…" The silver-haired soldier sighed. "But you're also smart, stubborn as all hell and fiercely determined. In another life I'd have been happy to have you in my team." Zero looked at his battered and bloody hands. "I'm sorry about what happened before, that was a mistake. I don't expect you to forgive me for it but…" Zero steadied himself with a long unsteady breath.

"I understand," Terra said. "I couldn't lead these men like you have. You've done well…"

"So that's it?" Billy spat. "You're just going to fuck off and leave. I guess you really are perfect for him. Grace was right, you're just as psychotic as Sharpe is." Billy pushed through the other soldiers without saying another word. Nobody tried to stop him and Terra honestly didn't care. She took out Sharpe's pistol, dropped the old empty magazine onto the floor, inserted the new one and pulled back the slide, just like she'd seen and been shown. She looked up at the others.

"So, does this mean I get a cool nickname as well?"

The men all looked around at each other.

"Sure," Wolfman said. "When you make it back with Sharpe."

"Good luck, kid."

"I pray for your success, Miss Kisaragie."

Zero just nodded. Wolfman and Terra shared a quick hug. She whispered "Thank you" into his ear so that the others wouldn't hear, then threw on the sunglasses and followed the single white arrow into the woods. To her credit she made it all the way to the edge of the trees before she looked back. Terra couldn't explain it, but somehow, she knew.

I didn't say goodbye. I know that I'll see you all again before the end. I have to believe that I will.

CHAPTER 14

◂▸

WHY ARE YOU HERE?

Terra was starting to feel a little proud of herself. She wasn't sure when but somewhere down the line she had learnt something from following the soldiers. She was getting very good at moving without making too much sound. The forest floor was bare but now some of the trees still had their leaves, though they were all turning brown as if ready to fall for the winter.

I wonder if seasons are actually a thing here?

It was a peculiar sight and detail that made her feel far safer in these woods. That and what the soldiers had said. Terra wondered if maybe she was just becoming desensitised to the emptiness of Limbo.

I'm not scared anymore, it doesn't even seem so dark to me.

There were a handful of Damned in the woods. Terra stumbled across a trio of the creatures; she reached one hand into her bag for her Glock but froze when one of the creatures looked straight at her. Terra didn't dare move, she held her breath as her fingers slowly curled around the handle of the gun.

The Damned made a strange hissing sound but Terra didn't move. Her body refused, though it wasn't fear this time. Something else held her in place. The Damned cocked its head as it studied Terra; still she didn't move. The Damned dribbled a little but after a painful few seconds turned back to the others and slowly hobbled away. Terra took a slow heavy breath.

Their vision is based on movement, so that's how he stayed alive out here on his own.

Terra only wished she'd learnt this sooner, but even so it was a helpful piece of information. She managed to slip past the Damned and continued to move unchallenged for at least an hour before she found something peculiar. The trees all abruptly stopped in a wide-open space. But it's what sat at the centre of that space that gave Terra a chill down her spine. There was a staircase standing there. A tall set of white spiralling stairs that should have led to the second floor of a building. Instead the stairs stood alone, and unsupported.

"What the hell?" Terra unintentionally voiced her thoughts.

"Not quite I'm afraid."

The voice was familiar to Terra. A low breaking voice of a teenage lad. Her gaze shot up to the top of the stairs and there stood the young man from her dreams.

"Eddie?"

"Only in likeness I'm afraid, girl," he replied.

Terra took a nervous step closer; she didn't realise it but she had already taken hold of her gun.

"What's with the stairs?" Terra asked cautiously.

"They're the highest point in… Limbo, I believe that's what you call this place?"

"Is that not what it's called?" asked Terra.

"It has many names, none of them matter really," Eddie's likeness replied.

"I'm looking for someone," Terra said with fragile confidence. "Have you seen a soldier come through here?"

Eddie's likeness gave her a toothy grin.

"I see everything from up here."

Terra held her ground.

"Are you going to tell me where he went?"

Eddie's likeness sat down at the top of the stairs and stretched out his limbs.

"Let's see, you're after the tall one with the blue eyes, yes?" Eddie's grin broke into a deep hearty laugh.

"What's so funny?" Terra hissed.

"Ow! I'd be careful, young lady, you're awfully easy to read when you wear your emotions on your sleeve like that. It's just as well he likes you too. Oh, don't look at me like that! You know it's true, even if you don't want to admit it." He broke into a laugh again.

I'm getting really pissed off with this prick's attitude.

"Come now, there's no need for such language, girl."

Terra froze.

He can read…

"I can, yes. I told you I can see everything from up here."

"What else do you know about this place? Terra questioned. "Do you know anything about the light?"

Eddie stopped laughing; he stroked his hairless chin a few times as he made a big show of thinking about it.

"A light? Is that what you see? Fascinating."

Terra cocked her head.

"You mean it isn't a light?"

"It is, yes, but it's also so much more." He chuckled again.

"Just wait until you see what it really is, oh my, if only you knew…"

"Knew what?" Terra snapped.

She raised the Glock to Eddie but as soon as she lined up her sights the young man vanished.

"The consequences of your actions."

Terra lowered her aim down at the base of the stairs. Eddie was standing on the first step. Terra put the red dot on his skull; she wasn't sure when it had happened but she couldn't have been any more than three paces away now.

Eddie just smiled.

"So, this is the first step. How interesting."

"I don't understand." Terra growled. "Explain what you meant by consequences."

Eddie shrugged.

"I can't do that."

"Why not?"

"Because you have to see it for yourself." Eddie started to laugh again; as the hideous twisted sound left his mouth the wind picked up around them. Terra's instincts screamed danger, every fibre of her being told her to run, but through gritted teeth and ferocious determination Terra held her ground and kept the gun aimed even as the wind started to blow her off balance.

"Tell me what you meant!" she shouted.

"One day you will understand."

Eddie leant forward until he was practically about to fall, then his face changed. The skin disappeared, leaving a fleshy, bloody, skinless face, oozing thick crimson blood from every inch of flesh.

"But by then it'll be far too late."

Terra pulled the trigger but turned away before she could see the result. Something warm and thick splattered the side of her face as she ran for the treeline. She battled against the blowing winds until her feet met the soft ground of the treeline's edge and the wind stopped. She looked back in bewilderment as if to confirm what she had seen. The staircase was still there, but there was no sign of Eddie.

Was any of that real? Never mind, I need to find Sharpe.

Terra made it up three steps before she sensed the movement beside her. She spun to the left raising her handgun. In the blink of an eye her arms were bent to the side and another smaller handgun was pressed into her chest. Terra looked up at the shocked expression of Sharpe.

"Terra?"

"It's me, Sharpe!" Terra yelped.

Sharpe took back his handgun and slid the weapon back into its holster.

◂▸

Billy's feet gave out from under him. Machine grabbed hold of his arm and heaved the lad back up. The team had been walking for a while and were making good headway towards the light. The white beam was becoming much thicker as they moved closer. The terrain however had begun to change from flat open plains to rocky hills and valleys, making visibility rather poor.

"Come on, kid, there'll be plenty of pussy where we're going," Machine chirped. He patted Billy on the shoulder and began moving back towards the others. Billy hadn't said a word since Terra had left; it was understandable but when they were this close to their objective, Machine just couldn't contain his excitement.

"All right so you got a thump from the girl because you ran your mouth a little. We've all been there, man, heck did I ever tell you what I said to Sam the first time we…" Machine stopped himself mid-sentence.

He'd noticed a peculiar black mark at the back of Billy's neck reaching up to his head.

"Hey, what's up with that tattoo on your neck? I've never noticed it before."

Machine made an effort to raise his volume to cover the sound of him switching off his rifle's safety.

"I don't have any tats," Billy murmured back.

Billy realised too late what was happening. Machine grabbed his rifle and slammed the stock into Billy's gut; he unclipped the strap and aimed it straight at Billy head. Machine stamped on Billy's right arm as he hit the ground. The other soldiers headed over as well.

"His mark has spread, it looks bad," Machine said firmly as Zero moved towards them.

Zero crouched down next to Billy. By the look of things Zero's mark wasn't doing too well either. Billy could see it beginning to spread to his hands, the veins in his fingers were starting to lose colour as was a little of his neck. Zero wiped his face. He held his head as he tried to think of what to do next.

"We're so close," Irish added. "He'll make it."

"If he turns with a gun in his hand, he could wipe all of us out," Zero replied. He turned back to Billy. "You should really have been keeping us informed about this."

"What about your mark, it's not doing too well either, is it?" Billy barked back. Machine and Irish turned their gaze on Zero.

"I'm firmly in control. You want to keep your gun? Fine. But if you so much as…" Zero was cut off when Wolfman started firing at something. The young soldier yelled "Contact" and the team snapped to a defensive position. The Damned had got the drop on them.

There were two dozen of the things sprinting towards the team. Machine moved off Billy and began firing his weapon. He scrambled back behind the soldiers as the creatures drew closer.

"Fuck, I'm out," Machine yelled.

A Damned had already selected him as its target. The creature tackled Machine to the ground before the soldier could draw his pistol. It tried stabbing at him with a clawed hand but Machine's strength was enough to hold the Damned back, though only just.

"Little help here guys!" Machine grunted as he struggled against the Damned.

Zero was busy jamming his knife into a particularly stubborn Damned that had swatted his rifle away, while Irish mowed down a bunch of the monsters with the little ammunition he had left. Billy used his borrowed rifle to finish a pair of Damned. This would have been fine if there weren't another five climbing over the hills to get to him. The first Damned was faster than the others. Its legs hadn't deformed to the same state and it ran with more freedom. It was three feet away from Billy when Wolfman's shoulder barged the creature away from him.

"Get out of here, Billy!"

Wolfman shot the Damned twice in the head as he called out to the student. The remaining four Damned, however, were already closing. Wolfman dispatched the first with a few precision rounds. The second took a chunk out of his arm. Wolfman swatted the creature away using his weapon as a club. Another was cut down by Machine who had managed to get his pistol on target despite the Damned he had been wrestling, literally chewing off his armour's shoulder strap. The fourth Damned, however, saw the opening and rushed towards Billy. Wolfman rushed to intercept; he tackled the Damned to the ground, shoved the barrel of his pistol into its mouth and pulled the trigger.

More Damned were coming. They were pouring out of the hills from all directions. Zero had managed to swap his rifle's magazines but was too busy holding off the creatures advancing from the rear to help his men.

"Don't let them separate us!" Wolfman yelled. "Stay together!"

The youngest soldier tossed his Glock to Billy.

"If you're going to stay then start shooting."

Wolfman drew his knife as another Damned raced towards him. He took a long deep breath as the creature approached. He moved fast; he flipped the Damned over his shoulder and onto the ground. He flicked his knife into the leg of the next. When the creature tripped and fell into his arms Wolfman snapped its neck with a sickly crunch. With no time to waste Wolfman discarded the disabled Damned and raised his fists for the next onslaught.

◀▶

"What the fuck are you doing here?" Sharpe hissed.

Terra and the sniper dropped down to their knees when something shuffled through the woodlands in the distance.

Without realising or communicating they each faced a different direction, covering one another's flanks as they bickered.

"I came here to bring your selfless ass back!" Terra snapped back.

"For fuck's sake are you trying to get yourself killed?" Sharpe growled.

"No but you are! Seriously what is it with you and trying to get yourself killed every fucking time we run into trouble!"

"Better me than you…"

Terra cut him off.

"Last time I checked you're a lot more useful to the people you're trying to protect if you're alive!"

As she turned over her shoulder to slam home her point, she spotted a Damned crawling out from behind a tree just a couple of feet away from Sharpe.

"Look out!" she yelled.

Terra grabbed one of the straps of Sharpe's uniform and wrenched him back. In the same motion she stepped over his body bringing her pistol to bear and fired two perfectly aimed shots into the Damned's face. The first shattered the creature's jaw, the second pushed its left eye through the back of its head. The back of the Damned's head popped, brains and grey matter splattered the trees behind the monster. The Damned dropped to its knees and sat there motionless. Terra, after taking a moment to remember to breathe, looked back at a stunned Sharpe.

Holy shit I'm a badass!

"If you're going to insist on protecting me…" she reached out a hand to help him up, "then I guess I'll have to protect you as well."

Sharpe took her hand, though he made sure not to put any weight onto Terra. He weighed over two hundred pounds with all of his equipment on. The Damned twitched behind them.

"Oh God, is it still alive?" Terra gagged.

"Just about. There's no brain function left, it won't last long like this."

Sharpe motioned to move on but Terra held her ground. She scanned the Damned; this one was still partially clothed, wearing some kind of old battered military uniform. It was hard to tell through the dried crusted dirt but the pattern seemed reminiscent of a tiger stripe.

"This thing used to be a person, right?"

"Yeah…" Sharpe croaked. "What of it?"

"We can't just leave it like this."

Sharpe studied the creature; he reached down for his bowie knife forgetting he'd lost that during his fight with the shimmer. Instead he took his regular combat knife from his vest, and moved towards the creature when a new thought struck him.

"If you're going to be out here covering me, you'll need to know your way around a little more than just that Glock I gave you." The sniper flipped the knife around holding out the handle to Terra. "I'll show you where to strike."

Terra took the knife into her surprisingly steady hands. Sharpe ran his finger across the creature's throat.

"In the movies they cut here, this'll work if you cut deep enough but your opponent will still be alive long enough to do some damage. I've seen someone do this in Afghanistan only to have the knife taken off them and stabbed with it themselves." Sharpe pointed to the creature's temple. "I don't care what they do in *The Walking Dead*, this is pure fiction." Finally, his hand drifted to the Damned's chest at the very base of the neck. "Strike firm, strike fast, it'll be clean and quiet."

Terra nodded. She took a firm grasp and plunged the knife down into the Damned's chest as hard and fast as she could. The knife slammed home, the tip of the blade slid through the Damned's thick skin. Terra felt cartilage and soft flesh rip and tear beneath the power of the blade. She pulled the knife back out while Sharpe held the Damned in place. The knife left the wound, bringing with it a thick lump of bubbling blood as the creature tried to pull air into its lungs. The Damned fell back gargling and choking, then fell very still and finally died after just a few seconds. Terra gagged fiercely but held down her stomach's contents.

"That wasn't clean, or quiet!"

"It's as close as you'll get. Knives are messy and loud, just pray you never have to use one in a fight, when there's someone bearing down on you. You don't get the chance to aim. You just have to stick it in wherever you can and hope for the best."

Terra's mind flashed images of Sharpe attacking the two men who'd found her upon her arrival in Limbo. The ferocity and speed... there was nothing clean there either.

"Come on, we should get moving before any more of them show up," Sharpe said.

As they moved through the trees a questioned wormed its way from Terra's mind to her lips in a subconscious attempt to break the silence.

"Did you see that thing on the stairs as well?"

"The stairs?" Sharpe croaked. "When did you see that?"

"Just before I ran into you, no more than half an hour ago," she replied.

Sharpe took a moment to consider that.

"I did see something weird on some stairs but that was months ago… what did it look like to you?"

"An old school friend…" Terra croaked. "It's weird though I feel like…"

"I saw the way you looked at that thing back at the cliff. It was the same person wasn't it?"

"I-I don't know what I saw," Terra lied. "It couldn't have been him."

"What happened to him?" Sharpe asked curiously.

"He died… but that was years ago, so there's no way…"

"Don't be so sure of that, time doesn't exactly mean a lot out here," Sharpe croaked in a much more sinister tone than he intended.

"And what does that mean?" Terra grunted.

I'm getting pretty fed up of all this cryptic shit.

"You don't know? I guess that makes sense actually."

"What do you mean?" Terra asked.

"You familiar with time dilation, Terra?" Sharpe asked.

"Something to do with black holes, right?" Terra's heart dropped. "Oh God, don't tell me those are in Limbo too?"

Sharpe chuckled. "Nah, time dilation is a theorised anomaly that occurs the closer you get to a black hole; basically the force of the black hole actually warps time. Theoretically speaking, time would move slower for you the closer you got to the event horizon."

Terra nodded slowly as she listened.

"And you think that there's something similar happening in Limbo?"

"Sort off, but less predictable," the sniper admitted. "When did you leave the group?"

"A couple of hours ago," Terra answered.

"Thought so… for me it's been about a week."

Terra stopped walking.

"Y-You can't be serious?"

"After everything you've seen, is it that hard to believe?"

That would explain how those guys caught up to us so quickly… and how he managed to get Sev's gun.

Terra scanned Sharpe's body. His bandages had all been changed or at least cleaned and his face did have a bit more colour in it than when she'd last seen him.

"So, what about the petrol station? That was about a day for me before I met you in the church but you looked like you'd really set up shop there."

Sharpe answered her with a completely straight face.

"About a month," he answered. "Give or take a week."

Terra just stood there staring at him completely dumbfounded.

"You okay, Terra?" Sharpe asked.

Terra shook her head; she actually laughed as her mind tried to make sense of Sharpe's words.

"There's no way. No way. What about the Damned mark? Why hasn't it taken you?"

Sharpe studied Terra for a moment, then he reached down for the base of his shirt with one hand and lifted it up. Sharpe revealed an unfairly well-toned stomach and a small patch of discoloured black skin coming up from below his belt line.

"Started out about halfway up my left leg and worked its way up. Still hasn't reached the right side yet so I've got a while before I need to worry about it."

Terra didn't actually hear what he said; her eyes were glued to his stomach.

Stop talking and take your shirt off.

"You okay, Terra?" Sharpe tucked his shirt back into his trousers.

Terra shook herself out of her dreams.

"Huh? Oh… yeah! Sorry, I guess I'm just tired."

Sharpe nodded slowly.

"Right," he affirmed. Luckily for Terra he didn't seem to understand what she'd been doing or if he did, he didn't show it.

The soldier waved a hand for her to follow and started moving through the trees again.

"We need to keep moving."

"Right!" Terra agreed.

A long walk later, the treeline ahead of them stopped. The landscaped completely changed. Terra and Sharpe were now walking down a dirt road flanked on either side by tall rocky mountains. Ahead of them was a scene of chaos. A large black SUV and an old sedan. Both cars were covered by a thick layer of grey dust. Terra rushed over to the cars while Sharpe hung back with his head held low.

"Cars! Actual cars, we could use these!" Terra called excitedly.

As she reached the first of the cars, she slowed her pace. The windows on the far side of the SUV were all shattered and destroyed. Large holes riddled the sides of the vehicles.

"Looks like someone shot these up. What do you think happened here? Sharpe? Are you okay?"

Sharpe approached slowly; he didn't need to look at the cars to answer her question.

"M2 fifty-calibre machine gun opened up from two miles away."

"That's… oddly specific…" Terra replied.

Sharpe pointed further down the road. Terra followed his gaze to a pair of pickup trucks, one was overturned and destroyed, the other was missing its windshield.

"They drove right into the kill zone, a sharpshooter up on that hill behind us opened up with an SR25 sniper rifle and cut them down."

"You were here, weren't you?" Terra stated more than asked.

Sharpe nodded.

"It was my last mission before the airport… the mission where Zero earned his position."

Terra looked around at the devastation.

"It seems more like you did all the work."

Sharpe managed a slight smirk.

"Well it was his plan, besides I'm not much of a leader. Give me a target, I'll give you results. That's what I do."

"So, what happened here exactly?" Terra changed the subject.

"An exchange was meant to take place between two rival militia. There was a friendly informant imbedded in one of the groups; he'd been discovered prior to the exchange and was set to be executed here."

Terra looked up at the hill.

"What information did he have?" Terra asked.

Sharpe sighed.

"Officially I wasn't supposed to know, but we found out a little later that a shipment of Russian gear heading to a base in Georgia was intercepted and disappeared. It was believed the militia had something to do with it."

"I'm going to take a wild guess and say a bunch of guns and black uniforms, right?" Terra questioned.

Sharpe smirked.

"You got it. Problem is the militia never got their hands on that gear, instead it ended up in Moi."

"Sounds like the plot for a Bond movie," Terra remarked.

"Yeah, sounds a little too perfect doesn't it? The Russians up to no good again."

Terra raised an eyebrow; something in his tone tipped her off.

"You don't think it was Russia that attacked us?"

The sniper didn't give the girl a direct answer, instead he winked.

"You'd be pretty good at this, Shorty."

"Are you offering me a job, soldier boy?" Terra battered her eyelids and for a second, she could have sworn the Sniper blushed.

Did he just give me a nickname?

"In another life, I just might." Sharpe cleared his throat as he set his mind back to his original task. "We'll be there soon. This should be the part where I tell you it's not safe for you but…"

Terra cut him off.

"But I won't listen and even if I did it would be just as dangerous for me to head back on my own anyway so I might as well stick with you."

Sharpe tried to hide his grin. He led Terra through the valley, past the vehicles. Terra wondered why they didn't try and salvage one of the truck's guns until she saw the size of the weapons.

"Those guns were designed to kill a man on the other side of a cinder-block wall two miles away," Sharpe said when he caught her looking. "No way in hell you could fire that standing. They weigh nearly as much a man and kick like a spooked mule."

"Ever tried it?" Terra asked as they continued.

Sharpe chuckled.

"There was one guy who tried, his name's Pyro. A tank on legs, to put it into perspective. This guy beat Irish in an arm wrestle. He managed to fire ten shots standing before he lost his grip. Didn't hit the target but he still did it."

Sharpe laughed.

"He was in Akira's team. That's Zero's brother."

"What's he like?" Terra asked, honestly curious.

"Imagine Zero but a little older and a lot wiser."

"That sounds… kind of terrifying actually," Terra said.

Sharpe agreed.

"He's the second most successful squad leader in the company," Sharpe continued. "And that's only because Boss's team has been going for longer…"

Sharpe's expression dropped, he clenched his fist.

"He'll be the one that gets sent after the guys who did this to us…" Sharpe lifted his head and relaxed. "That's enough about me though, what about you, Terra? Terra?"

Terra had stopped walking. They had cleared the valley and now something new greeted them. A raised platform sitting beside a long set of railway tracks. Sharpe raised his rifle as he moved towards the tiny building that was presumably the office of the station. Terra followed silently.

"Stay close to me, something's…" Sharpe tried to find the words. "Something doesn't feel right."

Terra understood.

"You feel the same way I felt back at those cars… you can feel something in the air. As if the motions of the people who were here are floating around you."

Sharpe looked back to Terra. She was hanging her head

low, her face hidden by the lack of light. She didn't look at him as she moved towards the platform. Sharpe hung back a few paces to give her some space.

"This place is from your past, isn't it?" Sharpe realised.

Terra pointed to the far side of the platform. As a shadowy figure stumbled onto the platform from the office, Sharpe's rifle was up and scoped in. But he couldn't find the target in his crosshairs. The figure was just a shadowy outline of a man, or rather a young man. The ghost paced back and forth holding something to his ear.

"That person I saw back there on the stairs… and the face on that thing…" Terra murmured. "His name was Eddie."

Sharpe lowered his weapon; he moved a little closer to Terra.

"We'd been together for about a year, he was my first… serious relationship, if you get what I mean?" Terra's voice was cracking but she held her composure well.

"Eddie wasn't well equipped to deal with school. But I was pretty adept. I got As in all of my GCSEs and I had my pick of universities and courses…"

The ghostly figure of Eddie continued to pace back and forth.

"He's calling you, isn't he?"

Terra nodded.

"I got accepted into a very nice arts school up north. But of course, I couldn't maintain my relationship with Eddie… He didn't take it well and we got into a fight."

They couldn't hear what Eddie was saying but Sharpe had the general idea.

"I was really mad…" Terra sniffed. "I didn't believe him when he said he'd come here. He said… he…" Terra dropped to her knees as the ghostly image of a train appeared on the tracks in the distance.

"I told him if he was going to be that stupid and weak, he should just go ahead and jump!" she cried.

Sharpe watched as Eddie stood at the edge of the platform until the train was entering the station. As he leant forward the ghostly images faded away, but this time they heard the sounds of the train roaring through the station, slamming on its horn, which of course was all in vain.

"That's why you're here?" Sharpe asked, "because you think you killed him?"

Terra looked up with eyes full of tears.

"I… I…"

Sharpe took off his hat and wiped his forehead. A great smile lit up his face as he laughed. He actually dropped down to his knees as he chuckled happily to himself.

"You… think this is funny?" Terra questioned, a flame of fury and despair boiling inside her.

Sharpe managed to compose himself; he met Terra's furious gaze with that same warm smile.

"This whole time I've been left wondering what it was you did to get yourself stuck here with us. I figured you'd killed someone or done something truly horrible, and yet… it wasn't you at all, it was just some stupid kid who ruined your life." Sharpe's expression changed as he pieced together the puzzle.

"His death hurt you so badly you had to up and leave the country to get away from him. Even after he was no longer a part of your life, he still ruined it."

Terra fought back against an ocean of tears.

"Yes! You got it!" she snarled. "That's my big secret and here you are laughing in my face about it…" She stopped herself as the guilt washed over her. “Go on then… laugh some more, I know I deserve it…”

Sharpe cocked his head.

“I’m not laughing because this is funny, Terra. I’m laughing because I’m relieved.”

“Relieved?” Terra spat.

“Yeah, relieved that the smart, beautiful girl I met in Moi airport is as innocent as I hoped she was.” Sharpe’s face relaxed back into a slight smile again.

“Huh?”

“Terra… you can’t blame yourself for this.”

She looked away, muttering something incoherent under her breath.

“You were young,” Sharpe continued. “You still are. All right so you got mad and said something you shouldn’t but even so, you didn’t push him! You didn’t make him jump. He did that. He did that because he was too selfish to live his life without you in it.”

“That’s so easy for you to say!” Terra sobbed. “You must be numb to death.”

Sharpe thought about it for a moment.

“I’m a soldier, more than that, I’m a sniper. I’ve killed people, a lot of people… so many people I’ve got pretty good at it. When you first pull that trigger it’s the easiest thing in the world. But that moment after he goes down is the hardest. When you see that lifeless limp body hit the floor you see a big piece of yourself die with them.”

“Your point?” Terra moaned.

She tried to look away but Sharpe gently pulled her chin back to his face so she had to look him in the eye.

“When I look at my teammates, I can see the hole that’s left, I can see the change. But when I look at you… I don’t see a killer. I see an innocent girl who's suffering for something that truly wasn't her fault, but she blames herself anyway."

Sharpe's face lit up as a new idea hit him. He took his hand away from Terra's face, reached up for his boonie hat and dropped it onto Terra's head, revealing the thick black hair that had been hidden beneath.

A short speech was never going to repair years of guilt and grief but right then and right there, it was enough. Terra jumped into the arms of the soldier and the pair held each other in a tight embrace as Terra cried. "I'm sorry! I'm so sorry I didn't… I didn't…"

Sharpe stayed there with her, on his knees, holding her close and he would stay there for as long as she needed. Secretly he knew as well as she did that sometimes it feels really good to cry.

CHAPTER 15

◀▶

THE BLOODY CRUCIBLE

Sharpe and Terra sat back to back in the office of the train station. They'd managed to salvage a pair of chairs so that they could more easily watch their sectors. Both of them wore their black sunglasses with the night vision mode enabled, extending their reach to the edge of the treeline around them. But alas, there had been no sign of the shimmering creature.

"I don't think it's coming," Terra said after a long bout of silence.

Sharpe didn't respond. The barrel of his rifle moved slowly just millimetres at a time as he scanned the spaces between the trees.

"Sharpe? Did you hear me?"

"Yeah, I heard you," the sniper mumbled. "If you're tired you can always take a nap."

Terra shook her head, not that Sharpe could see the gesture.

"Sharpe, there are just the two of us out here, if it really was following us it would have attacked us by now."

Terra's heart sank as her thoughts drifted.

Damn it, Sam. I think we could both use your company right now.

"Just a little bit longer," Sharpe said. "It'll come…"

"It's not coming, Sharpe," Terra said. "For all we know it went after the others, they could be out there fighting it right now while we're just sitting here."

"Damn it, I know!" Sharpe growled. He put down his rifle and threw his hands up behind his head in frustration. "No matter what I do, this fucking thing never comes out. No matter how many traps I set or where I go, it never comes out… It doesn't make any sense."

Terra took off her glasses.

"It knew you were expecting it."

"Huh?"

"Sharpe…" Terra said. "You've always been keeping an eye… looking out for this thing. And then the one time you didn't, when we were all relaxing in the cabin, that's when it showed up. Don't you get it?"

Sharpe turned back to her, confused.

"It didn't come because you were expecting it! It was only when we all let our guards down that it showed up."

"That's insane!" Sharpe exclaimed. "There's no way…"

"You're probably right about it being out there watching us but it won't attack because you know it's coming. Look what happened the last time it attacked us, you took off one of its faces and Irish took an arm!"

Terra tried to find a better way to explain it.

"It's hunting us, but a leopard won't attack prey that's aware it's there. It gets close, so close it can almost touch the prey, then when it least expects it…" Terra clapped her hands together, "it goes for the throat. It doesn't want to engage in a drawn-out battle. Even one on one, it knows how dangerous we can be. Sharpe, as long as you're looking out for this thing, it can't touch us."

"You might be onto something, Terra..." a new thought struck Sharpe. "Wait, the others!"

Right on cue, a faint but long burst of gunfire echoed through the trees. Terra's and Sharpe's eyes followed the direction of the sound until they fell on the beam of brilliant white light over the trees.

"Oh no," Terra moaned.

Sharpe jumped to his feet, and raced out of the office.

"They're in trouble, come on, Terra."

Terra had a hard job keeping up with him but she was able to stay relatively close to Sharpe as they ran through the trees. The gunshots were faint but they couldn't have been far off. Though they had stopped just a few minutes before, Terra and Sharpe cleared the trees and were greeted with a steep but low hill.

Sharpe reached the top first, then stopped and waited for Terra.

"What is it?" Terra panted as she climbed up after him.

When she reached the top, she got her answer. An ocean of dead Damned littered the dirt below them. The lights above reflected off spent bullet casings and the pools of crimson blood. Terra and Sharpe scanned the scene.

"I don't see any of the guys," Terra said hopefully.

"There's no way they fought off this many without someone getting hurt."

Sharpe slid down the hill to get a better look. He placed a hand on one of the creatures.

"Still warm, they can't be far ahead."

Before Terra could respond, Sharpe was moving again. She cursed as she forced her tired limbs to continue the run. Sharpe and Terra ran through several more hills, each littered with the bodies of the Damned, though they became less and less frequent with every step.

They found the other soldiers amongst the ruins of an old stone building. The building itself had long since been destroyed and was completely unrecognisable. Small stone walls littered the ground like a miniature maze.

"Oh shit, Sharpe!" Machine greeted as they approached.

"Saw your handiwork back there, looks like you guys had fun," Sharpe replied.

Machine's smile dropped, and Sharpe's heart sank with it.

"What happened?"

Irish stood up from behind one of the walls. Terra had just finished dragging herself up the hill; she dropped down to her knees as she sucked in a few deep breaths of fresh air. Sharpe paid her no attention; he headed towards Irish, followed by Machine's gaze as he walked. The oldest soldier was standing beside Wolfman, who was on the ground lying beside one of the stone walls. His neck was covered in blood, his assault vest was torn open. He was breathing slowly, but most of the colour had left his face.

"Hey… y-you came back," Wolfman croaked.

"Yeah bud. I'm back." Sharpe knelt down beside his friend.

"What happened?"

"You should…" Wolfman coughed, "see the other guy…"

"I did!" Sharpe confirmed. "You did good, brother."

Terra approached the men slowly. She caught a glimpse of Zero at the edge of the stone compound. Billy was talking to him about something that didn't look pleasant. His face lit up and then instantly dropped when he saw Terra. The young lad said something to Zero that the soldier didn't seem to listen to and came waddling over to Terra.

"Nice hat…" Billy groaned.

"Yeah, I'm thinking about keeping it, not sure about the colour though," Terra joked, but humour had never been her strong suit. "What happened?"

"A lot of things," Zero called back to them. "Your boyfriend abandoned us… and look what happened."

Terra saw Zero coming. She put herself directly in his path to block him.

"This can wait, Zero," she hissed.

Sharpe leant forward, gently putting his forehead against Wolfman's. He gripped the young soldier's hand in a tight grasp as Wolfman took his final breath. Irish lowered his head for a silent prayer.

"That's another one gone, because of you."

Zero's gaze was locked on Sharpe. Both Machine and Irish glared at him. Machine's hand drifted towards the handle of his rifle, while Irish sat atop a low wall watching him. Sharpe rose from Wolfman's body and advanced on his friend. Terra saw him coming; she ran into Sharpe wrapping her arms around him to hold him back but Sharpe gently pushed her away.

"It's okay," he said softly, "I think Zero and I need to have a talk."

Machine and Irish both approached, taking positions on either side of Sharpe.

"We all decided on this, Zero," Irish said calmly. "We're all to blame for this, not just Sharpe."

Zero shook his head violently as his composure failed him.

"Don't you dare! I said it! I said it right from the beginning and none of ya'll listened!" Zero pointed to Wolfman's body. "That's on you! You left us!"

"Zach…" Machine started. "Calm down, brother."

Irish caught something in the corner of his eye. It was slight but it was there, just behind one of the low walls towards the light. Irish raised his machine gun a split second after Bruce and his three surviving men popped up and opened fire. Irish pushed Sharpe and Zero over the wall closest to them. Terra and Billy dived down instinctively while Machine remained standing to return fire. A bullet tore into Machine's upper right leg and dropped the soldier to the ground.

"Shit!" Machine yelled, still spraying his rifle at their attackers as he fell. Sharpe jumped over the wall to pull Machine back into cover while Zero and Irish suppressed Bruce's men.

"Did ya miss me, fuckers?" Bruce screamed as he held his Kalashnikov over the wall and emptied its magazine. A few of the bullets caught Machine as Sharpe heaved him over the wall. Machine's left arm was immobilised but his vest saved him from death.

"God damn it, that hurts!" Machine growled through gritted teeth. Sharpe pressed his hands down on Machine's leg wound. Terra crawled on her belly to the two men.

"What can I do?"

"Put pressure on his leg!" Sharpe barked.

"Ah man, I get a hot Asian nurse?" Machine chuckled. "I should get shot more often!"

Sharpe moved into a crouch position; he took aim at a patch of wall where he suspected one of Bruce's men was hiding and fired three shots one after the other a second apart through the wall, spacing each bullet a foot apart.

Boom. Concrete. Boom. Concrete again. Boom.

Blood sprayed out in a thick mist from behind the wall; a man started screaming.

Irish was hunched low behind the wall, pushing in the last belt he had for the machine gun. He had maybe twenty shots left at most, which was enough for just a second of firing time.

"Zero! Machine's hit, we need to get him out of here!" the old soldier yelled as he slammed home the belt.

"Shit! We need every gun we have for this!" Zero retorted.

"Not me and Billy!" Terra yelled back.

A stream of bullets tore at the low walls, bullets ricocheted over the top of them.

"We can take Machine and slip down through the hills while you fight them off."

"Not happening," Sharpe growled.

"Yes, it is," Zero spat. "We'll cover you guys!"

"Sounds good to me!" Bruce yelled.

"Oh, I have had enough of your shit!" Irish roared.

All three soldiers stood up with weapons ready. Bruce's men did the same but the firepower advantage was well in the hands of the SOO soldiers. Another of Bruce's men went down as Terra, Billy and a wounded Machine slipped down into the depressions of the ground out of the line of fire. Sharpe vaulted over his wall to the next in the confusion. Irish sprayed his bullets over the top of Bruce's position. Zero was covering Bruce's last soldier but when the mercenaries stood up, Zero's rifle clicked empty. Sharpe stood up to fire, Irish turned his gun but not before the mercenary put a burst of sub-machine-gun fire into the old soldier.

"Irish!" Zero cried.

Sharpe finished Bruce's last man with the last bullet in his magazine.

"You all right back there, big man?" Sharpe yelled.

As quickly as it had begun the battle had fallen silent. The sounds of gunfire were now replaced by the moaning and shuffling of one of Bruce's men. The SOO soldiers all waited in silence, praying for a response from Irish.

"Thank God for body armour!" Irish wheezed. "You two finish this, I need a minute to catch my breath."

"Getting old, are we?" Sharpe joked as his shaking hands pushed in a new magazine.

"Ha ha, very funny," Irish retorted.

Zero nodded as he pushed in his last magazine, which at best was no more than half full.

"Hey, hey hang on let's talk about this like men!" Bruce called out, with just a slight hint of panic in his voice.

"Sure," Sharpe growled. "You stand up and my rifle will talk."

Zero moved to the side, flanking Bruce's position. The Australian had found what he thought was a solid piece of wall. Right up until that bloody sniper had put three .308 rounds straight through it into his subordinate who had just stopped groaning and started twitching spasmodically. He was a desperate man trapped in a corner like an animal. But he'd be damned if he was going to die quietly.

"Fuck it," Bruce growled.

The last mercenary's head had cleared the wall by six inches before Sharpe splattered his brains over the dirt.

"That's from Boss," Sharpe grunted as he moved to the wall, swinging his rifle back and forth, scanning for movement.

He inspected the bodies. One of Bruce's men was twitching but the others were all still.

"How you doing, Irish?" Sharpe called back.

There was no response.

"Irish?"

Sharpe made it back to Irish in seconds but he was already too late. Zero was crouching down beside the old man. A bullet had slipped into his chest just above his armour. He'd died just a few seconds before the younger men moved up.

"Damn it. You stubborn old bastard!"

"This is your fault…" Zero moaned.

Sharpe looked up from the bloody ground.

"Zero?" Something in his voice didn't sound right.

Silver hair covered his face as he looked down at Irish, but his voice didn't sound like his own. Zero slowly unclipped his rifle, showing a black misshapen hand; where he should have had normal fingernails he had long claws that seemed to have erupted from his fingertips.

"Zero… relax, brother," Sharpe reasoned.

The silver hair dropped to the ground as the face of the Damned looked up at the sniper. Sharpe raised his rifle with tears in his eyes.

"Please! Please don't do this to me, brother."

Zero, or rather the Damned he was becoming, hissed at Sharpe. The creature rose to its full height slowly, followed by the barrel of Sharpe's rifle. The slightest ounce of pressure and Zero's torment would be over, but Sharpe couldn't do it.

"You're my brother, Zero! I know that isn't you in there anymore… but I… I can't."

Sharpe slowly lowered the barrel of his gun and slung the heavy rifle across his back. The Damned watched him curiously as Sharpe reached across his chest and pulled out his standard combat knife.

"Even in this state, you deserve a fair fight, brother!"

Sharpe charged towards the Damned and the Damned towards him. They collided in a flailing mess of arms, blades and claws.

◂▸

Even while supporting the sizable weight of Machine, Terra still couldn't completely draw her attention away from the hill. The gunfight was still raging behind them. Billy was a few feet ahead of them, scanning the way ahead with his borrowed rifle.

"Billy…" Terra struggled. "I could use your help here."

"There could be more of them! We need a guard," Billy snapped in reply.

Machine's leg finally gave out; he collapsed to the ground taking Terra with him.

"Shit. Sorry, kid."

Terra was back on her feet instantly, trying to heave Machine back upright.

"You and the others have protected us this far, it's about time I repaid the favour." Terra managed to get Machine's arm over her shoulders. "Though this would be a lot easier if someone else helped…"

Machine nudged her in the ribs. He spoke quietly so Billy wouldn't hear.

"I wouldn't if I were you."

"Huh? I've known Billy for much longer than you guys." She raised her voice. "He can be really stubborn when he's feeling guilty."

Billy briefly glanced back over his shoulder. Machine grunted as he dropped back to his knees, once again pulling Terra down with him.

"Machine!" Terra cried. "Come on, we're so close."

Machine locked his gaze on hers; it was a cold, stern stare.

He fell on purpose.

"We weren't going to tell you this… but there's something you should know about Billy."

Terra cocked her head in confusion. Then the words from the petrol station hit her. What Sev had said just before he passed out.

You need to keep a better eye on him if she's here, he's becoming more unstable.

A sudden cold breeze carried the dread through Terra's body.

"Bu-But Boss and Sev weren't talking about…"

Machine pushed Terra away with all his might. Terra flew back a couple of feet as Machine drew his pistol. Before he could bring the gun to bear, Billy fired a two-second burst into Machine. Machine was shredded as a line of bullets ripped up his assault vest, into his arms and finally into his face.

"Machine!" Terra screamed. She went to draw her own handgun but Billy raised the smoking barrel of his gun in her direction.

"Uh-uh! Don't you even think about it," Billy growled.

Terra froze, her wide eyes locked on the smoking barrel of Billy's gun.

"B-Billy… What are you…" She struggled to form the words. Her blood was running cold with pure fear.

"He was slowing us down! I did what I had to do…"

Terra's shaking hands were over her mouth, tears were pouring from her eyes. She couldn't form words. Sev's last words were rushing through her mind.

You need to keep a better eye on him if she's here, he's becoming more unstable.

Terra's heart was racing; her body felt numb.

They weren't talking about Sharpe… All this time…

"H-He was going to shoot me!" Billy stuttered.

Terra fought against the urge to look at Machine. She knew it was too late, he was gone.

"Billy…" she said calmly. "Y-You need to put down the gun now… nobody else needs to get hurt."

"Don't tell me what to do!" Billy snarled, taking a firm grip of the rifle.

A black vein seemed to creep up to his lips from his neck like a worm. When it made contact, Billy gave Terra a sickly wide smile.

"I love you, Terra!" he confessed. "I have always loved you."

"Billy…" Terra croaked. "You're not well."

His face dropped.

"The only thing wrong with me is how I feel about you!" Billy roared.

Terra recoiled back a step. She raised her hands instinctively to cover her face.

"Okay, okay, I'm sorry I shouldn't have said that. That was wrong of me. I'm sorry. I know how you feel… I've always known," Terra admitted.

"But you never said a word!" Billy snapped.

"No!" Terra recomposed herself. "No… I didn't want to upset you, you're my best friend, Billy. I wouldn't know what to do if I lost you."

"Like you lost Eddie," Billy hissed.

Terra winced.

"Y-Yeah… Like I lost Eddie."

Billy's voice was starting to lose its tone.

"Well, you don't have to worry about losing me. I'm stronger than him. I won't abandon you like he did…" He paused. "Not like Sharpe did."

Terra stepped towards Billy. He raised the gun to her head.

"Get back!" he snapped.

Terra complied.

"Even now you're thinking about him, aren't you? About that pretty English cunt." Billy sighed. "Give me your gun."

Terra tossed the weapon to his feet, half hoping it would go off. Billy kicked the pistol out of reach.

"I tried so hard. So hard to make you like me," Billy started. "And then he comes along, shows a bit of muscle and batters his blue eyes at you and you practically bend over on the spot for him!" Billy growled. "Well, where is he now? Where is your pretty boyfriend now?"

Somewhere behind them, they heard a scream. Terra just knew it was Sharpe. She fell to her knees, covering her eyes.

"Huh." Billy shrugged. "Guess he isn't so tough after all." Billy chuckled. "And to think you were hanging on every word he said like it was God's law."

"That's what you do when you really like someone, Billy…" Terra murmured. "I listened to every word he said and it kept me alive; he taught us how to use that rifle you're holding, after all."

Billy raised an eyebrow. Terra looked up at him with tears running down her cheeks.

"And now he's gone too…"

Billy lowered the gun. He rubbed his face with a sweaty hand. "I'm sorry, I know this must be hard for you."

Terra nodded. She took a step closer to Billy and smiled. Billy returned the expression, slightly bemused.

"What are you smiling at?" he asked warmly.

"You," she replied.

Terra moved towards him slowly, moving one foot in front of the other, swaying her hips and bashfully hiding her eyes from Billy. The young man's face lit up with excitement. When she was just a few paces from him, Terra's satchel dropped to the ground and her smile dropped with it.

"You're out of bullets."

Billy looked down at his gun to find a smoking empty chamber showing him an empty magazine and then his eyes moved up to Terra's hand. She was holding a long black combat knife and was glaring straight at him.

◂▸

Sharpe swung his knife across Zero's chest. Zero, or rather the creature he had become, stepped back avoiding the strike and those that followed. A clawed hand flicked up at Sharpe, catching his arm. Claws tore into his skin. Sharpe grunted as he pulled away from the Damned. The creature snarled as it started to move in a circle around him. Sharpe panted as he raised his hands into a defensive position, keeping the tip of his blade aimed at Zero.

He's trying to knock it out of my hands. If I lose this knife I'm done for, but I can't keep this up for much longer either.

Sharpe faked to the right and dashed into Zero, hitting him with all of his strength. Sharpe and Zero slid back along the ground a few feet struggling against one another. Sharpe managed to take the Damned to the ground but Zero brought one of his legs up to keep Sharpe back. The Damned roared into Sharpe's face as it struggled to hold back Sharpe's arm holding the blade. The soldier screamed as he forced his arm down bringing the knife down on Zero's face. The creature struggled as the knife reached for its eye. Sharpe managed to free his left hand and grabbed the Damned's face. Zero stabbed his claws into Sharpe's side. Sharpe grunted as his armour took the hit and pushed the blade down into Zero's right eye. Zero shrieked as the blade broke through the soft meat with a vile squelch. Zero threw Sharpe off him with a hard shove. Sharpe staggered back as the creature pulled itself to its feet. Zero held one hand over the destroyed eye as he hissed at Sharpe.

"Fucking hurts, doesn't it?"

The creature charged Sharpe again. Claws and knifes flashed in a blur as blood was drawn from both fighters. Sharpe managed to drive the blade into Zero's side while Zero's claws sank into Sharpe's shoulder. They staggered back as Zero tried to bite at Sharpe's throat. In desperation Sharpe dropped onto his back bringing Zero with him. They each struggled to get on top of the other, sending them rolling across the ground, growling and snapping, until finally they tumbled off the edge of the hill.

Before Terra and Billy had a chance to move, Sharpe and a Damned tumbled down the side of the hill drawing the attention of both of the students. The Damned pulled itself upright and turned its attention on the students. Billy made a dash for Terra's gun.

"No!" Terra yelled.

Instinctively she rushed into Billy as he raised the gun. He managed to get off a single shot that skimmed just past Terra's ear. Terra collided with the young lad, unknowingly dropping the knife in the scuffle that followed. Billy managed to punch Terra in the nose, knocking her away from him. The Damned marched towards Terra with murderous intent in its eye. Suddenly Terra recognised who the creature had been.

"Zero?"

"Get away from her!" roared Sharpe.

The sniper dived onto Damned Zero, knocking him down to the ground just in front of Terra. Sharpe looked down only to see Terra's knife lying just ahead of him. Sharpe combat-rolled forward of Zero taking up the knife in the process. He jumped to his feet and roared as he tossed the blade with expert precision right into Billy's shoulder. Billy dropped the Glock pistol as he fell down to the ground desperately clawing at the blade.

"Ah fuck! Fuck, fuck, fucking hell it hurts! Oh God it hurts!"

Terra took the gun before Billy had a chance to recover. She took aim at his face.

"Wait, no!" Billy cried.

"Stay there!" Terra hissed.

She spun back around to Sharpe. Zero had recovered. He leapt forward tackling the sniper to the ground. Sharpe hit the dirt face first and had just enough time to roll over before Zero pinned him there.

Terra put the red dot on Zero's chest and fired. A bullet slammed into Zero's chest. Just as before, it wasn't enough to break the skin, but it did knock the monster back. Sharpe took the opening and rolled Zero down to the ground. Sharpe's fist came down on Zero's face like a hammer. Zero spluttered thick blood from his mouth as Sharpe hit him again and again.

"Damn. You. Zero!" Sharpe grunted between strikes.

Sharpe took a second to breath. Zero twitched and sputtered out more blood from his destroyed and broken face. Sharpe reached down for his boot and took out his spare blade.

"Why!" Sharpe growled. "Why did it have to come to this!"

The knife came down into Zero's forehead with a final crunch.

Terra closed her eyes just before the blade came down; she'd seen enough death on this journey. When she heard the body hit the floor she opened her eyes again. Sharpe was kneeling beside Zero's body, taking deep unsteady breaths. He was covered in fresh wounds, blood covered nearly all of his face and shredded uniform. His body armour had been torn open, showing Terra rows of small circular steel plates overlapping one another like the scales of a reptile. She couldn't tell if he was crying or if it was sweat but something was mixing with the blood as it rolled down his face.

Terra took a slow step towards him.

"Sharpe?"

The soldier didn't move.

"It's me… it's Terra, I'm going to take a look at your wounds now, okay?"

Sharpe's eye drifted up to meet her as she knelt down beside him. She jumped as he raised a hand to her face. His gloves had either been torn away or discarded; every knuckle was split and probably broken but he still had enough dexterity to cup her face gently. Sharpe's head dropped down onto her shoulder. Terra managed a slight smile as a single tear rolled down her cheek.

“Hey,” she mumbled.

Sharpe suddenly pulled back from her and jumped up to his feet. Terra spun around with him as Billy charged forward clutching the knife he had torn from his shoulder. Sharpe put himself between the students. Billy slid to a halt just outside of arm’s reach; he waved the knife at Sharpe.

“Fuck you, man! Fuck you! She was mine! Mine!” Billy growled.

Despite his injuries, Sharpe managed to keep his hands raised high and his face locked on Billy. The soldier shook his head.

“She… was never… anyone’s…” Sharpe panted.

A hideous smile ripped across Billy’s face. The lower half of his head up to his eyes had turned black; sickly thin black lines were slithering up the rest of the way as he spoke.

“And what exactly are *you* gonna do about it? You can barely stand up, let alone fight!”

Billy swung the knife at Sharpe’s face, barely missing him. Sharpe grabbed Billy’s arm and tugged as hard as he could. It wasn’t enough. Billy staggered half a step then tore the soldier back and punched him with his free hand.

He’s going to die.

Both men grunted from the pain. Sharpe went down first but pulled Billy down to his knees.

He’s too weak to fight.

Billy raised the knife high; he brought the blade down. Sharpe managed to grab his arm and hold him just a few inches away from his face with both hands. Billy grabbed the blade’s handle with his free hand and started pushing down.

“Terra…” Sharpe growled as he struggled against Billy. “Run!”

Sharpe managed to redirect the knife into his armour's shoulder strap with a sudden push. Billy grunted as he recovered and backhanded Sharpe with a sickly misshapen hand.

I have to do something.

Terra lifted the Glock pistol, expertly placing the dot on Billy's chest.

"Get off him, Billy!"

Billy tore the knife free from Sharpe's armour. He barely even glanced at Terra as he raised the blade.

"I'll deal with you when I'm done with him!" Billy snarled.

The knife came down but Sharpe caught the blade in his already bloody hands. He grimaced as the knife started to push deeper into his skin.

Shoot him.

"Billy, stop!" Terra cried.

If you don't then Sharpe will die.

Terra pleaded with Billy again.

"Please, Billy, don't do this!"

The knife drew closer as Sharpe's strength failed him.

Do it!

"No!" Terra screamed.

Two gunshots rang out. Billy took one to the chest and another right between his eyes. The back of Billy's head exploded. He fell limply to the side of Sharpe, who rolled back to his knees and reached around for his rifle, only to stop short when he realised where the shots had come from.

"Terra?"

Oh no…

The gun fell from her hands.

"No. Oh no. No, no, no!"

Terra screamed so loud and for so long she felt her throat begin to tear. Sharpe managed to make it to the terrified young woman and took her in a deep embrace as she cried.

"Billy! No. I'm sorry! I'm so sorry, Billy! Oh my God what have I done!"

Sharpe looked down at Billy's lifeless body, then his gaze drifted to Machine.

"That wasn't Billy, Terra... it might have looked like him but I promise you that it wasn't."

Terra buried her face into Sharpe's chest; she felt hot sticky blood on her skin as it soaked through her clothes, but she didn't care. She didn't care about anything anymore.

It's because of me... it's my fault.

Sharpe's grip loosened on Terra. He dropped back from her with one hand holding his head as he groaned.

"Sharpe!" Terra shrieked. "Oh my God are you..."

"Fine, there's no major damage, just a little blood loss." Sharpe had regained his breath and managed to wipe away some of the blood from his face.

"The fuck do you mean, a little blood loss?"

A Damned wandered out from behind the hill as its eyes were caught by the glowing white light. It screamed and recoiled, and it was only then that Terra realised just how much brighter it was here.

"We need to go." Sharpe heaved himself to his feet. "Come on."

Terra's gaze fell on the bodies around them.

"Terra..." Sharpe sighed. "We can't do anything for them now."

"I know..."

Terra staggered past the bodies of Billy and Zero until she fell to her knees beside Machine. Sharpe watched silently; he unslung his rifle that had by some miracle remained across his back during the fight. Although the scope was scratched and it needed a clean, the weapon was still in usable shape. Terra took up Machine's hand in hers.

"Thank you… all of you."

Terra rose back to her feet and went with Sharpe towards the light.

Sharpe's exoskeleton suit creaked and groaned as he staggered forward. The device was dented, bloody and covered in dirt, yet it still kept moving. Terra just knew that without that suit there was no way Sharpe could have remained standing. After ten minutes of walking or rather, steadily limping through the low valleys and hills, the ground opened and the light was so close and bright it was almost blinding. The pair had to hold up their hands to shield their vision. Sharpe tried to find his sunglasses only to find they had been lost during the fight. Terra found hers crushed into several jagged pieces. Sharpe muttered something about German engineering at this discovery.

Soon the hills gave way to what seemed to be the edge of a wide crater; the ground shot up six feet into the air in a sudden almost vertical mound of dirt.

"Oh, for fuck's sake, what now?" Terra groaned.

Sharpe held up a hand to silence her.

"Hear that?" he asked.

"Hear what?"

"Stay here," Sharpe said. "I'll go take a look."

Terra shook her head. When she spoke, her voice was barely a whisper.

"No. We go together."

Sharpe agreed. Together they crested the embankment, slid down the other side and froze. Before them they saw exactly where the light fell. A bright white beam reaching down from the heavens; all of the purple lights they had seen along their journeys converged into the centre where they joined with the beam. But the light didn't hit the ground. Instead in fell into a vast open lake. At the heart of that lake, where the light fell, floating just an inch off the water, was a very old, very basic wooden door.

CHAPTER 16

MARIA

"W-Wait! P-Please don't shoot!"

That was roughly what the girl was saying. Sharpe was nearly fluent in Russian, and conversational in German. French, however, was not his strong suit. It also didn't help that the young woman he had in the crosshairs of his weapon had just been attacked by a couple of very strange humanoid creatures with black skin and long claws.

"Calm down!" Sharpe growled.

The girl kept crying. She was on her knees just ten feet in front of him holding out her hands to shield her face.

"Speak English! *Anglais, Anglais! Je suis Anglais!*" Sharpe spat.

The girl started to compose herself. "*An-Anglais?*" she stuttered.

"*Oui, Anglais!*" Sharpe nodded as he cautiously lowered his rifle. "Do you speak English?"

"*Oui*, um, I mean yes, though I am, how you say, a little under-practised?"

Sharpe kept his rifle in the low ready position, meaning the barrel was pointed at the ground but the stock was still pulled into his shoulder, ready to be fired.

"What's going on? Ten minutes ago, I was at Moi International Airport, next thing I know I'm… wherever the fuck this place is with these fucking things."

The girl wiped her eyes; with a few ragged breaths she was able to compose herself a little more. She was pretty, blonde, about average height and thin. She'd probably have been a lot more attractive if her eyes weren't strained from her tears.

"These creatures, they are called the Damned. This place, as you call it, it is called Limbo."

Sharpe shook his head.

"Limbo?" he snarled. "As in, what, fucking purgatory?"

The girl nodded. "I am so sorry."

Sharpe's gaze drifted up to the black sky. Thousands of thin purple lights streaked through the darkness, all slithering like distant snakes. Every single light moving in the same direction. Sharpe dropped to his knees; he planted the rifle's stock into the ground to give him something to lean against.

The girl rushed over to him.

"I am sorry, monsieur. But you have died."

The soldier knelt there staring at the ground, his thoughts racing; his eyes drifted to the dead Damned lying on the ground.

"Are there… are there any more of these things about?"

The girl nodded frantically.

"They're everywhere," she said. "They're not that fast or clever but if you run into a bunch of them… you will not have good day."

Sharpe looked up to the girl.

"Do you have a place to stay? A camp or a hideout?"

She nodded.

"Yes, though it is best not to stay in one place for too long. My name is Maria, by the way."

Sharpe shook himself out of his thoughts. He forced a smile.

"Sharpe; under any other circumstances I'd say it's a pleasure to meet you."

◀▶

"Where do you think they go?" Maria asked out of the blue.

The pair were lying on a dirt hill looking up at the purple lights. Sharpe lay with his hands behind his head for support.

"I'm not sure they're going anywhere," he said. "They seem just as pointless as everything else here… Ow!"

Sharpe grabbed his arm where Maria had pinched him. She waggled her finger in his face and tutted smugly.

"No, monsieur! Everything is here for a reason, all the buildings and the trees, and even the Damned. These lights are no exception."

Sharpe sighed. "I'm glad you're an optimist, one of us needs to be."

Maria smiled at him. "I have been here a long time. It is that optimism that has kept me alive."

"I meant to ask about that, how is it you've managed to stay here so long?" Sharpe asked. "If those Damned things are the result of being in Limbo for too long, why haven't you turned yet?"

Maria shrugged.

"I am not entirely sure of how it works, but I guess it's maybe because I haven't given up? Or maybe because I have something that is, ah! I do not know the word for this."

"Anchoring," Sharpe said. "You feel like there's something holding you here, like an anchor."

Her eyes lit up.

"Yes! That is the word. Anchoring! Because I do not give up, I will be here for as long as I need to be. Besides this place isn't all that bad really."

Sharpe sat up.

"What? This place is hell! We have to watch our backs every damn second in case one of those things shows up, nearly every building seems to be haunted! And the longer we stay in one place the more likely we are to have all of these things come down on us. Name me one good thing about this place, Maria!"

The young woman smiled. She reached out and tapped the tip of Sharpe's nose.

"I have you, don't I?"

Sharpe actually blushed.

◂▸

Keeping track of time was near impossible; fortunately, Sharpe's 'magic glasses', as Maria liked to call them, had a built-in clock that was counting the days in real time so they could keep track of their sleep schedules. So far, the pair had been together for a little over three months. They had also found themselves a place to hole up. A small caravan that was sitting in the middle of a dense petrified forest. The caravan was old, covered in rust with one of its windows cracked but it was better than nothing, and it didn't seem to be harbouring any ghosts. The pair of Damned that had stumbled across it, though, were a slight issue. The two creatures clumsily staggered through the woods three metres apart. The leader and the larger of the pair reached the caravan first. It sniffed the air loudly as it tried in vain to find the scent of the humans. The Damned felt the impact of a boot first as its right leg buckled from behind, and then before it could recover a cold pain tore across its neck as the knife struck home.

Maria yanked the knife free as the creature fell to the ground trying to clutch at its throat, but its disfigured arms prevented its hands from coming anywhere near the wound.

"I did it!" Maria cried in success. "I got him!"

Sharpe was busy pulling his larger bowie knife free of the second Damned that lay twitching spasmodically at his feet.

"You're really starting to get the hang of this. I'd expected a pretty girl like you to be a lot more squeamish," he congratulated her.

"Hey! I'm not some little girl who needs to be protected," Maria mocked. "And we are the same age!"

"Yes, but I have years of training and experience behind me," Sharpe explained. "You were too scared to pick up a knife when I first met you. I honestly don't understand how you managed to survive out here alone for so long."

Maria moved to the caravan door and took hold of the handle as she spoke.

"I never said I was alone out here before you. I had friends with me for a while."

Sharpe moved to the other side of the door. He raised his blade to the ready position.

"What happened to them?"

Maria hid her sadness behind a smile.

"They… moved on."

Sharpe nodded understandingly.

"Ready?"

With a nod, Maria tore open the door and the soldier raced inside. The caravan was disgusting; the ground was littered with mouldy pizza boxes and Dorito packets. The kitchen was covered in God knows what and a strange smell hung in the air. Maria pinched her nose as she followed inside.

"Still not the worst place I've slept in. You can have the bed," Sharpe offered.

"Aww, aren't you a true English gentleman?"

Sharpe grinned.

"Trust me, sweetheart, there's nothing gentle about me."

◀▶

Maria leapt out of bed with a ragged gasp. She couldn't remember what happened in the dream but she could tell from the sweat running down her face that it wasn't a good one. She reached across the bed for her phone to check the time. The phone wasn't always reliable, but luckily the battery never seemed to decline or if it did it was incredibly slow. The screen told her it was 6.35am, which wasn't overly helpful since the sun never rose but it did mean she was about due to get up and take her turn on watch.

"Hey!" she called out. "Why don't you come in here and get some rest, I'll take my turn early."

There was no response.

"Oh, come on! I know you haven't been sleeping well… Sharpe? You all right?"

Maria picked up the handgun and combat knife Sharpe had given her and cautiously made her way outside the caravan. She poked her head out of the open door where Sharpe should have been and found him crouching down beside one of the trees a few metres away.

"If you need to take a shit, just wake me up; it's no big deal you know!"

Sharpe slowly raised a closed hand and Maria fell silent and very still. After a few seconds he opened his fist and waved his fingers forward, beckoning her over. Instinct told Maria to be cautious; clearly something was wrong. She moved as carefully and quietly as possible until she was just behind the soldier.

"What is it? A Damned?" she whispered.

Sharpe didn't respond; then again, he didn't need to. Maria saw what it was he had found. It couldn't have been any more than four metres away from them; it was low to the ground with its head down and staring back at them but that did nothing to hide its impressive size.

"Oh my God!" Maria mimed.

Before her, almost completely hidden in the darkness, was a fully grown and very impressive Siberian Tiger. The colossal cat took a steady step towards the pair of humans. Maria started to lift the handgun, only to find it caught in Sharpe's hand. He didn't look at her; his eyes were locked on the tiger. Sharpe just shook his head slowly, more for Maria's sake than his.

"Trust me," he whispered. "It's all right."

Maria was thinking a lot of things about the situation, but "all right" was definitely not one of them. Sharpe didn't even have his rifle in his hands. The weapon was leaning up against the tree beside him. Maria's eyes darted between the rifle and the cat. She'd seen a few documentaries on this animal, and knew that even if Sharpe had his gun to hand, he wouldn't stand a chance at this distance.

The tiger took a step towards them, it was barely two and a half metres away from them now. Maria put her hands over her mouth to hide a silent whimper. Then her gaze darted back to Sharpe. The sniper made a bizarre noise that sounded halfway between a huff and a purr.

"What are you doing?" she whispered.

The tiger stood motionless, studying the pair of humans for a moment, then Sharpe made the sound again. The tiger lifted its head and took another step closer.

"Oh my God!" Maria mouthed more than spoke.

Sharpe made the same strange huffing noise one more time, and then the tiger did the same. Keeping his eyes locked onto the cat's, Sharpe turned his head slightly to Maria so that she could see his expression.

"It's all right, he doesn't mean us any harm."

"Oh yeah, sure! He doesn't look hungry at all!" Maria retorted.

"If he was, Maria," Sharpe whispered, "we'd both be dead already. Just relax, okay?"

"How can I relax?" she hissed. "It's a fucking tiger!"

"Just think of him as a big house cat; he's curious and wants to see what we're about. Just follow my lead and trust me."

With that Sharpe put his head down and faced the ground. He moved both his arms forward and placed his hands on the dirt in a half praying position. Maria looked at the tiger, which was now watching her, completely undeterred by the human's strange noises.

"I swear if I get eaten because of you…"

Maria slowly knelt down and assumed the same position. They heard the sounds of footsteps, until Maria could see the tiger's feet before her. She held her breath as she felt the cat's wet nose brush against her hair. The cat inhaled slowly, taking a long breath of her scent. Sharpe made the huffing noise again and the tiger reciprocated. The cat switched over to Sharpe and smelled him too.

"See?" he whispered. "We're nice humans, though I don't think this is the first time you've met nice people, is it?"

The tiger huffed again, almost as if it understood Sharpe's words. After a few seconds the cat pulled away from the humans. Maria kept her head down as she listened to the footsteps slowly fade into the trees. After a few seconds, they both lifted their heads and looked at each other. Sharpe was grinning from ear to ear like an excited schoolboy. Maria looked as if she was about to have a heart attack.

"What?" Sharpe asked. "I'm a cat person."

◂▸

After a couple of weeks, the Damneds' presence became too much for the two survivors to handle, and they were forced back on the move again. This time they had cleared the forest and were now walking across what felt like an endless open plain of dry dirt. There were no shrubs or bushes, no trees for cover, just a rise in the ground some distance ahead of them.

"Are you sure we couldn't have brought the bed with us?" Maria complained.

"I said if you wanted to bring it, feel free, but you didn't want to carry the bloody thing," Sharpe retorted.

Maria pouted. "I thought my big strong soldier companion would be able to help with that!"

Sharpe laughed. As they walked, he tilted his head back

and looked up at the purple lights. Still there was no change in their movements and no sign of convergence.

"The longer this goes on, the more I'm starting to think we aren't getting anywhere," Maria groaned behind him.

"That's not very optimistic of you!" Sharpe mocked. "I'm supposed to be the cynical one here."

Maria shook her head; her voice was low, lacking her usual bubbly energy. "Yeah, I'm sorry. I guess I'm just tired."

"Couldn't sleep?" Sharpe asked.

Maria shrugged. "No, I slept pretty well. Probably the lack of sunlight getting to me, I guess."

Sharpe raised a closed fist and they stopped moving. After five seconds they dropped to one knee. The soldier had seen something. He raised his rifle and started scanning in the direction of the movement.

"You only say 'I guess' when something's bothering you."

Maria sighed. "I don't know, it's not like we're stuck in purgatory or anything…" she groaned.

Sharpe found his target. "What the fuck?"

"What is it?" Maria asked.

"Come take a look at this." The soldier leant to the side so that Maria could see through his scope. Even through the powerful optic it was difficult to make out, but the Damned in the crosshairs seemed to be wearing some kind of medieval plate armour. The purple lights caught what was left of a mangled breast plate and if they stayed quiet enough, they could hear the faint clattering of chainmail as the creature moved closer.

"Holy shit!" Maria exclaimed.

"Yep," Sharpe agreed.

Maria, anticipating what came next, backed away from Sharpe's scope and pushed her fingers into her ears.

"I'm ready," she said.

Sharpe put the crosshairs over the Damned and hit a button on top of his scope. A number appeared just above the crosshairs.

223 metres.

Sharpe took a moment to feel the wind. There was a slight breeze in the air blowing left to right; the soldier adjusted his aim. He lifted the scope up so the crosshair was just above the Damned's head. Then slightly to the left, just past the creature's face. With a slow exhale he pulled the trigger and the bullet ripped through the chest plate with ease.

"It's down, let's go check it out."

The creature was still alive when they reached it. It tried to reach out one of its hands towards Sharpe but the soldier stood safely out of reach. Maria sat down on the opposite side of the creature as it lazily thrashed his claws at the soldier.

"Poor bastard," Sharpe croaked. "He must have been out here for centuries."

"No," Maria disagreed. "Probably not, time isn't always relevant in this place."

"What do you mean?" Sharpe questioned.

Maria nodded to his legs.

"In my time soldiers wear armour like that, but it covers almost all of their bodies."

Sharpe stared at her in bewilderment, completely oblivious to the struggling Damned at his feet.

"What year was it?" he asked anxiously.

"2074," Maria answered.

"No fucking way!"

"What about you?" Maria asked, completely ignoring the soldier's comment.

"2030," Sharpe replied.

Maria's expression changed. She did a good job of hiding it, but she suddenly looked much sadder than before. Sharpe thought about asking but decided it would be best not to.

"Forty years… that's incredible! Hey, who's the president of the United States? Oh, what about the UK, did they ever leave the…"

Maria shook her head solemnly.

"I can't tell you that," she croaked.

Sharpe threw his hands out in protest.

"What? All right, fine, tell me something else about the future!"

Maria gave him a stern cold glare.

"I can't…"

Sharpe shook his head in confusion, he walked around the struggling Damned and sat down on the ground beside Maria.

"Why can't you tell me anything?"

"Because I asked her not to," came a voice from behind.

Sharpe and Maria both spun around. Sharpe raised his rifle and took aim instinctively, but then he froze in place. Before them was a tall spiralling white staircase. At the top of that staircase was a young man in what looked like school blazer and trousers, though peculiarly he wasn't wearing anything on his feet.

"That's a nice trick, friend," Sharpe yelled. "What do you want?"

The young man chuckled.

"I like this version of you better than the next one. Confident and fearless!"

"Maria get behind me," Sharpe ordered, but the girl didn't comply.

"I've seen this before," she murmured.

"What?" Sharpe spat.

"Your weapon isn't going to do you any good, soldier, you might as well put it down."

Sharpe narrowed his vision.

"I've seen some weird shit in my time here, and none of it can't be killed by a well-placed bullet or two."

The young man on the stairs shook his head in disappointment.

"Yes, I guess you would say that, wouldn't you?"

"I'm sorry, can we help you with something?" Sharpe growled as his finger started to squeeze the trigger.

"No," the young man said. "I'm not here for you, *hero*, I'm here for her."

Maria gasped. Sharpe's rifle thundered into life as the sniper fired three perfectly aimed shots at the young man. They hit nothing but the air behind him. The young man had disappeared and reappeared at the base of the stairs. Sharpe dropped his rifle and produced his bowie knife. Before he could take a swing, Maria had grabbed his arm in a firm grip.

"It's all right," she said. "He won't hurt us. He just wants to talk."

Sharpe glared at the young man, but lowered his knife.

"Oh, I do so enjoy that spark of yours, Sharpe. That's what's going to keep you alive out here." The young man turned to Maria; his expression twisted into a scowl. "You, young lady, should know better than that."

"Hey buddy, she didn't tell me anything…"

"She told you enough!" barked the young man. "I thought I made it clear that your actions here have serious consequences, smaller slips than yours have caused great trouble during these *fragile* moments."

Sharpe glared at the young man.

"What the fuck are you talking about?"

Maria, however, seemed to understand perfectly. She hung her head low in shame. "I'm sorry," she croaked.

The young man sighed. "Yes, I'm sure you will be."

"Mother fuc..." Sharpe roared as he lunged towards the stairs, but the mysterious young man and his staircase had disappeared before he could make any contact. Sharpe stumbled forward into the empty space. Maria held her ground staring down at the dirt with tired eyes. Sharpe turned back to her with his arms extended to either side of him.

"Care to explain whatever the fuck that was about?"

Maria kept staring down at the dirt.

"Well?" Sharpe growled.

"The last time I saw him, he told me something, something very important. I'd actually forgotten all about it until now..." She trailed off.

"What?" Sharpe hissed.

Maria shook her head.

"I need some time to think, all right?"

Sharpe rubbed his fingers against his temples; that was enough crazy for one lifetime.

"Whatever, you can think while we walk."

◂▸

"Out of the field and back into the trees," Sharpe sang aloud to Maria as they walked. It had been hours since their run-in with the stairs and Maria had remained silent the entire time. They were back in the woods again, only this time the trees weren't petrified. They actually had leaves, though granted these leaves were sickly and brown and really should have fallen to the ground by now, but for the two travellers it was something new at least. The trees soon gave way to a small but not unwelcome lake. It wasn't the first body of water they had seen, but it was exactly what Sharpe thought they needed right then and there.

"Sharpe," Maria croaked after a long silence.

The soldier turned back to her expectantly.

"You're a soldier..." She paused for a brief second to compose her sentence but the sniper interrupted her.

"I am, anything else new?"

Maria glared at him. "This is serious, Sharpe!"

"Then talk to me!" the soldier retorted. "Cut out the dramatic pauses and tell me what's wrong. You can talk to me, Maria, nobody's going to hurt you, you're safe with me."

Maria winced.

"If you knew that you could do something to help someone you cared about... would you do it? Even if it meant something really bad would happen to you."

Sharpe rolled his eyes.

"Maria, that kid or whatever it was freaked me out too." The soldier approached the frightened young woman and took her hands into his. "You're safe with me. No matter what happens I'll protect you."

Maria fought back her tears.

"Promise me," she said.

Sharpe smiled.

"I promise I'll protect..."

"No!" Maria ripped her hands out of his. She grabbed the soldier's collar and pulled him in close; she looked up to him with tears rolling down her pale cheeks.

"Promise me that no matter what happens, you'll survive until the end, promise me that no matter what happens or what you face you'll save someone from this nightmare, even if it isn't me!"

Sharpe pulled away from the girl.

"Look, Maria, you're tired. It's been a long stressful journey, I get it, but..."

"No, you don't get it!" Maria sobbed. "There's a way out!"

Sharpe's eyes lit up.

"What?"

Maria released her grip on him.

"That boy on the stairs... I saw him before I met you. He told me there's a door, if you follow the lights for long enough, you'll find it."

Sharpe's excitement left him as quickly as it had come.

"And you believe him?"

Maria nodded. "He told me I'd meet you, and here you are."

Sharpe sniffed.

"Finding a mercenary in purgatory isn't much of a gamble if you ask me."

Maria looked down at the dirt by her feet. The soldier forced a smile.

"Hey, come on, that water looks like exactly what we need, you go wash up and I'll come join you in a bit, okay?"

Sharpe started to walk towards one of the trees but Maria grabbed his arm.

"Promise me," she demanded.

The soldier rolled his eyes.

"All right fine, I promise, Maria; now go wash up, I need a piss."

Maria released his arm and started towards the water. Sharpe watched her for a few paces before turning back towards his chosen tree. He only caught a glimpse of the creature in the corner of his eye as he turned, and by the time he had, it was too late. The Damned was larger than any he'd seen before, faster as well. The creature leapt out of the water like a crocodile attacking a zebra, only Maria was the zebra. She had no time to react; a clawed hand ripped across her body, cutting open her stomach and chest, sending a cloud of blood into the air as she screamed in horror.

"Maria, no!"

Sharpe had his rifle up and had started blasting before Maria had hit the ground. The Damned took the brunt of five shots to its chest. The creature staggered back but kept standing. Sharpe lowered his rifle slightly so that he could get a clear look at the creature. It was only then that he noticed the monster had three heads attached to a grotesquely wide body. The creature made a low hissing sound and Sharpe raised his rifle again. He brought his scope to bear on the monster's central face but just as he squeezed the trigger the creature vanished, seemingly engulfed by a veil that twisted and distorted light. Sharpe was able to track the shimmering beast long enough to fire another four shots before it broke from his line of sight and disappeared into the trees.

The soldier threw his gun to the side as he dropped to the ground to help Maria. The Damned had sliced through her stomach releasing her entrails into her hands. Her clothes were almost completely torn away along with the flesh around her chest. Maria clawed desperately at her stomach trying to force everything back inside.

"Maria! Stay with me, hey look at me! It's all right, you're going to be okay!"

Sharpe fumbled through his pouches with shaking hands until he produced a bandage which he pressed down onto her stomach in a desperate attempt to stop the bleeding. Maria gasped as she fought against the urge to scream.

"Stay with me, Maria! Please!"

Sharpe could see the colour leaving her face as blood poured out of her; already his bandage was soaked and doing nothing to slow the bleeding.

"I'm going to give you something for the pain!" Sharpe said as he started to search through his pouches for his morphine, but Maria's bloody hand fell on his arm, pulling him back to her.

"I-It's okay," Maria stuttered. Her hands had fallen to her sides and she wasn't struggling anymore, her voice was calm and controlled. The pain was starting to leave her body.

"You need to carry on alone now."

"Shut up!" roared the sniper. He recoiled his head and screamed as loud as he could. "Help! Someone please help us!"

A bloody hand touched his face. He felt the warm blood mix with the cold tears on his face. He looked down at Maria to see her smiling at him.

"There will be others, others who need your help. You will need to be strong for them."

"No!" Sharpe growled defiantly. "It's you and me out here, Maria! I promised I'd protect you!"

Maria struggled to take in a breath.

"You have protected me," she croaked. "I never would have made it this far without you."

"You're going to make it a lot further too!" Sharpe sobbed. "But you have to keep your eyes open and stay with me!"

Maria managed a frail smile. Sharpe wiped a hand over her delicate face, smudging blood across her cheek.

"Thank you," she whispered. "Thank you for being my anchor..."

Her hand dropped to the ground and her eyes closed.

◂▸

Six months to the day, or rather the night since he had arrived in Limbo, Sharpe was lying on top of a small wooden market stand roof looking up at the purple lights. He wasn't sure why there was a random market stand in the middle of the woods, and he didn't really care. The half a dozen Damned that were trying to climb up to reach him also didn't bother him. Sharpe didn't know how long he'd been up there for either; for all he knew it could have been days. He felt the timber frame of the market stand begin to creak and give way as one of the Damned started gnawing through the supports. A hand clawed at his boot, which was just overhanging the roof, breaking him out of his thoughts.

"Can't I just have a minute?" Sharpe groaned. "Can't you all just fuck off for a bit and chase someone else?"

Sharpe had his rifle lying across his body and a full magazine loaded ready for a fight.

"What's the point...? It's been three months, Maria. And I'm still alone out here. I guess I'll die alone as well."

Just before the first support broke a hail of gunfire engulfed the creatures below the soldier. After just a few seconds of machine-gun fire the Damned were all gone. Sharpe had jumped up to a low crouch position and readied his rifle in the direction of the gunfire. He couldn't see his saviours in the darkness of the woods.

"Hey! Put the gun down, we're friendly!" a low masculine voice called out.

"That's what the last one said," Sharpe growled in response.

Sharpe's ears picked up a variety of whispers as his saviours conversed about him.

"Hey!" a new voice called out, this one female and familiar. "Say that last part again!"

"Why should I?" Sharpe called back.

A woman walked out of the woods with her hands held up in the air. She wore a black flat cap over blonde hair tied neatly into a bun. But it was when Sharpe spotted the SOO uniform that he lowered his weapon.

"Because your big sister told you to!" Sam yelled up to him.

Sharpe dropped down from the roof of the market stand. They stood there staring at each other for a moment, Sharpe remaining tense.

"It's good to see you again, bro," Sam greeted as she took a step closer, but Sharpe raised his weapon to her.

"How do I know it's you?" the sniper growled.

Sam held her ground; she met his cold tired eyes.

"If you don't believe her," came a voice, this one with a distinctive Irish accent, "then what about me?"

Irish stepped out of the woods into the light, with his machine gun slung over his shoulder.

"Or how about me?" said Boss as he too stepped into the light.

Sharpe lowered his rifle slowly, his eyes darting around the trees as the rest of his fire team stepped out into the light. The exhausted sniper dropped to his knees and into the open arms of Sam as she raced forward to embrace her brother.

"I'm sorry," Sharpe croaked as he buried his head into her shoulder. "I've been out here for so long. God, the things I've seen, Sam..."

Sam held him a little tighter.

"It's all right, you're not alone now, you're with us. You're safe."

CHAPTER 17

◂▸

THE DOOR ABOVE THE LAKE

"Oh my God," Terra croaked.

Sharpe didn't say it, but he agreed.

Before them stood a door. A door in the centre of a brilliant white light.

"Where do you think it leads?" Terra asked.

Sharpe shook his head. "It doesn't matter," he said firmly. "We're going through."

Terra turned back and looked at the way they'd come. They weren't really there but, in her mind, she could see the town, and the petrol station, she saw the ravine and the cabin; the faces of everyone who'd been lost along the way.

"It has all been for something," she whispered. "You should be proud of your men, Boss."

Sharpe wiped his eyes when he was sure Terra wasn't looking. He took a long, deep breath and readied his rifle. The mission wasn't over yet.

"Right then. As the last soldier standing, I'm in charge," he asserted. Terra looked up to him and then finally out at the door.

"You're going through first," he croaked. "I'll stay here and cover you."

Terra went to say something but Sharpe gently pressed a finger over her lips.

"No buts!" he ordered. "The Damned will have heard the commotion from before. They'll be coming for us and we won't be able to outrun them in the water. You go through and then I'll follow you."

Terra shook her head in defiance.

"Who will cover you though?"

Sharpe shrugged.

"I'll be fine on my own. If we go together, I won't be able to keep them away from both of us. If I stay up here, I'll have all the time and space I need."

Terra shook her head again.

"No!" she cried. "Sharpe, I don't want to lo…"

Sharpe placed a hand on her face, pulled her in close and they kissed. His hands held her waist, gently pulling her into his body. Terra went willingly into his embrace. Their lips slid across each other; Terra's arms were wrapped around his shoulders and instinctively she had risen to her tiptoes so that she could get as close as possible. Just a few precious seconds later, it was over.

Sharpe pulled back and flicked the rim of the boonie hat down, which Terra had forgotten she'd been wearing.

"Keegan." He gave her the warmest, most honest smile she had ever seen from him; her heart melted. "My name is Keegan Monroe."

Terra was too high on endorphins to form a proper response. She made a few sounds that were almost words but even she didn't know what she was trying to say.

From somewhere behind them they heard the almost-human cry of a Damned. Sharpe nodded to the door.

"On your way, girl, quick as you can now."

The soldier climbed back up to the top of the embankment and took a knee. He turned back when he realised Terra hadn't moved. She was still there staring at him, her eyes begging him for one last piece of reassurance.

"The longer you take to get through, the harder it'll be for me to follow."

Can't argue with that.

Terra approached the water. She pulled the strap on her satchel so it hung high and tight to her body.

I can do this. She has to do this.

No, I… I have to do this.

Terra took a long, deep breath and stepped into the water. She gasped as the icy cold liquid washed over her feet and ankles, though after a moment she felt slightly refreshed. She estimated the door was only about one hundred metres away, but she'd be slow if the water got deeper.

Terra heard the snap of Sharpe's rifle barking to life behind her; the sound seemed to echo into the darkness. She wasn't sure what he had seen but it had to have been on the other side of the lake from her.

"Move your ass!" Sharpe yelled.

With a nod of determination Terra moved deeper into the water. Eighty metres from the door the water was up to her waist. A Damned sprung up out of the water just a few feet ahead of her. Before it could make a sound, its skull split open leaving Terra's ears ringing from the sound of the gunshot. His shots were becoming more frequent now. Terra looked over to the side as a pair of Damned climbed over the embankment.

Only the first one reached the water's edge before it felt the slam of the bullet to the chest.

"Damn, Sharpe you're... ah!" Something hit Terra in the chest with the weight of a hammer, knocking all of the air out of her lungs. She was sixty metres from the door but lost all of her momentum.

"Terra!" Sharpe yelled.

Shocked and confused, Terra looked around her as she tried to find the source of the strike. But there was nothing. Terra shrugged off the pain and gave a thumbs up over her head to signal to Sharpe as she moved on.

Something just hit her... Me! Something just hit her...

Terra wrote off her bizarre thoughts as being down to stress. Sharpe drew her attention at fifty metres when he fired three shots in rapid succession. Again, Terra felt the force of a hammer hit her, only this time it was much stronger. She dropped down to one knee, barely able to keep her head above the water.

What is happening to her?

Have I been shot?

No there isn't any wound... she's... I'm okay.

Terra's head was pounding with pain; disorientated, she looked around as she tried to find the source of the pain. Her body was unscathed; she was cold, but she wasn't wounded. In her frantic state Terra caught a glimpse of something shining to her side. There it was, stalking towards her. She only saw the creature because of the way it distorted the water around its legs. The shimmering beast let down its camouflage revealing its sickly humanoid shape.

"Oh no!"

Terra pushed herself harder; at forty metres she stumbled down again. The creature was almost on her.

She's not going to make it.

In a futile effort to defend herself, Terra drew her pistol and raised it to the monster, but again she felt the weight of the hammer hit her chest. Terra dropped the gun into the water, losing it in the cloud of silt and sand her feet had kicked up.

"No!" she cried.

The creature was almost on her. The Damned, or whatever it was, had regrown one arm but was now down to just two heads; the one that had looked like Eddie was missing. It reached out a hand towards her. Suddenly the hand was violently pushed away in a cloud of blood as a bullet tore into its wrist.

"Maria!" Sharpe shouted. "I know you came here for me!"

Sharpe looked past the creature at Terra. He held his conviction.

"Well, here I am!"

The beast made a hideous sound that was equal parts anger and excitement. The soldier was in the water now. He wasn't far in but he was far too close to be safe.

"Sharpe, what are you doing?" Terra yelled.

He's going to die.

"Don't worry about me! I'll be right behind..." A Damned sprang out of the water behind him. It leapt onto Sharpe's back in an effort to drag him under the water.

"Sharpe!" Terra screamed.

He's strong.

Again the hammer hit Terra. She stumbled forward. Sharpe managed to throw the creature over his shoulder into the water and was busy slicing its throat as he called out to Terra.

"I'll be fine! Just go!"

He can't defend himself with you here.

"Damn it!" Terra grunted as she rushed towards the light.

There's nothing I can do.

At ten metres she turned back to see more Damned rushing into the water towards Sharpe, who had his rifle up firing into the creature he called Maria as it rushed him. Terra watched in horror as a Damned pulled the barrel of the rifle to the side and Maria raised its hands to strike the sniper. Sharpe screamed into the faces of the monster. With tears in her eyes and knowing there was nothing she could do, Terra turned back to the door. To her shock and surprise the door was opening. It creaked and groaned as the timber seemed to protest against the movement. On the other side Terra could see something peculiar. The door seemed to open to a large grey room. The image was hazy and blurred as if she were looking through water, but it was clearly a square room. At the centre two figures stood watching the door's opening. Terra could hear sounds like distorted voices as the two strange figures conversed. They seemed to be wearing some kind of uniform but it was difficult to tell.

"Terra, watch out!"

Terra turned back to see the Damned that had been attacking Sharpe racing towards her. Dozens of creatures tore through the water and even each other to get to her. Terra opened her mouth to scream but once again felt the impact of the hammer on her chest. She staggered back until her heel caught the edge of the door and she fell through into a pit of total darkness.

◆

Well, this seems familiar.

Terra was falling again, falling through that same dark, empty abyss as before, when she first arrived in Limbo. Just as before, her body was numb, but as time passed, the feelings in her extremities returned slowly. Except in her lower left leg; for some reason that was still numb. She reached out to find it but couldn't feel anything. She didn't even know if she really had a physical form anymore. Terra felt a sudden rush of hot air flow past her; she heard the rushing of wind and suddenly felt a hard surface beneath her as she hit the ground.

Terra sprang upright sucking in a lungful of air. Her lungs burned as if she hadn't taken a breath in hours. She held up a hand to shield her eyes from a ferociously fierce light. Her ears were overwhelmed with the sounds of thousands of voices and cries. She could feel an immense heat radiating from behind her but her fingers felt numb. A force landed on her chest and pushed her down.

"Miss! It's okay! You need to stay still," demanded an unfamiliar voice.

The voice belonged to a woman but the accent was impossible to place; it sounded almost German but not quite. As her eyes adjusted, Terra felt her head being lifted by something soft and then something was wrapped around her face covering her mouth.

Damn that sun is so bright… wait…

Terra was staring up at a brilliant blue sky, with a big yellow sun shining down on her. Then she realised the device around her mouth and nose was in fact an oxygen mask.

"Oh my God!" Terra cried as realisation set in. She looked over at the woman tending to her. She was wearing the same SOO urban camouflage uniform, but the face was someone new. With dark hair and hazel eyes, the woman was pretty but older than Terra; she must have been around thirty.

"Please relax," the woman said. "My name is Witcher. I'm here to help."

"Y-You're SOO, right? Like Sharpe?" Terra croaked. Speaking was hard and her throat felt so dry.

"That's right," Witcher answered. "Listen, you've been in an accident, you hit your head and inhaled a lot of smoke, you'll be okay but try not to move too much."

Terra rolled her head to the side and her eyes fell on a scene of chaos. People raced around the burning terminal of Moi International Airport. Armed soldiers and wounded civilians were everywhere. A thick cloud of black smoke reached up into the sky and drifted out towards the ocean. A fighter jet roared as it screamed overhead at immense speed. She felt a sudden rush of pain shoot up her left leg; she grunted as she hoisted herself up to see what was happening.

Witcher was wrapping a bandage around a bloody wound just below her knee.

That's right. I was shot!

"You were lucky," Witcher said. "The bullet ricocheted off the bone, it'll hurt like hell for a bit but you'll be able to walk.

A ricochet? Damn, how the hell did Sharpe deal with actually getting shot?

"Sharpe…" Terra croaked. "Where's Sharpe?"

Witcher's face dropped. Tears formed in her eyes and Terra's heart sank.

"I'm sorry… he and the others haven't been found yet."

Before realisation could set in two men raced over carrying the limp bloody body of a soldier in that same SOO uniform. One of them, as well as carrying a more standard AR-15, was carrying a very familiar sniper rifle.

"Witcher, I need help here!" The voice was southern American and came from a soldier who looked almost exactly like Zero, only this man was older.

They put the body down on the ground next to Terra.

Terra tried to yell but choked instead. The body was male, almost completely covered in blood from multiple open wounds; his armour had been torn away along with his left eye, but it was unmistakably Sharpe. The silver-haired soldier leant over Sharpe and tore open his shirt.

"He's not breathing!" the other soldier who had carried him over cried. Witcher set about attaching the pads from her defibrillator to him.

"Clear!" Witcher yelled.

Sharpe's bloody lifted as the electricity shot through him but he didn't wake up. Terra reached out a hand towards the soldier as she prayed.

"Please! Please wake up!"

"Clear!" growled Witcher again.

Again, Sharpe was hit with the electric shock but nothing happened.

"Stubborn bastard, wake up!" Witcher roared.

She slammed the pads home and shocked him again.

Nothing happened.

"Sharpe… please!" Terra croaked.

"Come on Sharpe!" roared the silver-haired soldier.

"Keegan…" Terra mumbled.

Witcher reached over for the defibrillator and cranked the dial up to the maximum voltage. She began vigorously rubbing the pads together as the device powered up.

"I don't know who this girl is but she's really cute and seems to really like you, so do us all a favour and wake the fuck up!"

The pads were slammed onto the soldier's chest. Sharpe almost completely left the ground as he was hit with the final charge. His one remaining blue eye opened as he coughed up a mouthful of blood.

"Sharpe!" everyone cheered.

"He's not out of the woods yet, we need to get him to the hospital," Witcher ordered.

"Chopper's on the way to pick up the next load, get him on it," replied the silver-haired soldier.

Sharpe's eye slowly drifted towards Terra. He reached out a weak, unsteady hand towards her but soon realised he couldn't quite reach. A large black helicopter swooped in seemingly from nowhere.

"There it is!" barked the silver-haired soldier. "Witcher, Frankie, get Sharpe on that bird, I'm going back in!"

"Akira, wait!" Witcher yelled.

"Zero's in there!" Akira yelled back. "I need to get him out!"

Terra tried one last time to reach for Sharpe's hand as the sniper was lifted onto a stretcher. Keegan Monroe slowly coiled his finger around into a thumbs up and then mustered the strength to form a phone signal with his thumb and little finger as he was carried to the helicopter.

We did it, Keegan. We made it.

"So," Witcher had to partially yell to be heard over the sounds around them, "you want to explain how you know Sharpe's name?"

Terra managed a smile. "It's a long story."

"*Look over there!*"

"Huh?" Terra looked around at Witcher, confused.

It couldn't have been her – that voice was whispering – but where…?

"*No, look over there!*"

This time the voice seemed to come from her right. Terra followed the sound of the voice, but Witcher seemed to have spotted whatever the mystery person had seen first.

"What the fuck?"

Terra stared out across the chaos as three men approached the helicopter at a steady walking pace. Two of them wore what Terra recognised as some kind of military uniform, probably belonging to the local force. The middle man however was far more surprising. He was tall, bald and wore what had once been an expensive suit, which was now covered in blood, though the man himself didn't seem to be injured.

"Nathan Kebal?" Terra said out loud.

How is that possible?

"Come on, girl, we need to get you somewhere safe."

Witcher pulled Terra to her feet slowly, but Terra refused to pull her gaze away from Kebal.

"How is he alive?"

The helicopter… everyone there was killed… everyone…

"*No.*" The voice was louder now. "*Boss was also standing right next to him but he was with the other soldiers… he must have blocked their aim.*"

A second voice, this one much more distinctively male and unfamiliar.

"*Wouldn't the soldiers have been more of a prime target? After all they damaged the helicopter just a few seconds later.*"

Maybe…

Witcher's gaze darted between Kebal and Terra as the bald man came closer.

"It's a miracle, right!" Witcher yelled excitedly. "The most valuable and loved man in Africa, maybe the world, survived."

She looked back at Terra expecting her to be surprised, which Terra was, but not in the way she expected.

Nathan Kebal suddenly changed course and lightly jogged over to Terra, whose gaze locked onto his face as he slowed to a halt before her.

He doesn't even have a scratch on him. Not a drop of that blood is his.

Terra clutched her hands to her head as her thoughts started to get away from her. In her mind she played out the events she had witnessed again and again. The whole time, the voices, which she was now convinced were in her head, commented on everything.

"*He was right there next to Boss and Professor Marcos. But Boss was alive after the first pass, he was in the line of soldiers that fought back.*"

"*Then he must have blocked the shot at Kebal.*"

"*No. If that were the case they would have just shot through Boss.*"

"Come on, kid, we need to get you out of here!" Witcher snapped Terra back to reality.

Terra resisted Witcher again but this time the soldier was able to pull her towards the helicopter; Terra still clutched one hand to her throbbing headache.

"Is she okay?" Kebal yelled over the thundering rotor of the helicopter.

Terra managed to look up and see his face just a foot away from her.

"She's in shock but she'll be all right, sir!"

"H… How are you…?" Terra struggled.

Kebal turned to face her; he placed one hand on her shoulder and in that moment, Terra's mind suddenly cleared.

They didn't miss.

"Don't worry… the people responsible will pay for what they did here."

They missed him on purpose.

"Yeah…" Terra agreed. She nodded so that Kebal could understand her. "They will."

EPILOGUE

◂▸

Four broken ribs, a gunshot to the upper arm, multiple shrapnel wounds and of course one missing eye. That's what it took to finally keep Keegan down. The young soldier lay in a soft clean bed on the fourth floor of Mombasa Hospital. Keegan had been in that hospital for a week and had spent the first few days in the intensive care unit before being transferred out to his own private room, partially due to his own demands. The pain was kept in check with medicine and his injuries seemed to be healing steadily. What he hated was knowing he was taking up a perfectly good hospital bed that could be given to a patient who actually needed it. The bed was far too soft and comfortable, but that's just how you feel when you spend most of your days sleeping on mud or a hard wooden floor if you were lucky. Boredom was a slight issue, but Keegan had been given a couple of books and a tablet by some of his fellow soldiers who had come to visit.

The young soldier also had a good view; outside his window he could see the city of New Mombasa and beyond that the ever-so-inviting ocean. The first thing he wanted to do when he was released was to jump into that soothing cold water and just float there, with the sun on his face.

Or maybe there's something else I need to do first.

"Mr Monroe, there's someone here to see you." The nurse's English was impeccable.

"Who is it?" Keegan asked. His voice was croaky from smoke inhalation from the airport.

"She said she came to collect on your offer," the nurse responded.

A smile crept across Keegan's face.

"Send her in."

The nurse stepped to one side; as she did Terra Kisaragie stepped into Keegan's room. She walked with a slight limp and held a crutch under her left arm but seemed to be moving well without it. Terra's skin was slightly paler than when Keegan had last seen her; her jeans clung to her hips by a belt that she hadn't needed before. Terra's gaze clung to the floor as she entered the room. Slowly and with great hesitation her gaze lifted to Keegan's bedridden state. Her expression changed; colour flooded her face as tears welled up in her eyes. She threw her hands up over her mouth, dropping her crutch to the floor. Keegan managed a smile.

"Hey, quiet girl."

Terra took a moment to compose herself. She sniffed and wiped her eyes, smudging black make-up across her face.

"Hey," she whispered.

They stood there looking at each other for a long quiet moment. The nurse decided it best to leave them alone, and that was when Terra joined him at his bedside, clutching one of his hands in hers.

"You're a hard man to find, Keegan Monroe."

Keegan chuckled. "Yeah, I guess I probably should have given you my number, but in my defence, I was a little preoccupied."

Terra couldn't quite look him in the eye as she spoke.

"H-How much do you remember?" she asked.

"Before or after the explosion?" Keegan spoke again before she could respond. His words turned the warm summer's air icy cold and sent a shiver down Terra's spine. "Before or after Limbo?"

She surprised Keegan then. He was expecting a flood of tears; he was expecting the frightened young girl to throw herself into his arms and cry, and when she did, he would hold her and comfort her. But that's not what happened. Terra gave him an honest smile and a breath of relief.

"I thought I was crazy. I have all of these memories that I didn't dare share with anyone… and then there are the voices."

"The voices?" Keegan asked cautiously.

Terra nodded slowly.

"The doctors called it 'stress-induced psychosis.' They say it'll pass in time but I'm not so sure. What about you? Did you come out of there with anything like that?"

Keegan thought about it for a moment.

"I've been on some pretty heavy-duty painkillers since the attack. I've only really been conscious for the last few days and everything is still hazy."

Terra's eyes worked their way across his body, scanning his injuries. Keegan was covered in bandages, and even the parts that weren't bore dozens of tiny scratches and bruises.

"You must be in agony," Terra mumbled more to herself than to him. "I'm so sorry."

"It's my job, Terra," Keegan said. "I knew the risks, as did everyone else. I'd do it all again and give up my other eye if it meant you'd get through that door."

Terra's expression changed; she remembered something then.

"Keegan. Just before I went through the door, I saw something, something I can't explain."

"A big dark room like a prison cell, right?" Keegan interrupted.

Terra stared at him in awe.

"Y-Yes, what about the people?"

"People?" Keegan questioned. "I didn't see anyone."

"I saw two people standing there on the other side of the door," Terra added.

"What did they look like?"

Terra shook her head. "I couldn't really see them, the image was distorted, it's hard to tell but they looked like men, big guys maybe? I'm sorry I'm really not sure…"

"But definitely people. Humans, not Damned?"

Terra nodded. "Yes, a hundred per cent. Two people, probably men. I think they were wearing white."

"The Damned went straight for it as well," Keegan added. "That's how I got out. I gunned the lot down as they rushed the door and slipped past Mar… the big one."

"All of them?" Terra asked.

"No, just the ones that attacked you, then I ran through the door with the others on my tail."

"It's a good thing they didn't follow you through!" Terra exclaimed.

Keegan looked out of the window. "Does beg the question though, doesn't it? Where did they go?"

Terra cocked her head.

"What do you mean?"

"That door," Keegan murmured. "I don't think we actually went through."

"That must be the painkillers talking," Terra said.

"No, hear me out." Keegan took a long breath, he looked around the room as he tried to string together his thoughts. "Witcher hit us both with a defibrillator. Those were the impacts you felt when you were in the water. After you went through, I had the same thing. Now, granted we both stepped through that door but I don't think we made it all the way through to the other side."

Terra threw up her hands to stop him.

"Keegan, this is all very confusing, what are you saying?"

The young soldier held a hand to his missing eye. He strained as if the very idea was causing him pain as he spoke.

"Terra, what if the door wasn't so much an actual door, but more of an opening or a bridge. What if… and I know how this sounds… but what if being closer to the door is what allowed us to be resuscitated?"

Terra groaned; her head was starting to hurt too now.

"I don't get it," she snapped. "Are you saying we didn't go through the door at all?"

Keegan nodded excitedly. "Exactly! I think we may have just been in the right place at the right time. Somehow, despite the weird time zones of Limbo, we arrived at the door at the exact moment in this world that we were being resuscitated." He gave her a wide grin.

Terra smirked. "That is definitely the meds talking," she laughed. "That's one hell of a coincidence, Keegan."

He gave her a more serious look.

"After everything we've seen, is it really that hard to believe?"

Terra swallowed hard.

"You make a good point."

Keegan smiled; he turned and looked out of the window again. Terra followed his gaze, her heart sinking as her mind also wandered in the same direction as his.

"Where did the door come from?" Keegan asked.

"More importantly," Terra added, "where does it lead?" They both shuddered. Terra took Keegan's hand back into her own. Her mind wandered as she tried to think of something to talk about besides what had happened, but all of her thoughts were on Limbo. Well, almost all of them.

"Nathan Kebal survived," Terra mumbled. "I keep playing it out in my head, the helicopter and those men, and I just don't see a way he could have survived unl—" Keegan threw a hand over her mouth. He whispered gently into her ear.

"Think about where you are, Terra; you don't know who's going to be listening."

Terra pushed his hand away from her face.

"Oh right, yeah, because talking about the fucking afterlife wasn't crazy enough already!" she snapped.

"Nobody would believe or even understand us talking about that, but Kebal is different." Keegan looked around the room. Satisfied, he whispered to her again. "I saw him escape, he ran right past those guys in black and they acted as if he was fucking invisible. There's no way guys of that calibre would miss a target like him, not that close."

"The voices said something about that, come to think of it, they pointed it out to me," Terra added.

Keegan took note of that.

"The voices did?"

Terra nodded. "Yeah, is that unusual?"

"For psychosis, it's not unheard of, but it's rare."

Terra shook away the worries and anxieties trying to struggle their way into her head.

"You don't think he was connected, do you?"

Keegan groaned as he strained to look around again as if he was looking for an invisible watchman.

"I don't *think* he was, Terra, I'm damn sure he was."

Terra swallowed.

"What do we do now?"

Keegan shrugged. "About Kebal? Not a whole lot, there will be an investigation; the CIA and I'd wager MI6 will get involved in that. In the months and probably years to come I expect my company will get a good chunk of work out of this." Keegan's expression changed as he thought of something. "As for you, however, you have some serious thinking to do."

Terra cocked her head.

"Huh?"

The sniper smiled, his eyes lighting up with excitement.

"Have you ever considered a job in the military?"

They spent the rest of the night talking, and the next day, Terra came to visit Keegan again, and the day after that. Keegan Monroe and Terra Kisaragie had survived and escaped the nightmare world that was Limbo. But deep down neither of them could shake the feeling that somehow it wasn't over. Eddie's warnings hung in their minds, and never strayed out of reach.

"*Oh my, if only you knew… the consequences of your actions.*"

Matador

Lightning Source UK Ltd.
Milton Keynes UK
UKHW020639190820
368484UK00015B/1048